Margaret Yorke lives in B
past chairman of the Crime Writers' Association and
her outstanding contribution to the genre has been
recognized by the award of the 1999 CWA Cartier
Diamond Dagger.

THE HAND OF DEATH

Margaret Yorke

WARNER BOOKS

A *Warner* Book

First published in Great Britain in 1981
by Hutchinson

This edition published by Warner Books in 2001

A CIP catalogue record for this book
is available from the British Library.

ISBN 0 7515 3115 4

Typeset by Derek Doyle & Associates, Liverpool
Printed and bound in Great Britain by Clays Ltd, St Ives plc

Warner Books
A Division of
Little, Brown and Company (UK)
Brettenham House
Lancaster Place
London WC2E 7EN

To my friends in the police,
with admiration and respect for the job they do

1

He closed the magazine and put it under the pile of newspapers. Then he shut the drawer and locked it, placing the small brass key in a chipped china mug which stood on the desk. He stacked a number of ball-point and felt-tipped pens and some pencils in the mug on top of the key: such a simple hiding place. For a while he sat with his eyes closed, allowing his imagination to range over what he had been looking at; at last he rose, and climbed the cellar steps.

He washed at the small sink in the scullery at the back of the shop where the electric kettle and tea things were kept. In the mirror he checked his reflection: his face was a trifle flushed but that would soon fade. He took a comb from the pocket of his fawn corduroy jacket and slicked down his thick, greying hair. He straightened his brown silk tie. Then he switched off the last remaining light and let himself out by the back door, which he locked with a key from a ring he kept in his pocket.

A fine drizzle was falling as he walked quickly down the alley behind the shop to Church Lane, where his van was parked. It was an elderly Morris

Minor, maroon, with *Nanron Antiques* painted in neat white letters on the door. He never parked outside the shop, except to load or unload.

He paused on the corner. To the right lay Tellingford, and home; to the left, the High Street and the Plough Inn. Occasionally, after a Friday evening's work on the books, he would go into the Plough. It was a small gesture of independence which Nancy accepted with no more reproach than a resigned smile and some words about the meal having dried up in the oven. But whatever the hour, the food was always perfect. Nancy was an excellent home-maker.

He still felt excited. Those spread limbs, that mane of tangled hair and the wide inviting mouth that he had been staring at in the magazine remained in his mind. It would be prudent to delay his return, allowing his pulse to slow and his thoughts to settle. He always made out that his weekly book-keeping took longer than it did, to win time he need not account for.

He turned left towards the Plough. As he opened the door, a warm wave of smoky air and a buzz of noisy talk surged to greet him. The inn, on the road between Tellingford and Middletown, was a tempting stop for commuters on their way home from Tellingford station, and local businessmen.

Ronald Trimm, dealer in furniture, clocks, china and bric-à-brac, squared his fawn corduroy shoulders, put on a cheery smile, and walked briskly up to the bar.

George Fortescue sat wedged, thigh to thigh, between two other men in the railway compartment.

There was no space to spread a newspaper between the elbows of his neighbours; in George's hand was a paperback book, a tale of high adventure on the seas. For the length of his journey to Tellingford station, George was not a man beset by domestic problems, nor aware of the hot, airless train, but aboard a man-o'-war seeking the Spaniards with a cutlass in his belt. At stops along the line people got off the train, brushing past his knees, knocking into him with their briefcases, stepping on his toes. Through it all he remained detached, navigating the Atlantic.

He had developed a routine, always getting into the same compartment which delivered him by the footbridge over the line at Tellingford, so that on wet nights he need not trudge along the platform. Often there were familiar faces on the train, but no one from his office caught the same one and even if there was a breakdown or the train was otherwise delayed, conversation was not encouraged by the regular commuters. Sometimes a pair of younger men, euphoric after concluding a successful deal, would talk in excited tones throughout the trip, but the older ones shut themselves off with book or crossword, or in slumber, recouping themselves for their next round of human contact when they reached their families.

On just such a damp, cold night as this, three months ago, George had learned that Angela had left him, after twenty-two years of marriage. He had reached home to find a note on the mantelpiece and a stew in the oven for his dinner. He had not been able to understand her action then, and he understood it no better now. She had said she was wasting her life.

'She had everything she wanted,' George had said to his son Daniel, who was reading mathematics at Fletcham University. When Angela had not returned after two days, George had driven to Fletcham, forty miles away, to see if Daniel could explain.

'Tough luck, Dad,' said the embarrassed Daniel. 'She just wants to be her own person, I expect.'

'What does that mean?' George asked, no wiser.

'Well – not your wife – not my mother. Just herself,' said Daniel.

'She told you, then?'

'Just that she was going away. She didn't say much,' said Daniel, and then added, awkwardly, 'There's no one else. At least I don't think so.' He turned the idea round in his mind. Surely there wasn't?

'Do you know where she is?'

'Staying with Jean,' said Daniel promptly, glad to produce a fact. 'She's going to find a place of her own later.'

What's she planning to live on? Will she expect me to keep her? Who's going to look after me? What about clean socks and shirts? My meals? Questions milled round in George's head. And what would everyone say?

'She reckons I'm off your hands now, Dad,' said Daniel, in his mercy not adding that she might otherwise have departed sooner.

His father looked as if he had had a punch in the guts. His rather sallow face was pale; there were large

4

bags beneath his eyes. The whole thing was embarrassing to Daniel.

'I don't understand,' said George.

'She thought we took her a bit too much for granted – meals, the washing – all that – making it easy for us to follow our own interests and not bothering about her having any,' Daniel said. He felt an impatient pity for his father.

'She had all day to herself,' said George. 'And evenings too, quite often.' For George himself was a great committee man, a member of the Lions, on the parish council with aspirations to the county when retirement loomed, and secretary of the Liberal Association. He was frequently at meetings, and he played golf most Sundays.

That friend of Angela's, Jean, was to blame, George decided, driving home from Fletcham after his talk with Daniel. Jean had a job in public relations and a flat in Wandsworth which George had never seen; she went alone on holidays abroad and for years had been having an affair with a married man. George had never approved of her, and now she'd talked Angela into this mad adventure.

She'd soon come back, sheepishly apologetic, he reasoned, rallying after the first shock; after a time he'd agree to forgive her.

But she hadn't. She'd found a flat of her own and a job in a big store over Christmas, in the toy department. Now she was working in a travel agency, so Daniel said. He admitted the flat was more of a bedsitter but said she seemed well and happy.

George and Daniel had eaten Christmas dinner

with Bill and Eileen Kyle; Bill Kyle was George's solicitor and a golfing partner. On Boxing Day Daniel had left to stay with his girlfriend, Vivian, and meet her parents for the first time. George was alone for the rest of the holiday. The empty house still felt strange, and so did the empty bed.

He found a village woman, Mrs Pearson, to clean the house until Angela came to her senses, which must happen in the end. Meanwhile he filled what spare time he had with activity.

So now, when he reached home from the office, he adopted a strict routine. Soon after Angela left, he had noticed an increase in weight; he'd taken to having a good lunch at midday, since he had to prepare his own evening meal and depend on Mrs Pearson for the shopping. He ate mainly from the freezer at night, popping boil-in-the-bag dishes into pans of hot water. To combat the weight problem, George had taken up jogging. He'd begun by going out early in the morning, before breakfast, but had given that up after a few days; it was too cold and bleak at half-past six, when he must set out if he was to catch his usual train. Now he ran in the evening, in a dark tracksuit and, on very cold nights, with a woollen cap he wore for golf on his bald head. He did not run every evening, because of his committees and other meetings; he had added more interests to his life, the preservation of rural England and of Crowbury in particular being the latest. But most evenings, now, he would enter the house and, instead of automatically pouring the large whisky he'd drunk straight off in the first days after Angela's departure, following it with a second, he would go upstairs and put on his jogging outfit. In fifteen minutes' time he would be loping round the village roads. He was already fitter, and ran further and faster each week. After his run he would have a shower and change into sweater and slacks, eat braised kidneys or whatever the evening's dish might be. He'd watch television till eleven or a little later; then he would go to bed. George always slept well.

Ronald Trimm didn't enjoy beer all that much, unless he was very thirsty, but drinking it aided, he felt, the masculine image he sought to project. Tonight, he ordered half a pint of bitter – a pint was too much volume – and looked around the bar. He recognized a number of people. There was the manager of one of the Tellingford banks, and the senior partner of a firm of estate agents; they were sitting in a corner talking intently. Ronald knew neither of them personally but had been at furniture sales where the estate agent conducted the auction. There were some young, smartly turned out couples, the women perched on stools by the counter or standing by the hearth, their well-tended bodies displaying an unconscious confidence, the men often with an air of arrogance about them. Ronald looked at a dark-haired girl in black velvet pants and a red shirt; he imagined her spread in a revealing pose as illustrated in one of his magazines. What must it be like to be married to her? Exciting, he thought, but frightening too. He hovered on the fringe of a group, wanting to join their brisk, bright talk, but not bold enough. He noticed none of its brittleness, nor the falseness in the repartees. The landlord, to whom he sometimes talked, was too busy taking orders for much conversation. Ronald sipped his beer and gazed about, trying to seem at ease, a man of poise.

Then Dorothea Wyatt came up to the bar and ordered a double gin and tonic. Ronald had never got used to seeing women buy their own drinks, although why not, if they earned good money and claimed other types of equality with men? He was surprised, now, to see Mrs Wyatt, who collected china jugs and sometimes bought from him, apparently here alone.

Noticing him, she said, 'Why, hullo, Mr Trimm,' and swayed a little, waiting for her glass. She was a small woman, somewhat on the plump side, wearing an off-white wool skirt and matching polo sweater, with black beads round her neck. She wore long black boots, and her reddish hair was, Ronald knew, too dark to be natural at her age; he noticed the small vertical lines around her mouth and the thin skin on her hands.

'Good evening, Mrs Wyatt,' he said. 'Damp, isn't it?'

'Damp?' Dorothea Wyatt giggled, spilling her new drink. 'What – the gin? I hope so.' She drank some of it, then set the glass down and fumbled in her large handbag for her purse. She thrust a five-pound note across the counter.

'I meant the weather,' Ronald said. 'It was raining just now. Well, drizzling.'

8

'Oh yes – an awful night,' said Dorothea. She took her change from the landlord and stuffed it into her purse. 'Cheers,' she said, and spilled more of her drink, this time on her sweater. 'I'm sitting over there,' she added, gesturing towards the window, and ignoring the drips she set off across the bar towards a banquette seat.

Was she suggesting he should join her? Ronald took a step to follow her, watching her off-white wool back as she wove a course past the fireplace, stumbling over the toes of some of the younger customers and being set upon her way with a firm hand on her elbow by one young man. Reaching the bank manager and the estate agent, she stopped. Ronald saw her put her drink down on the table and pull out a spare chair.

'Well, what are you two wicked men plotting?' she inquired, and almost fell into the seat between them.

The estate agent paused in mid-sentence. The bank manager drew himself upright, leaning away from her. Dorothea smiled from one to the other and leaned across the table towards the bank manager, who answered stiffly.

'We were having a business talk,' he said.

'Pooh – business,' said Dorothea, waving a hand on which she wore a large sapphire and diamond ring. 'This isn't the time for dull business, is it, Mr Trimm?' and she looked at Ronald, who was watching her in amazement. He'd always thought her so dignified; she wasn't, now. 'Join us, Mr Trimm,' she cried gaily. 'We're all friends here.'

She moved her chair closer to the bank manager,

and Ronald saw her ringed hand disappear under the table. A horrified expression came over the bank manager's face and he shrank away from her, moving his chair. Incredible though it seemed, Dorothea Wyatt, widow of the managing director of a small engineering business and owner of the Manor House, Crowbury, was very drunk and was making unseemly overtures to a respectable citizen in a public place.

She had to be stopped from disgracing herself.

'You'll be more comfortable over here, Mrs Wyatt,' Ronald said in a firm voice, indicating the window seat. 'I'll take your glass across.'

'Oh – isn't this more cosy?' Dorothea protested, but seeing her glass departing, she took her hand away from its dangerous position, stood up unsteadily, and saying, 'Too bad, darling,' to the bank manager, wavered away with Ronald.

Ronald gave a quick nod to the other two men. The bank manager looked extremely relieved; a fine perspiration bedewed his brow and he mopped at it with a large white linen handkerchief. The estate agent merely shrugged. There were one or two titters from the group about the fireplace but they were mainly too intent on their own conversation to pay much attention to outsiders. Ronald steered Mrs Wyatt to the banquette and perched beside her, tensely. He was deeply shocked by the fact that a woman of her standing was on the brink of making a spectacle of herself. She had already almost finished her drink.

'Finish your beer and have a drink on me, Mr

Trimm,' she said. 'You can get me another gin, too.'
She began fumbling in her bag again and pulled out
several pound notes. 'Get yourself something
stronger. Have a scotch.'

'Not just now, thank you, Mrs Wyatt,' Ronald said
primly.

'Well, get me a double gin and tonic, there's a
lamb, and don't look so stuffy,' said Dorothea.

Ronald took a deep breath.

'I think you ought to be getting along home now,
Mrs Wyatt,' he said.

'Who wants to go home?' said Dorothea. 'There's
no one there. There's nothing to go home for.' She
moved closer to Ronald. 'It's so sad,' she said.

She looked now as if she might weep. Ronald cast
a worried glance round the bar, but there was no help
coming. Everything depended on him.

'I'll take you home,' he said. If she'd come here in
her car, he must drive it, and walk back later for the
van. A drunken woman was, at any time, a most
distressing sight, and a drunken lady, which Mrs
Wyatt was, was infinitely worse. She must be rescued
from herself. 'Come along,' he said, standing up. He
was good at ushering time-wasting non-buyers from
the shop, able after years of practice to pick them out
from genuinely interested browsers, and he used the
same masterful technique now, waiting for her to
rise.

She did.

Nancy Trimm was fond of saying that she and Ron
did everything together and had no secrets from each

other. Even in the hours when they were apart, she knew where he was, and if he was not in the shop she could reflect that he was bidding at an auction, visiting a dealer, or collecting or delivering goods for repair or renovation from one of his outworkers. Nanron Antiques had begun as a market stall in Middletown, run by Nancy while Ronald went on working in menswear in Middletown's large department store; now it kept them both.

They lived in Tellingford, at Number 15, Sycamore Road, a bungalow with a bay-windowed living area that led to a dining recess off the kitchen; the main bedroom at the back overlooked the neat garden with shaved lawn, beds for annuals, and productive vegetable patch. Tellingford, originally a small market town, had grown since the war and now included two industrial areas, one on each side of the river that ran through the centre. To house those who worked in the factories, estates of modern houses in various price brackets had been built wherever planning permission could be granted, and villages in the surrounding areas had expanded too. Crowbury, three miles away, was now considered exclusive; property there fetched high prices. The road through the village had been widened and improved; quality shops had opened, and there were now a specialist delicatessen shop as well as an old-fashioned general grocery; two butchers; a dress shop; a hardware store; a shop selling children's clothes, knitting wool and haberdashery; a greengrocer; a newsagent and tobacconist; and Nanron Antiques.

There was no parking problem in Crowbury,

where just off the High Street there was a large, tree-lined square facing the church, and drivers on their way to Tellingford or Middletown often stopped to shop there. Weekend motorists, seeing the pretty shop fronts, some timbered under thatched or old tiled roofs, would pause to browse. There was talk of a tea shop opening in what had been a forge; and Clematis Cottage, now being renovated, had been sold to a potter. Nancy had seen, when they opened the shop, that Crowbury was a coming area; one day, she planned, she and Ronald would live there.

When they met, Ronald was a carpet fitter at the Middletown department store where Nancy worked in the gift department. She made up her mind to marry him quite quickly, but first she set about improving his qualifications for the role of her partner, guiding him away from carpets to menswear when there was a vacancy. His appearance soon smartened up. Nancy aspired to a husband in business on his own and, because she had a mild interest herself in restoring china, which an aunt of hers had done as a hobby, she thought of antiques. They had class.

Reluctant though she was to leave Ronald's side, soon after they married she left the store and went to work part-time for an antique dealer. She started to pick up small objects at sales, and stored them in a cupboard at the flat where she and Ronald lived. Meanwhile, Ronald acquired some good clothes at staff discount, and a polished manner under the supervision of Mr Golding, head of menswear for the past fifteen years.

At her market stall, Nancy began selling items

13

individually priced which she had bought in job lots at auctions; she made a considerable profit. When her mother died – her father was killed in the war – her small inheritance went into a deposit on the bungalow, a year's rent on the shop in Crowbury, and more stock.

Ronald disappointed her by showing no aptitude for mending china or restoring furniture; he was not neat-fingered enough, and he wanted results too quickly. But he learned to buy wisely, and developed connections with local dealers, particularly one specializing in clocks, so that a good part of their business was outside the shop. Nancy sent Ronald out knocking in those early years. He soon knew enough to spot a bargain, and the manners he had learned in menswear inspired confidence in the gullible householders he called on in villages fifty and sixty miles away. Occasionally, even now, he would visit a hamlet in search of old women who might not yet be wary of door-to-door callers. Ronald, in any case, in his good clothes and with his nice way of speaking, was very different from the rough, tinker-like knockers who had spoiled the market. If he came upon some choice object worth a special effort, he would pay several visits over a period of weeks, doing odd jobs for the old person who owned the desired article – usually a clock – like fixing a shelf or wiring a plug, turning himself into a trusted friend. Then he would offer twenty pounds for some valueless thing – probably junk – adding that he'd pay a fiver for that old, shabby clock. After his careful groundwork, he was never refused.

14

Nancy looked after the shop when Ronald was on the road. Buses which ran between Middletown and Tellingford every hour stopped at Crowbury, so she could travel independently. She had never learned to drive; somehow or other there had never been time. It didn't matter, in the excellence of their partnership; perhaps it was even good for Ronald, she would fondly reflect, to maintain supremacy in this traditionally masculine area. A man liked to feel strong.

2

In his black tracksuit, George Fortescue blended into the scenery as he jogged round the streets of Crowbury in the dark. Sometimes he kept to the residential areas, where the streets were lit, and at other times, if there was a moon, he ran along the lanes. If a car approached when he was pounding down a road, he would be warned by its lights and would move on to the grass verge while it passed.

At first, George had found that all his concentration was needed for the sheer physical effort of lifting one foot after the other, but as the days passed he began to pay more attention to his surroundings. He noticed aspects of life in Crowbury which he had never thought about before: through lighted windows he saw families at their evening meal, or the flicker of a television screen; he met people out with their dogs, often elderly men with a terrier on a lead. Battered cars, driven by youngsters on their way to Middletown for a night out, would roar by, and as he passed the various pubs their assorted clientele would be arriving or departing.

On this damp Friday, George padded down the

short drive of Orchard House and into Church Lane. The soft drizzle soon beaded his face and clothes, but as he ran on he forgot about it, concentrating on his breathing, trotting along at a gentle pace. He circled the chestnut tree in the square in front of the church and ran on down a footpath linking Church Lane with the High Street once more. As he approached the Plough, the door opened and a couple came out on to the pavement. They crossed the road ahead of him, and he had to slow up to let them pass. He did not glance at them deliberately, for he felt no curiosity; one thing about jogging was that it detached your mind from life's trivia. But he recognized Dorothea Wyatt.

The Manor House, Crowbury, was never in fact the domicile of the lord of the manor but had once been a farmhouse on the estate of the neighbouring manor of Fordwick. It had been extensively renovated when it was sold off many years before, and the Wyatts had improved it still more. It was a pleasant, long, low house made of local stone, with an old tiled roof, set in four acres of land, most of it meadow which Dorothea let for grazing. A public footpath ran across the field at the end of the garden, and beyond, less than a mile away, was the river. There were trees round the house, a beech and larches, but the elms at the boundary had died and been cut down, leaving stark stumps by the fence.

Ronald helped Dorothea out of her car, a Saab, which he'd enjoyed driving and he'd managed it well, unfamiliar though it was and much livelier than his van.

'Have you got your front-door key?' he asked.

'It's too big to put in my bag,' said Dorothea.

She went round the side of the house to where a water butt stood on bricks under a spout, and fumbled beneath it, coming up with a long iron key.

The front door was made of solid oak, the original one dating from when the house was built. Dorothea had some trouble fitting the key in the lock, but she managed at last, opened it and went in, and Ronald, who still held the keys of the car, followed. There were lights burning in the hall in which they now stood, coming from a room on the left where the door was open, and shining down the stairs from the landing above. The wireless was on; light music played loudly.

'Shut the door, for God's sake,' said Dorothea. 'Don't let in the cold.'

Ronald obeyed. He put her keys down on a gleaming oak dresser which must have been well over two hundred years old. He saw a fine oak carved cupboard against one wall, and a little spinning wheel by the hearth in which stood an iron basket grate and firedogs. A solid fireback spanned the chimney wall. A Windsor chair stood at the other side of the fireplace. Ronald, twitching almost visibly like a hound on the scent, went to look at it; it was made of yew. Such pieces rarely went through his hands; they were too good, too perfect, fetched too high a price.

'Come along,' Dorothea was calling. She had disappeared through the doorway of the room from which the music was coming.

Ronald thought about his van, still parked in Church Lane, and the damp walk he would have to fetch it. He thought about Nancy and their meal. Then he went into Dorothea's sitting room.

It was not large. It was comfortably furnished with a modern sofa, but one easy chair was Edwardian; another, wing-backed, earlier still. They had been re-upholstered in velvet. There was a mahogany tallboy between the two windows at which hung full-length gold brocade curtains. A sofa table, heaped with magazines, stood against a wall. Ronald saw a posset pot and a pair of Worcester vases on top of the the tallboy.

'You've got some lovely things, Mrs Wyatt,' he had to remark.

'Yes. Most of them belonged to my husband's family but I've picked up one or two myself,' said Dorothea. 'I keep my jugs and some more china bits and pieces in the other room.' She gestured towards a door on the right.

Ronald had sold her a Coalport jug which Nancy had repaired; she'd noticed the neat mend at once, and he'd reduced the price. After that, whenever she had looked at an object in his shop, he had always pointed out any blemish, however expertly restored. It would not do to deceive a woman like Mrs Wyatt, who was one of Crowbury's leading residents.

Dorothea turned down the radio.

'I always leave this on when I'm out, to frighten the burglars,' she said. 'And it makes the house nicer to come back to. I don't like the silence. It's horrid, living alone, especially at night. I haven't got used to it yet, and my husband died three years ago. That's why I go to the Plough, when I can't take it any more.' She seemed to have sobered up now. 'How about a drink, Mr Trimm? Won't you join me?'

Ronald glanced at a plain brass carriage clock on the mantelpiece. It was just after half-past seven. Another five minutes wouldn't make a lot of difference.

Nancy Trimm had made beef olives for dinner. She never called the evening meal by any other name; supper was a snack, or a late-night repast after some festivity. The table was laid with the plated cutlery they had always used since she had picked up the tarnished and incomplete set years before, and good glasses – not matched goblets but odd ones, not worth much if put in the shop. Nancy liked things nice.

To follow the beef olives, there was apple amber. Fruit was good for the health, and there were plenty of apples from their own Bramley tree stored in the shed. When they had bought the bungalow, one of its attractions had been the large garden; houses and bungalows being built now had no space for fruit trees in their minuscule plots. With their freezer, Ronald and Nancy kept themselves supplied with vegetables for most of the year. It did Ronald good to get out there in the garden on a Sunday, no matter what the weather, and when the evenings were light he'd put in an hour or so after work most days. Never on a Friday, though; and when he was at a sale he might return too late for even half an hour's hoeing. Apart from the garden's usefulness, working in it made him tired: too tired for any of that unpleasantness.

At first, Nancy had to endure it. They'd been going out together for some time – to the cinema, walks in the park on Sundays. Working in the store, as they both did, Saturday had been a full day like any other. He came to tea to meet her mother; he had no family of his own now; like her, he had lost his father when he was very young and had been brought up by his mother. This was a bond for them; another was the fact that they were only children. Ronald's mother had died when he was seventeen. When Nancy and he met, he was living in digs in Middletown; he was only twenty when they married, but she was twenty-eight and getting anxious. Nancy had been out with several young men before Ronald came along, but sooner or later they all wanted one thing and, when this was denied them, that had been the end of it. But she must marry: to be unmarried was to be a failure, to advertise that one had been passed over. That was before Women's Lib made it possible, even admirable, to choose independence, or to say that one had chosen it.

In the end, Ronald had wanted the same thing as the others. The kisses he planted on her reluctant lips grew more demanding; she felt, one evening after her mother had gone up to bed, hard urgency in his body pressed to hers. She'd let it happen, at last, on a summer's day when they were in the country. Ronald, carried away, had not noticed her own lack of enthusiasm as he moaned and heaved, then lay inert upon her. The pain had been severe, too. She

21

was reluctant to permit it again but, when she did, it wasn't so bad, and after a while she was even able to detach her mind and pretend it was happening to someone else.

He didn't talk of marriage, so she made him. That was before the Pill. After the wedding, she pretended she'd had a miscarriage. For quite a long time she convinced him that the doctor had decreed restraint, and after that she made him take precautions on the few occasions when she allowed him contact. It never happened now; she made quite sure of that.

Apart from this aspect of it, which Nancy preferred to ignore, she favoured married life. Ronald had proved an apt pupil in all she set out to teach him, and his appearance had improved as his coarse, sandy hair became flecked with grey. He was not tall, but not short either; and he had kept his figure. They were respected in their circle of acquaintances, intimate with nobody, but on friendly terms with neighbours and fellow traders.

Nancy kept the bungalow impeccably. When Ronald walked through the door in the evening, his slippers would be waiting on the mat and he would leave his shoes in the hall. This was not for his comfort, but lest he bring mud indoors. His dinner – always ample and tasty – would be ready. Afterwards, if gardening was not possible, there might be catalogues to consult, or a small woodwork repair too minor to be passed on to the cabinet-maker he used. Ronald was not encouraged to help with household tasks. The kitchen was Nancy's territory and he was not welcome there; once, he had almost attacked her at the sink, coming up behind her and grasping her round the waist, his body tight against her. He'd been drinking before he came home; she'd caught it on his breath. She'd managed to get away that time, and she'd taken care that such a thing never happened again. All that was quite unnecessary. Mutual support in the business, a respected position in the neighbourhood, and modest comfort in the home were the things that were important; shared interests were essential to a good marriage, and the business gave them those. Besides that, a man must be well looked after, as was Ronald. He could have no cause for complaint.

She knew he often went to the Plough on Fridays, and would be ready with her tactics for physical evasion when he returned, though for years now she had been unmolested. Providing he kept to just the one evening and did not stay long at the pub, she was prepared to overlook this little failing.

But he was always home by eight, and this evening, when the hands of the functional electric clock on the living-room mantelpiece said eight forty-five, Nancy did begin to wonder what had happened. She went to the window more than once to see if the van was in view. Perhaps it had broken down. Not for the first time, she wished the shop was on the telephone, but there was a box nearby and Ronald used that if he needed to make calls. In this business, the telephone was an expensive luxury. Surely it was impossible for him to have an accident between Crowbury and Tellingford? He knew the road so well.

He came in at nine forty.

He had thought out his story as he walked back to the van, deciding in the end that a version of the truth was the only solution, for if he made out that the van had broken down or that he had had a puncture, Nancy might find him out by checking at the garage where his repairs and servicing were done.

'I popped into the Plough and Mrs Wyatt was there,' he explained. 'You know – Mrs Wyatt from the Manor House.' This should impress Nancy. 'She collects jugs – we've sold her several,' he reminded her. 'She wasn't feeling very well, so I took her home. I couldn't leave her until she seemed all right, as she lives alone,' he said. Then he rushed on. 'A lovely place it is, and she's got some stuff, too. It's a wonder she hasn't been burgled.'

There'd been a beautiful walnut commode on the landing; then, in the bedroom, a fourposter, the curtains white with little sprigs of flowers on them.

They'd had drinks first, sitting on the sofa – he'd had a scotch, half a tumbler of it poured from a cut-glass decanter, just splashed with soda. She'd had two large gins herself, one after the other. Then she'd turned off the lights, all except a lamp on the table by the sofa, and told him how lonely she was.

'After nearly thirty years of married life, being a widow isn't easy,' she'd begun.

Ronald had nervously gulped his drink down, intent on leaving, but she had poured him another, and one for herself, then sat close to him. She wore some sort of flowery scent. Ronald forgot the lines and imperfections on Dorothea's well-made-up face.

24

He knew only that her hand, as earlier in the Plough, was straying, and this time he was the target.

'We'll be more comfortable upstairs,' she'd murmured quite soon, and had led him there. She'd left one soft light on in the bedroom and finished undoing his shirt. His tie had gone already. Without any apparent effort her own clothes seemed to come off, even her long zipped boots. He saw pale, naked shoulders, and breasts that were large and soft. Everything that happened after that was a dazed memory, as in a dream. She was asleep when he left, stepping round the room collecting his clothes, remembering his tie from the sitting room. He'd locked the front door from outside, posting the key in through the letter box that was fitted in the post at the side of the door. A place like that shouldn't be left unlocked, easy prey for thieves.

He looked at Nancy now. She had been a pretty girl, and was still good-looking, but she lacked something that Dorothea Wyatt had in abundance. Style: that was it. And something else, too, was missing: the power to give and receive intense physical pleasure; yet the potential must be there, locked up in her compact body. He thought that there could be no two more different women. The experience he had just had was like nothing he had imagined, even when poring over his magazines.

'Mrs Wyatt,' Nancy was saying consideringly. 'The Manor House – mmm. You did right, dear. Did you call the doctor?'

'No. She insisted that it wasn't necessary,' Ronald said. 'I left her as soon as I could.'

He'd covered her with the white quilt, as she lay there breathing through half-parted lips.

He'd go back, of course. She'd be expecting him. She had told him that he was wonderful, and indeed he had felt that he was.

'I said I'd value some of her pieces for her,' he said, amazed at how easy it was to invent. 'The insurance may need stepping up.'

'You might look for things for her, if she collects furniture as well as jugs,' said Nancy. 'It could be quite useful.'

'That's what I thought,' said Ronald smoothly. 'I hope you weren't anxious, dear, when I was so late?'

'Oh no,' said Nancy. 'Why should I be? I knew it couldn't be anything serious.'

3

Ronald woke early the next morning. He felt instantly alert, eager for the day ahead. He looked forward to Saturdays, because for nearly a year now, Lynn Norton, the daughter of Hilda and Keith Norton who lived next door in Number 16, Sycamore Road, had helped in the shop each week. Ronald and Nancy had known her and her older brother since they were small children.

Lynn was nearly sixteen now, and had grown into a pretty, quiet girl, neat in her school uniform of navy skirt and white blouse. She drew well, and wanted to study art; she was saving her weekly pay towards a trip to Italy. Sometimes Ronald would give her a lift to school in the van. Her brother was now in the Merchant Navy and seldom home; Hilda Norton had a job with a building society in Tellingford and Keith Norton went to Middletown every day, where he was manager of a firm of builders' suppliers. He left home before his wife and daughter, for his office opened early.

It was Nancy who had suggested Nanron's, when she learned that Lynn wanted a Saturday job.

'It would give me more time at home,' she said. 'I could get the place straight for the weekend, and catch up with repairs.' She was skilled now, and did them for other dealers too, but the work was slow and needed space where objects could be spread out, propped up while they set. The small second bedroom was given over to it, with bench and glues and mixes.

Help in the shop was essential on Saturdays, for Ronald had to go out then to see the dealers who were not available during the week.

Lynn had thought of a coffee bar or a dress shop as a suitable place to earn money for her travel fund, but when she was offered a job at Nanron Antiques she took it at once. She liked working among the old pieces in the shop, and would wonder who had owned a cup and saucer, or a fan, or an elegant chair, before it reached the sale room. She was learning about the stock. Ronald liked it when she asked questions and he took trouble to explain. Sometimes they looked things up together in the large reference books he kept in the cellar on the flat desk where he did the accounts.

He'd slept so soundly last night! He lay for some minutes in his single bed, separated by a wide bedside table from Nancy's, recalling what had happened the previous evening. It was like a dream, one of the solitary fantasies he indulged when he looked at his magazines. He'd assumed that most people's marriages settled into a routine like his and Nancy's. She was a wonderful wife, he knew. Without her, the business would not exist. She was a faultless housewife and was always bandbox-neat herself in modestly becoming clothes. Her life pivoted around him. If there were times when he felt that something important was lacking, he pushed such disloyal reflections from his mind.

Their intimate encounters had always been disappointing to him, joyless, and soon over. Now he knew how different things could be! But it was impossible to imagine Nancy abandoned, as Mrs Wyatt was last night. Mrs Wyatt: Dorothea. He tried the name in his mind. He'd use it next time. He'd called her 'Darling', he recalled with pride, but had not used her first name.

Meanwhile, there was the day ahead with little Lynn, whose shape was filling out; whose arm or thigh he sometimes brushed against; whose hair, if they bent together over some object in the shop, or to consult a reference book, smelled fresh and fragrant; Lynn, who was like a daughter to him.

That Saturday morning, Dorothea Wyatt was woken by the telephone. It had rung several times before her groping hand managed to find and lift the receiver. The caller was her daughter Susan.

At first, Dorothea could not understand what Susan was saying; she felt as if she were surfacing from some long submersion a great way from reality, and her head was pounding. But at last she understood Susan to be telling her, with impatience now, that she was coming for the weekend.

'I'll be there for lunch, Mummy,' she heard, in a cross tone. 'I said lunch, Mummy. Mummy? Are you there? Can you hear me? I can't hear you.'

'Lovely, darling,' Dorothea managed. 'Lovely to see you. What train will you be on?'

'I've told you already, Mummy. I'll catch the twelve twenty.'

'All right, darling. I'll be there to meet you,' Dorothea said. 'Twelve forty-five it arrives, doesn't it?'

'Of course, Mummy. It always has. I'll wait, if you're late.' Susan, replacing the receiver, sighed. You'd think your mother would be pleased to see you, she reflected, whereas hers had sounded strange. At this hour she couldn't have been at the gin. Susan had decided to make this duty visit when Leo, her current boyfriend, had revealed that he meant to spend the day tinkering with his Porsche, which needed work done on the carburettors. Leo loved his car – more, she feared, than he loved her. He drove it in races for standard cars which she had to watch from the pits, half deafened. She was not sure that their relationship was secure enough to become permanent.

'Oh dear,' said Dorothea aloud, hand to head. Now she must get up and root round for something for lunch. And be at Tellingford station by a quarter to one. But it would be lovely to see Susan.

She sat up. Immediately, her head throbbed harder than before. Round her, the bedclothes were in disarray, the sheets crumpled. What a restless night she must have had.

Then she remembered that she had woken in the night with her body, for once, at peace. Someone had been here with her. It had happened before; one of Harry's business friends had needed no invitation, and there was Colin Hampton, married to her own childhood friend Molly, who had been in her bed more than once. Who was it this time?

Dorothea had crawled out of bed in the night, dragged on her dressing gown and gone downstairs. Every light was on and the radio was playing. She checked the front door and found the key on the hall floor.

'Must have dropped it,' she had muttered to herself, pushing home the heavy bolts.

She had felt hungry. Had she eaten any supper? She couldn't remember. She went into the kitchen, found some bread and buttered it, and cut a slice of cheese. As she ate, she tried to remember who her visitor had been.

She'd been to the Plough, she recalled. Who'd been there? Faces swam before her, but none seemed to fit. She had a vague memory of diffidence, of uttering encouragement. He'd had crisp, wiry hair on his chest. She'd always liked hairy men: Harry had a forest of dark hair on his chest.

Then she remembered.

'My God! Mr Trimm!' She said it aloud. She often talked to herself. Sometimes she pretended Harry was there, and talked to him. With an effort she conjured up in her mind a picture of Mr Trimm with his neatly brushed sandy hair, streaked with grey – pepper and salt, almost – the corduroy jacket he always wore in the shop, his polite manner. Then she began to laugh. 'Well, at least he always looks clean,' she told herself.

She had stopped laughing quite suddenly.

'Oh, Harry, Harry,' she mourned, starting to weep. How could she go on without him?

Harry had seemed dull to some people, but he was her tender lover and her dear companion, who had brought her joy through so many years, their first ardour only heightened by the comfort of familiarity. He had died so suddenly, with no warning and no chance to say goodbye.

To bring Mr Trimm into Harry's bed had been a terrible betrayal.

Still sobbing, Dorothea had dragged herself across the hall, back to the sitting room and the gin bottle. In the end, she'd taken the gin up to bed with her.

And now she had another day to face.

Lynn enjoyed Saturdays at Nanron's. She liked seeing what was new since the week before, and what had been sold. Stock changed all the time.

Uncle Ron would set off at about half-past nine on his various errands.

'The business is in good hands when you're in charge, Lynn,' he would say, and would pat her shoulder.

The shop premises had once been part of an inn. There was a narrow front room with a bow-fronted window on to the High Street, where the best items were displayed. Upstairs was another room, where china and glass less immediately striking and other oddments were shown. At the rear was a scullery, with an electric kettle and small geyser for washing up mugs and teacups, and downstairs was the cellar, where the book-keeping and other paperwork was done.

Furniture restoration and repair work was done by

Will Noakes, to whom Ronald took broken chairs to be given new backs, damaged chests and tables and sometimes pieces whose sole use was to supply wood for renovation. These were the quality jobs, but often at the back of the shop Lynn would see a shabby painted chest or a chair or table. Some weeks later the same items would reappear, the paint stripped, the surfaces smoothed and polished to show the natural wood. Valerie Turner did these for Ronald in the garage of Primrose Cottage, in Ship Lane.

Nanron's customers, in the main, could not afford perfect pieces; they were happy with old furniture that was reasonably priced, even if the legs were wrong or there were other flaws; it would match their renovated cottages.

In a sense, Lynn relaxed on Saturdays. The rest of the week, it was off to school as soon as she finished her cornflakes and then it was all go, but in the shop there was no pressure. The customers never hurried, and Uncle Ron was nice to work for. He'd told her to call him Ron, now that she was his colleague, but somehow she couldn't do it. She managed by not addressing him directly; if she needed his advice for a customer, she would say, 'I'll just ask Mr Trimm.'

He was very cheerful this morning. Perhaps it was because the weather was better.

Lynn began dusting the stock as soon as she'd hung up her coat at the back. She always did this, and polished the horse brasses which hung on a beam; they were in constant demand. There was rarely a customer until getting on for ten o'clock, for food shopping was the weekend priority and only when that was done did people find time to saunter. On Saturdays, Nanron stayed open through the lunch hour, catching people on their way to or from the Plough, which did a brisk trade in bar lunches.

Mr Fortescue came in that morning. Lynn knew him by sight; she and Uncle Ron had seen him several times when they were walking to the van after locking up on a Saturday evening; he'd jog by in his black outfit, seeming old to Lynn because he was bald, his arms bent to his sides as he lolloped along. Uncle Ron knew that he lived at Orchard House.

He wanted a present, he said. Something easy to post.

'For my wife. She's gone away,' said George. 'Left me. After twenty-two years of marriage. It's her birthday on Wednesday. I can't just ignore it, can I?'

Lynn felt very embarrassed at hearing these personal details and a blush spread up her neck and over her face, but George did not notice. He had a compulsion, these days, to make people aware of his circumstances; he'd nothing to be ashamed of, after all; it was Angela, not he, who had behaved badly. Every year since they married, he had given her a bottle of Chanel No. 5, the size increasing with his salary, but he couldn't post scent.

'Would you like to look round?' said Lynn. 'I'll ask Mr Trimm what he can suggest.'

'Mm – thanks,' said George and began prowling about the shop, peering at china ornaments and pieces of silver while Lynn murmured to Ron who was rearranging objects in a glass case.

Ronald conducted George Fortescue to the open

case. Within, some pieces of antique jewellery were set out: a garnet brooch, amethyst earrings, a cameo pin, various pendants. There was an old locket, still containing plaited strands of faded hair.

George thought that macabre.

'Someone's mother,' Ronald explained. 'It was quite usual once to wear a locket like this after the death of a relative. They make pretty ornaments. You could take the hair out. Lynn, my dear, would you put this on to show Mr Fortescue?'

Lynn stepped forward, and Ronald slipped the locket, which was on a narrow silver chain, over her head. She lifted her heavy hair to let the chain slide round the back of her neck. The locket rested on her softly rounded bosom, shining against the severe navy sweater she wore with her school skirt.

'Very nice,' said George. 'But I hardly think—'

'Try this,' said Ronald, motioning to Lynn to remove the locket. He picked a piece of amber on a gilt chain from the velvet tray in the case, and slid that over Lynn's head.

There was no doubt that the silver locket looked better on her than the irregular lump of amber, but the amber would be more appropriate for Angela, who had a dress that sort of colour, George recollected. He could not have described her clothes with any accuracy, but had a vague sense of prevailing browns and greens.

The amber pendant was not as expensive as the silver locket. George paid for it by cheque.

4

Ronald was seeing everything through new eyes.

Though the weather on Sunday was chill, the skies grey and the air raw, he perceived beauty in the pale spears of bulbs thrusting through the cold ground. There were snowdrops in bloom under an apple tree. It was dry enough to do some digging, Nancy had pointed out at breakfast, and he obediently went off to clear the patch where the sprouts had been.

While he dug, his thoughts could roam.

It had been a good day yesterday. He was glad to be rid of that amber pendant; it had been in the shop some time, too large for most people's taste, and it wasn't good to let stock linger. He'd bought it, with some other jewellery, from a house clearance. He had an arrangement which worked well with a couple who cleared houses, buying from them china and porcelain objects which needed repair, battered chests and chairs, and obscure grimy ornaments which often turned out, when cleaned, to be attractive pieces of jewellery. The amber pendant had been dull, covered in dust and grease, when it came his way, and the silver locket was black.

The locket had looked well on Lynn. He wondered if she would like it for her birthday. He knew just when it was – the fourth of May – and she would be sixteen.

He lit a bonfire later. The smoke spiralled straight up, then drifted across the Nortons' garden, but that didn't matter today because the Nortons had gone to visit Hilda's mother.

Ronald thought about Hilda and Keith. He supposed their life was much like his and Nancy's, although Nancy knocked spots off Hilda where housekeeping was concerned. In the Nortons' bungalow you'd find the sewing machine on the dining-room table and meals being eaten in the kitchen. There would be magazines, or even books, left face downwards on the sofa, keeping the reader's place. Hilda and Lynn were always reading. He and Nancy had no time for that, apart from what was required in the way of business, and his own little cache at the shop.

In the Nortons' bungalow, washing up was stacked to be done later; meals were not dished up properly but were served straight from saucepans, and had an air of being flung together. But it was nice visiting: you needn't worry about a bit of mud attached to your shoe, for Hilda never noticed such things and anyway the floor probably needed hoovering; she only cleaned up once a week, whereas Nancy dusted every day. She thought Hilda very slovenly.

The Nortons slept in a double bed. Nancy said it

was disgusting, at their age. That Sunday morning, Ronald wondered if Hilda and Keith got together still. Older couples did. He'd learned that.

He'd visit her on Monday. She'd be expecting him. Dorothea. He said the name aloud to a wizened sprout stalk.

He'd tell Nancy he had promised to price a bureau for her.

His heart sang as he counted the hours till Monday evening.

Susan Wyatt slept late on Sunday morning. When she came downstairs, her mother was sitting in the kitchen in her dressing gown, drinking coffee. She looked haggard, old; even ill.

'You all right, Mum?' Susan asked sharply.

'A bit hung over,' Dorothea admitted.

She'd produced a good meal for Susan, the evening before. She'd taken some chicken joints out of the freezer and casseroled them in wine sauce from a tin, adding more wine. There were raspberries, also from the freezer, and cheese, and she'd opened a litre bottle of chain-store claret, which they'd finished between them. They'd watched an instalment of the latest television costume series, then a comedy show which Susan had thought puerile but at which Dorothea had laughed a lot. Then Leo, Susan's boyfriend, had telephoned, and after that Susan had gone off to bed. Dorothea had stayed up late, drinking gin. Susan would be horrified if she discovered that her mother often carried the remnants of a bottle up to bed with her, so this time she poured a generous measure into a tumbler and bore that off; it looked as innocent as water. Now her head was bursting.

What was to be done about her, Susan wondered. She felt exasperated pity; she loved her mother, but was frightened by her visible deterioration. Daddy had died three years ago, after all; by now she should be coping. Other people did. It was tough, of course, and had been very sudden. Susan had been dreadfully shocked herself, and sad; she still missed him, though it had been better since Leo appeared. It would be a good thing if her mother would re-marry, remove the worry on to someone else's shoulders. Surely there must be some kindly widower about? On the other hand, older people grew set in their ways and might find adjustment difficult. But in later age one probably didn't expect so much from another person. Once or twice recently her mother had been difficult to understand on the telephone. She was drinking much too much – that was evident.

'Have you seen the doctor lately?' Susan asked.

'There's no need,' said Dorothea. Her doctor had prescribed sleeping pills and tranquillizers after Harry's death, but the last time she had seen him he had said she must wean herself from sedatives. She could not tell her daughter that the rest of her life, stretching ahead for perhaps twenty years or more, was something she could not bear to contemplate. 'I'm fine,' she said brightly.

'If only you'd get a job,' sighed Susan. 'It might be fun.'

'But what?' said Dorothea. They'd had this conversation before. She had no real qualifications. She'd

39

done a secretarial course, way back, but had met Harry and married him before it was over; she could type a bit, but couldn't do shorthand to save her life and thought herself far too old to learn. She'd never been the least bit clever.

'A hotel receptionist,' Susan said, inspired. Her mother's poise and social know-how would be of use in such a post.

'I'm too old,' said Dorothea. 'They want young, pretty girls, like you. Besides, it would be such a tie. I wouldn't be able to get away to visit Mark and the children.'

But she hardly ever travelled to Yorkshire to see Mark, her son. She didn't get on all that well with his wife. She didn't seem able to make any sort of effort. Susan guessed that her friends must be losing patience with her.

There seemed no way that Susan could help. At least, though not exactly rich, her mother was quite nicely off, which saved a lot of worry, though perhaps if she wasn't and had to do something about it she'd pull herself together. Mark didn't want the responsibility of their mother; he meant his sister, the daughter, to shoulder the load.

One day the house would have to go. It was much too big for one person, but they all loved it, and at the moment Dorothea could afford to run it. Mrs Simmons came in to clean four times a week and Joe Cunliffe did the garden, leaving rose pruning and a few minor tasks to Dorothea. It all went on just the same as when Susan's father had been alive, but there was this great gap where he had been.

Her mother was only fifty-two, not really old at all. She did Meals on Wheels occasionally, and a few other village things from time to time; or had done. There was less talk of that lately. But then fêtes and things didn't happen in the winter.

Susan decided to drop the subject of her mother's problems. She told her that Leo was coming to lunch. On the telephone the night before he'd said he missed her and he'd come to fetch her.

Dorothea hadn't faced the thought of Sunday lunch yet. She'd feel more human later. She rather liked Leo, who had fixed the sticking windscreen wipers on her Saab the last time he had come down. And it was always nice to have a man in the house.

There was a shoulder of lamb in the freezer. If she put it in water, maybe it would thaw.

After lunch, Leo washed Dorothea's car. The lamb had been rather pink about the bone, and not exactly tender, but heaped with gravy and redcurrant jelly, and surrounded by peas and roast potatoes, it was not too bad. Dorothea had found some mince pies left from Christmas in the freezer, and had opened each of them and spooned in brandy to buck them up.

'He's very energetic, isn't he?' she remarked, looking out of the sitting-room window to where Leo was vigorously leathering the Saab. He wore Harry's gum boots, and the sleeves of his guernsey sweater were rolled up, revealing strong, pale arms.

'Mm.' Susan was flicking through a colour supplement. 'Doesn't like sitting still. Doesn't read much. Likes to be up and doing,' she said. 'He's very physical. He'll probably want to go for a walk when he's done the car.'

Dorothea would have liked a sleep herself. Her eyes felt dry and hot, the eyelids heavy. She piled a log on the fire. 'He's nice,' she offered.

'Mm.'

Dorothea sighed. She remembered other young men who had been produced: there was a suave one in advertising whose manners had been just too good, and during whose brief reign Susan had her naturally wavy hair done Afro style and taken to wearing tall boots and skin-tight pants with a bright green belted shirt, looking, her mother thought, like a fugitive from Sherwood Forest. She had reverted, now, to what still seemed uniform – blue jeans and a bulky sweater, with her hair falling softly to her shoulders. She looked very pretty. Dorothea wondered if she was happy; she wanted to mention it, but feared to be intrusive.

'It's kind of him to do the car,' she said. Leo seemed to her like a puppy, eager to please, and full of energy that might explode if it were to be suppressed.

When the car was done, just as Susan had foretold, Leo suggested a walk. The sun broke faintly through the clouds as they set off over the garden and climbed the fence into the field beyond, to join the public footpath, which linked up eventually by means of stiles with Church Lane.

'Why don't you get a dog?' asked Leo, who had a problem over what to call Dorothea. Somehow he could not bring himself to use her first name, though instructed to do so, yet addressing her as Mrs Wyatt seemed so formal. So far, he'd managed not to call her anything. Dorothea had noticed his difficulty; it had not been shared by Susan's other young men and it made her feel antique.

'They're a tie,' she answered. She'd had a spaniel which, old and smelly, had had to be put down shortly after Harry died. She'd had no heart to get another.

'You could take it for walks,' Leo persisted.

'It's a good idea, Mummy,' said Susan, who had already thought simply of appearing with a puppy.

'I'll think about it,' Dorothea said. 'When the summer comes.' A puppy would need training. She could not tell Susan that sometimes she slept so heavily, and so late, that a puppy might whimper for a long time and be unheard.

Striding out in her green wellingtons, she resolved to pull herself together when the summer came. She'd cut out the gin and take up some healthy sport: swimming perhaps, or even tennis; she was not too old. There was a club in Tellingford. But she knew she wouldn't really do it.

When they climbed the stile into Church Lane and worked their way back to the High Street, they met other walkers out enjoying the thin winter sunshine. There were parents with children in pushchairs and dawdling toddlers, and new babies snug in prams.

'I don't know any of these people,' Susan said.

'Nor do I, really,' said her mother, who had been replying to friendly 'Hullos' from some of them, and smiling at others whom she recognized from shopping trips in the village. 'They're from the new estates,' she told Leo. 'People have been selling off their gardens, and up spring bright brick boxes. Crowbury is growing.'

'It's a smart place to live if you work in Tellingford or Middletown,' said Susan.

'I like seeing them about,' said Dorothea. 'The young people.'

But they made her feel old. It was so long since Susan and Mark had been pram-bound, and she rarely saw Mark's children, so the solace of granny-dom she'd heard lauded by contemporaries was not really hers; though she was fond of the children, she didn't know them properly as individuals. Besides, the fact of their existence emphasized her conviction that life had no more to offer her of her own. Maybe it would be different when Susan married and had a family. But she might move further away even than Yorkshire: Saudi Arabia, for example. Leo, however, seemed firmly rooted in his city bank; it made her warm to him as a potential suitor, and he seemed to be a kind young man.

Susan paused to gaze into the window of Nanron Antiques. 'Bought anything from here lately, Mummy?' she asked.

'Not since you last came home,' Dorothea said.

Could she ever go into the shop again? It would be too much for Mr Trimm; he'd be horribly embarrassed. Besides, his wife might be there, that neat woman with the helmet of hair, every strand in place. She had thinly plucked eyebrows and wore shiny dark lipstick. Dorothea wondered fleetingly how Mr

Trimm enjoyed kissing that sticky-looking mouth. He had kissed rather nicely, as she recalled. She'd enjoyed it all at the time.

What would these young people think, if they knew? She laughed at the idea.

'What's the joke?' Susan asked.

'Oh, nothing,' said Dorothea.

'Does the shop do well?' asked Leo.

'Seems to,' said Dorothea. 'It's been here for ages.'

'I wonder what his turnover is,' said Leo.

'Oh Leo, how soulless you are,' said Susan. 'He can't go anywhere, Mummy, without wondering how much capital there is behind a thing, and if it's running at a profit.'

To Dorothea, this didn't sound like a character defect at all. Leo would be a safe provider as a husband. But Susan showed no sign of wanting one; she earned a good salary herself, working with a multi-national oil company.

They walked on, and met a running figure dressed in black.

'It's George, isn't it?' said Susan. 'Does he even jog on Sunday?'

'It seems so,' said Dorothea. 'Hullo, George,' she called, as the runner approached.

The black figure slowed and began running on the spot; his breath clouded round him in the clear air.

'Leo Kent – George Fortescue,' Dorothea introduced. 'We didn't think you did this mad thing on Sundays.'

'Oh yes, unless I'm playing golf,' said George. 'My partner cried off today.' He went on marking time.

45

'Must keep going, Dorothea, if you'll excuse me,' he panted.

'Don't let us stop you,' said Dorothea. 'Come in for tea, though, if you like, on your way back.'

'Thanks, I will,' said George, and went pounding on.

'He'll undo all the good of his jogging, having tea,' said Susan.

'He won't. He says he can eat like a horse and never put on an ounce, with all that exercise,' said Dorothea.

'You should try it,' said Susan to Leo, hitting him gently in the stomach. Leo was quite well fleshed.

'I get my workout on the squash court,' said Leo repressively. 'Isn't he getting on a bit for jogging, though? Your friend? He might have a heart attack.'

He shouldn't have said this: Susan's father had died of one. But the women took the comment calmly.

'He does it to fill in time,' said Dorothea.

She and Susan gave Leo the details of George's domestic history as they walked home.

'Maybe she'll come back?' said Leo. 'His wife.'

'She was bored to tears with him,' said Dorothea. 'He's a dull man, but I'm very sorry for him. He's lonely and he feels humiliated. He left Angela on her own a lot, with all his meetings and things. I don't think they could talk properly to one another. I miss Angela.' They'd sometimes had coffee together, or snack lunches, putting the world to rights. But Dorothea was surprised when Angela left.

They had a cheerful time at tea. There was a packet

46

of crumpets in the freezer, and there were some scones and blackcurrant jam. George ate four crumpets and Leo ate two, and they finished all the scones and a packet of bourbon biscuits.

Susan and Leo left for London directly afterwards, and George, in his tracksuit still, begged a lift the short distance to Orchard House; he was stiffening up; it was a mistake to have had tea before his shower.

Dorothea was alone again by six o'clock.

5

On Monday evening, Ronald Trimm stood expectantly on the Manor doorstep, listening to the jangling of the bell.

He'd gone home first and had his meal: curry, it was, made with leftovers from the Sunday roast. Afterwards, he went upstairs and cleaned his teeth thoroughly, to make sure no spicy flavour lingered, then ran a hand over his jaw. It was stubbly; she'd mentioned, jokingly he thought, his five o'clock shadow, last time. He swept his electric razor swiftly, guiltily, over his chin, wondering what to say if Nancy caught him. But she didn't. She was washing up.

He'd told her he would be going to look at Mrs Wyatt's bureau, and she'd made no demur beyond saying, 'I hope she won't expect you there often, Ronald. There's plenty to do here, in the evening.' There were always the repairs; she sometimes persuaded him to do the simpler part like stripping old glue from badly mended ceramics.

'I know, dear, and I don't like to leave you, but it's doing her a favour, you know. She does buy. I watch out for jugs she might care for, and she always buys them.'

'Yes – well, don't let her take advantage of your good nature,' Nancy warned.

He shot out of the house now, in case she noticed he had changed his shirt.

'I'll not be long,' he said.

The Manor doorstep was made of stone hollowed by the tread of centuries. Ronald waited patiently. The lights were on in the house, and the garage doors were closed, so he thought she must be in; the doors of the garage had been open when he brought her home on Friday. Only two days had passed since then! It seemed an age away. He rang again.

After some time, a light came on above his head, the bulb mounted in an old iron lantern. Then the door was opened a fraction, held back on a chain. Dorothea peered through the gap.

'Who is it?' she asked.

Ardent and eager, Ronald stepped closer.

'It's me – it's I – Mrs Wyatt – Dorothea—' He hovered, changing his weight from one foot to the other, searching for the right words. He'd been rehearsing on the way over but forgot his prepared speech now. She'd unfasten the chain in seconds, pull the door wide and enfold him to her. In his mind he'd anticipated the moment many times since Friday. Tonight he'd need no coaxing; his passion would amaze her. He stood there, feeling it mount.

But the door opened no further.

'I can't see you now, Mr Trimm. You must go

49

away,' said Dorothea. She had recognized her caller with a shock of sick dismay.

'But Mrs Wyatt – Dorothea – we – I—' Ronald floundered, unbelieving.

'You must go away,' said Dorothea again. She hadn't expected this. She must stop it at once; a curt response and he'd get the message. 'How dare you call like this, without an invitation? What are you thinking of?' she said, and closed the door.

Ronald stood there, staring at the ancient, faded oak. The outer light went out. He raised his fists and beat against the door, calling her name again, incredulous. How could she speak to him like that after what had happened?

He should have telephoned first. Perhaps she had someone with her. That must be the explanation. He'd apologize and arrange another time. He rang again.

The door remained shut. He heard music in the background; she'd turned the radio up loud. Her harsh words echoed in his head.

In the end he drove away. As he turned out of the gate, he picked up a lone figure in his headlights, loping towards him: that jogging Mr Fortescue.

Perhaps she was expecting him to call. He'd be let in, all right. He lived in Orchard House, not a bungalow in Tellingford. He went to London every day and didn't keep a shop. He drove a Rover, not a shabby van. The stuck-up bitch! But he'd been good enough for her ladyship on Friday evening, when she was feeling randy and was all set to make a spectacle of herself in the Plough.

Such behaviour! It was quite disgusting.

He couldn't go straight home; Nancy would know something was wrong. He drove about for an hour, heedless of where he went, round lanes and by-ways, cursing aloud some of the time, more angry and distressed than he ever remembered being in his life.

When at last he turned into Sycamore Road he saw a couple standing under a tree near his own bungalow. They were tightly clinched, but drew apart as the headlights of the van fell upon them. The girl, the boy's arms still round her, turned her face, and Ronald saw that it was Lynn. His heart gave a lurch. That was Peter with her, he supposed, a boy, still a schoolboy, who was sometimes waiting for her on a Saturday, when he brought her back from the shop. Hilda and Keith approved of him, Ronald knew, and let Lynn go out with him; yet look at the pair of them now, carrying on for all the world to see.

It was everywhere; all around – even that lovely little Lynn knew all about it. Only he, Ronald Trimm, had been sold short.

But Lynn was just a child.

Ronald made a business of locking the garage door before entering the bungalow, to give himself time to calm down. Nancy would notice, if he seemed upset.

'It's all right,' Lynn was saying to Peter, in the road. 'It's only Uncle Ron.' She kissed him again, lightly, on the mouth, and then ran in to her own home. They'd been at a rehearsal for the school production of *The Tempest*, in which she was involved with the scenery and stage-management. Peter, with homework to do, had no time to come in this evening for a cup of tea, as he often did when he brought her home.

She thought no more about it.

Nancy took care of the shop the next day while Ronald went to an auction. It was an executor's sale held in a large old house some miles beyond Fletcham, the county town, and he had marked down some furniture likely to go cheaply, as well as several boxes of oddments, the sort of things with which Nancy had begun her stall and which could still be sold profitably as individual items. Now that stripped furniture was so popular, he bought chests, chairs and cupboards that were unsuitable for dipping in a caustic bath because they were made of oak, which would discolour, or were glued and so would fall apart. He paid Valerie Turner a fraction of what it would cost to have them dipped to strip these things by hand.

It was hard work, as Ronald knew; he had done it himself until Valerie came into the shop one day with a plated teapot she wanted to sell. She had been disappointed at the price he offered, and he had realized that she needed money badly. At the time she came in, he was waxing a newly stripped chest; she admired it and a few minutes later she had agreed to take over the work. At first she was very slow, but that did not worry Ronald since he paid her by the item. She had two young children and wanted work that she could do at home and in her own time; there was a brick garage, once a stable, at Primrose Cottage, where she lived on the outskirts of the village, and that became her workshop. Ronald's own time was better spent visiting dealers or sales than stripping furniture.

Driving to Fletcham in time to view the items he had marked in the sale catalogue, Ronald still burned with anger at his treatment from Dorothea the previous evening. He'd heard young men in the Plough talking about bored young wives on housing estates. You had a fine time if you were a well-set-up young representative, calling in the afternoon; you could take your pick, he'd learned. The young men would laugh about it, and Ronald had joined in, trying to show camaraderie, declaring envy. Not all the eager ladies were so young, he'd been told, slyly.

It was the truth. And if Dorothea Wyatt could behave like that, so could others.

He enjoyed the sale. He always did. There was a thrill in bidding quietly, up to his limit, not a penny more, and finding his judgement so precise. He had a feel for things, there was no doubt of that; Nancy had said so, all those years ago when she first tutored him. The auctioneers knew him now and were ready for his bids. At first he'd driven straight home, eager to show Nancy what he'd bought and win her approval, but then he found other dealers would stop off for a beer on the way back, and he began to do it too. He liked snatching time when he was accountable to no one. Nancy never went to sales with him, for she had to be in the shop.

Ronald wore a muffler today that Nancy had knitted. She always had knitting on hand to do when not otherwise busy; she had made Ronald several warm garments and had a small stock of gloves and caps and scarves for when she was asked for donations by organizers of charity bazaars. Ronald knotted his muffler and tucked it into his jacket after writing his cheque to the auctioneer. Then he began loading the van.

There was a woman in a dark green leather coat at the sale; she seemed to be a dealer, but Ronald had not seen her before. She bid against him several times, and bought a small oak chest with a damaged back that Ronald had been after, outbidding him by only two pounds. He, however, had outbid her for a walnut veneered writing box. If they clashed again, it might be worth their while to get together. Ronald saw her packing the disputed chest carefully into her Cortina estate.

She came up to him just as he was about to start the van, and mentioned the writing box. She wished she had gone on. She smiled, saying this. She was a small woman with very fair hair worn rather long.

'Well, I'm open to offers,' said Ronald.

She named a price which would give him a small profit.

'Very well,' he said. 'But it's packed in one of the chests I've got in here. It'll take me a few minutes to unload the van.'

'Oh dear,' she said.

A week ago he would never have done it, but the new Ronald had more nerve and this was an attractive woman.

'Why don't we stop and seal our bargain over a drink?' he suggested. There was a pub down the road where some of the buyers had gone for lunch, though Ronald himself had sandwiches made by Nancy, and his flask of coffee.

The woman hesitated and looked at her watch.

'Is it really right inside the van?' she asked.

'Yes. I'll have to get everything out,' said Ronald.

Vans and cars were moving all round them as the sale packed up; the auctioneers had almost finished; her Cortina was already blocking the way for another car.

'Do you go through Fletcham?' she asked.

'Yes.'

'Would you mind stopping off at my place, then? It's only just off the main road. I've got to get home,' she explained.

'Certainly,' said Ronald. 'Shall I follow you?'

'Please,' said the woman.

She got into her car, and Ronald, who was ahead of her, drove slowly off, pulling into the side of the drive to allow her to pass when she came up behind him. She drove rather fast, and he had to push his old van to keep on her tail as they travelled along the twisty lane towards the main road.

She turned off at traffic lights on the outskirts of Fletcham and he followed her through several residential streets until she turned again, this time into an estate of small new houses, where she stopped outside one of them. Number 7, Ronald noticed. He had expected to be led to her shop. Maybe she didn't have one, but operated from home. Plenty of dealers did.

'I'll go ahead – you come in when you've got the

box out,' she said, and hurried up the path to the house.

By the light of a nearby street lamp, Ronald took out most of his load, found the box, and replaced everything else. Then he walked to her front door, which he found on the latch.

It was a clear invitation to enter, which he did, with the box.

The narrow hall was carpeted in dark green, the carpet continuing up the stairs. There was a small Regency mirror on the wall, over a folding-top mahogany card table. Ronald saw framed prints above the staircase.

'On your right – go in – I won't be a minute,' called the woman. Her voice came from upstairs.

Ronald went into a sitting room which, though tiny, reminded him of Mrs Wyatt's. There were long apricot-coloured curtains at the window and good rugs on the floor. He saw a mahogany Pembroke table and two nice rosewood chairs. There were more prints on the wall. He was looking at them when she came in.

'Sorry about all that,' she said. She had taken off her coat and was wearing a white polo-necked sweater. She bent to switch on an electric fire in the grate. 'The heating's come on but it hasn't really warmed up yet. Now, that cheque. But a drink first.'

She crossed to a bow-fronted cupboard from which she took two sherry glasses and a bottle of Harvey's Amontillado. When she had poured each of them a glassful, she took a cheque book and ballpoint pen from her handbag, and sat on the small velvet-upholstered settee which faced the fireplace.

'Who shall I make it out to?' she asked.

Ronald told her.

The cheque was soon written, and she held it out to him. Ronald took it and put it in his pocket without looking at it. Then, with barely an instant's hesitation, he sat on the settee beside her, and raised his glass.

'Cheers,' he said.

He posed no obvious threat as she stretched her legs out. She wore dark corduroy trousers and tan boots.

'I'm tired,' she said. 'I always enjoy a sale, but it's nerve-racking. Still, I'm pleased with today. I'm glad I've got that box.'

'I think we came out about evenly, all told,' said Ronald. 'We seem interested in the same things.'

'Yes.'

'We must have an understanding, if we clash again,' he said, regarding her over his glass. She was gazing ahead at the electric fire, but she had invited him into her house and they were alone.

'I've just moved down here from London,' she said. 'I've got a shop in the town but I've had a bit of trouble getting reliable help for when I have to go to sales and things. My partner has a job and can't help.'

'I see.' Ronald saw her partner as another woman like herself, perhaps dabbling in antiques as a hobby before retirement. This woman was older than he'd thought; the fair hair was, in fact, greying, and her thin hands were veined.

He thought back to last Friday. They had sat on the sofa together, just like this.

Ronald put down his glass, now empty, and carefully laid his right hand on her thigh. That was how Dorothea Wyatt had begun.

In less than two seconds she had lifted it off, not roughly but extremely firmly, and was standing up.

'I have to go out now,' she said. 'And you must go. Goodbye.' She looked at him hard, not smiling any more and suddenly looking a great deal older and very stern.

'Well – yes—' Ronald's voice was a croak. His heart thumped and he felt a hot choking feeling in his throat. 'Goodbye.'

He almost ran from the room and out of the house.

Felicity Cartwright closed the front door after him and leaned against it.

'Phew!' she said aloud and, safe now, began to laugh. Fool, she berated herself, for taking him at face value. He certainly seemed harmless enough. Perhaps it was a compliment to be thought worthy of a pass at her age.

She finished her sherry, poured another, and went into the kitchen to see how the oven was doing. The automatic timer had gone wrong and that was why she had been in a hurry to get home. A casserole was warming up, and soon her partner, Hugo Morton, whose wife was crippled with arthritis, would be here to share it with her. He had been her lover now for twelve years. She wouldn't tell him what had happened.

Ronald had to make several attempts to start the van, he was so put out. She'd seemed as though she wanted it, like the women those other men talked

58

about, but then she'd turned haughty. He was in a very bad temper by the time he reached home and read her name on the cheque.

6

Dorothea knew that she had behaved badly, but she had also been inept. Mr Trimm, after all, had good reason to expect a welcome. When he rang the doorbell she had been alarmed, for she was not expecting a caller and did not like opening the door in the dark. It had been an anti-climax to find Mr Trimm on the doorstep and her immediate reaction was anger. The next day she thought it rather comic; he had obviously expected to carry on where they left off on Friday.

Idly, she played with the idea of an intrigue with Mr Trimm. How the village would enjoy it, and they'd be sure to discover if he parked his van at her door, or even came and went on foot. In fact, two and two would be made into five even if the visits were innocent. But she did not want her name and Mr Trimm's linked by gossip. Dorothea had a feeling that she had been more than a little sloshed in the Plough that evening; she had been there alone before, when very depressed, but hadn't overstepped the mark, as far as she knew. Mr Trimm had driven her home in her own car so he may have saved her from

60

disgracing herself. At any rate, he didn't deserve the treatment she had given him; she'd heard him pounding the door after his dismissal.

She must make some sort of amends.

On Tuesday morning, after her usual slow start to the day while her head cleared, she went up to the village on foot. She called at the butcher's and the greengrocer's, and then sauntered on to the antique shop. Peering through the window, she saw Mrs Trimm, neat in her pinafore, inside. She was polishing something.

Dorothea smiled and waved in vague greeting. Mrs Trimm graciously inclined her smoothly coiffured head.

Dorothea moved on. She could not see Mr Trimm in the background, but anyway it would be a mistake to go into the shop while his wife was there; he might be even more embarrassed. She'd call another day.

On Wednesdays, Ronald made his regular calls on Will Noakes, the cabinet-maker, and Valerie Turner who did the paint-stripping. Sometimes he went further afield to see dealers, and then Nancy would go early to the shop, but if it was an easier day she would come out on the midday bus in time to join him for lunchtime closing. She would bring cold beef and pickles, or a home-made pie of some kind, to make a change from sandwiches, and would brew coffee in the scullery. She liked this time together with him and would catch up on the morning's news.

He looked tired today, she noted, inquiring how the morning had gone.

'Someone was asking about that yew dresser,' Ronald told her. 'I don't know if she was really serious. Said she'd ask her husband.'

'Who was it?'

'No one I recognized. A young woman with a couple of children.'

She'd left her children in the car, and they'd shrieked and blown the horn. The woman had been tall, long-legged. Ronald had imagined touching her as she stooped to open the dresser drawers, jeans tight on her slender thighs. She was too lean, too tall, too pert – that was the word for her, he had decided, whilst replying politely to her remarks. She had a wide mouth and good teeth.

He noticed them all. He could have given an accurate, detailed description of every woman customer, whether he'd made a sale or not.

He liked the older ones, the ones who were less aggressive, more assured. In the magazines, those exciting young ones with the pouting lips looked as if they might eat you.

The business with Will Noakes was soon done. Ronald delivered some of the things he had bought the day before which needed attention, and collected what was ready. Will had made a good job of fitting a new leg to a mahogany cupboard. He'd matched a missing strip of inlay on a small table, too. He was a skilled craftsman; it was Nancy who had found him, hearing another dealer talking about him, and had persuaded him to work for them although he was already very busy.

Valerie Turner, rather less satisfactory, was not one

of her discoveries, and she often fell behind with the work.

Today, a chest for which Ronald already had a buyer wasn't ready.

'I'm sorry, Ronald,' she said. She'd asked him to call her by her first name as soon as she began working for him, and responded the same way. He liked it, though it made rebuking her less easy. 'Timmy's had earache,' she explained. 'He's been at home for a week and I can't really get much done when he's around.' The garage was cold, though there was a paraffin heater; some of the materials she used were inflammable and the caustics were dangerous, so the children were allowed in the garage only when she was sanding and polishing and all her other equipment was stacked safely on a shelf above their heads.

'I've got a customer for it, Valerie,' said Ronald. 'She's coming in tomorrow.'

'Oh, I'm sorry. Look, I'll finish it tonight, when the children are in bed,' she said. 'I really will, Ronald.'

Things weren't easy for her, with the two children to manage and no husband, Ronald reflected.

'I'll come and pick it up tomorrow, then,' he said. He mustn't relent, though he could easily put the customer off for a day or two.

'I'm going to see my parents tomorrow,' said Valerie. Her mother had recently had a serious operation, and her father had retired early because of a heart attack. They lived in Middletown. 'I'll leave the garage unlocked and then you can just come in and take it.'

'All right,' said Ronald. No wonder she never had things done in time if she allowed herself to be deflected by visits to her parents. She wasn't well organized. He'd been in the house for a cup of tea once, finding it shabby and cluttered up with children's toys. He'd got jam on his sleeve. 'I've got some more for you,' he said. 'I'll bring it all in.'

'I'll help you,' she said, and pulled off the stained rubber gloves she wore to protect herself from the strong chemicals. The sleeves of her thick sweater were rolled up, and her forearms were white and rounded.

Ronald looked at them as they laboured together, carrying in the things he had bought at Fletcham, his own hands warm in his leather gloves.

She wasn't stuck up, like Mrs Wyatt or that woman yesterday. And she lived alone, apart from two small children.

Nancy fried cod for their meal that night. On Wednesday afternoons a mobile fishmonger parked in the church square, and mothers collecting their children from school would call at the sea-green van, with its name, The Lobster, painted on the side. Nancy would go out as soon as it drew up, when there wasn't a queue, and be back in time for the two o'clock opening of the shop. Wednesday afternoons were seldom busy, as the other shops were closed, and she was able to polish the silver and do whatever else in the way of cleaning was required, apart from the floor, which she did after locking the door at five thirty. Ronald would come for her soon after that, his visits done and specialist sales concluded with other dealers.

Tonight he was not hungry, and had a struggle to finish his fish. He did not want to upset her by leaving it.

'Not out of sorts, are you, dear?' Nancy frowned, remembering he had not looked himself that morning.

'No – no. I've got a bit of a headache, as a matter of fact,' said Ronald.

'I hope you haven't caught a cold.' He might have, at yesterday's sale; he'd seemed tired when he came home, and had less to say about it than usual. 'Better gargle tonight,' she told him. If Ronald fell sick, the business would suffer for, though she could manage the shop, she couldn't get round the dealers, and that was how money was made.

While she was washing up, he went into the workroom where, among other things at varying stages of repair, there was a lustre jug Mrs Wyatt might like. Its handle needed rebuilding but Nancy would make it like new. He picked it up, suddenly wanting to hurl it across the room and smash it into tiny fragments. But he set it down again, the impulse suppressed; an act of such violence cost money, and would have to be explained in some way to Nancy as an accident.

Women were such cheats. Those girls in the magazines, spread out so shamelessly, would clamp their legs together and say no, like Nancy, if you met one of them and tried to touch her. Dorothea Wyatt hadn't, but she'd been drunk. He pictured her lying on her big, soft bed. Felicity Cartwright, in her neat Fletcham house the evening before, had sprawled on the settee, trousered legs stretched out. Valerie Turner had exposed bare, soft arms; she had wide hips in shrunken, faded jeans. They were cheats, all of them, blatantly setting out to seduce and then crying 'Hands off!' All women were the same, even little Lynn in her Orlon sweater and pleated skirt, promising all sorts of things to young Peter and leading him on, and then when he couldn't hold back any more she'd cry 'No'. Maybe they'd let you, once or twice, but that was only to gain power; that was what they wanted: power over you, the man.

Valerie Turner would be working in her garage now. She'd be finishing that chest, sanding it down, the stripping done. She'd be dressed in that sagging old sweater she always wore; he could swear she hadn't a stitch on underneath.

Ronald went into the kitchen. Nancy was putting away the last spoon. She never let Ronald help her; she didn't like to see a man with a tea towel in his hand.

'Would you mind if I went for a little spin in the van, dear?' he asked. 'It might clear my head.'

She might offer to come with him. He almost hoped she would.

'Oh, do you think that's wise? Wouldn't an early night and a couple of aspirins be a better idea?' said Nancy. 'Poor dear, is it bad?'

'Just a nasty throb,' said Ronald, and it was true. What had been an excuse had become fact: his head was pounding.

'Well – wrap up well,' said Nancy. 'And don't be long.'

'I won't,' said Ronald.

He went into the bathroom and washed his hands very carefully. In the bedroom, he looked among his clothes, and took out a woollen scarf and the bala-clava helmet Nancy had knitted for him to wear in the garden when it was very cold. It was dark purple, almost black. He removed his shirt and tie and put the shirt in the linen basket. Then he pulled on a black roll-neck sweater and replaced his corduroy jacket. He wore the scarf but he pushed the helmet inside the jacket, against his body.

'Just off, dear,' he called in the hall. She might still come.

But Nancy had some ironing to do. Ten minutes later Ronald was in Crowbury.

Valerie had read to Timmy and Melissa after their baths, and answered demands for an extra kiss. She had refused biscuits or sweets in bed because the children had cleaned their teeth. At last they settled, and she did the day's washing-up, watched by Truffles the spaniel from his basket.

She must finish that chest for Ronald Trimm. He was coming to collect it next day. If she went on being late with things, he'd stop bringing them. The work was satisfying in that the pieces of furniture looked good when she had done them; she liked to see them, pale and gleaming, and run her hand over the smooth, sanded wood. At first she'd sandpapered them by hand, but now she had an electric sander which, in her own view anyway, gave a more even finish. She liked that part. What she didn't enjoy so much was daubing them with stripper; scraping off curling paint; rubbing with wire wool after washing the pieces down with methylated spirit. It all smelled a great deal, and there were piles of waste which had to be disposed of carefully because they would so easily catch fire. She wrapped them up, first in newspaper and then in polythene bags, and the dustmen removed them with her other garbage. She was afraid of bonfires, with the thatch, though she cautiously burned garden rubbish on still days, water handy in a can and bucket.

What she would really like to do that evening would be to watch an undemanding programme on the television and perhaps be made to laugh by some cheerful character on the screen. She shouldn't be working for Ronald at all; if she had any true initiative, she would seek out these tatty bits of furniture herself, and sell them for her own profit when she'd tarted them up, not someone else's. But she had no transport to go and find them in, nor any spare cash to invest in making such purchases.

She rented the cottage from Bob Mount of Fell Farm, further along the lane. He'd had the thatch mended but, when the cold water cistern began to leak, it was her responsibility to pay for a replacement. There was always some expense, from shoes for the children to a new element for the electric kettle. Bob was very good; he'd let her have logs from diseased elms cut down on the farm at a very cheap rate, and the rent was, by current standards, not excessive; but he wasn't a charity and she didn't expect special consideration. Other women were in a much worse plight than she was; Nigel at least paid something for the children.

On cold winter nights, like this one, with an empty purse and the thought of difficult years stretching ahead until the children were grown up, Valerie could be reduced easily to tears. But, when the weather was good and the children well and cheerful, she was often happy. The ship she sailed was small and patched, but it was her own. She no longer had to pose as the sophisticated wife of a sharp executive on his rapid way to the top. No longer need she try to keep her weight down while giving smart dinner parties for people Nigel was eager to know. He had found the right sort of wife the second time round, one who would enjoy administering the material possessions he was steadily acquiring – the large house with the two-acre garden and swimming pool, and the kitchen straight out of a magazine, according to Melissa. He'd end up as chairman of the company.

With all this, it was a great pity he didn't hand on more to her. How could she have a well-paid job herself, when she had to be at home for the children? She wouldn't turn them into latch-key kids. His payments were often late, as well as meagre; she suspected she had been outsmarted over the arrangements.

Timmy and Melissa enjoyed visiting their father. They liked the big garden and the swimming pool, and they seemed quite fond of their father's new children, twin boys. Perhaps, one day, they would find the contrast too great, and prefer the splendours of Sunningdale to the simplicities of Crowbury.

Sighing, she went to the garage. Truffles raised his head as she passed his basket, gave a wag of his tail, and decided to stay where he was.

'Sensible fellow,' she told him.

Her father had given her the sander. At first she'd run it from an extension lead plugged into the kitchen but, as the days grew shorter, she had had to have the garage wired. Bob Mount had made no objection. His wife, Pearl, and Valerie had grown quite friendly through meeting at the school, and the children played together sometimes now. Pearl often picked Timmy and Melissa up in the mornings, and Valerie tried to repay this kindness by collecting all of them some afternoons. You got prickly, she had noticed, about accepting benefits when it was difficult to make some return.

A single powerful bulb hung on a flex from the tiled roof of the garage. The chests, cupboards and chairs waiting for Valerie's attention stood about, casting shadows. Valerie had her back turned to the door, the noisy sander in both hands, pressing it on the top of the chest she was finishing, moving it round and round, the fine dust flying.

Standing outside, he could hear the noise. Carefully, gingerly, he lifted the latch and pulled the door towards him. He peered round and saw her, her arms moving, her legs braced a little apart, quite unaware. He stepped inside and closed the door.

He'd pulled the chin part of the balaclava up over

the lower part of his face, the brow bit down to his eyes. Then he'd wound the scarf round even his nose. His corduroy jacket was in the van which was parked off the road in a copse down the lane. This one was going to say yes, and no mistake. He'd stopped at the shop on the way and collected a large folding knife with a bone handle which he kept in his desk for odd tasks like cutting twine. The knife was in his hand now, the blade exposed. He'd given no thought at all to what would happen afterwards; he was intent upon just one thing: getting hold of the girl.

Screaming wouldn't help her, Ronald thought exultantly, with the sander making such a din. He needn't try to stop her mouth. He wanted both his hands.

Valerie felt heart-stopping terror as sudden pressure on her shoulder forced her down over the chest, the sander jerking away from her and crashing to the ground. She drew breath to scream, and saw a knife held before her face. She tried to twist away and to kick out at her attacker, but the man stood up against her, stronger, by far, than she was.

She heard the sander whirring on through all that happened as she fought and struggled; she could see it on the floor when she stopped resisting because he threatened to hurt the children.

7

It was all over very quickly. When he had gone, leaving the garage doors open to the night and the cold air, Valerie could not move. She thought she was literally going to die of fright as her heart pounded and fluttered and then thudded in her ears. The sander was still whirring away, lying on the floor, and at last she managed to make the effort to reach the switch and turn it off. Her mind fixed on a single thought: the children. The cottage was unlocked; he could have gone in there first, before attacking her. Truffles was more likely to have greeted him with a wagging tail than fierce snarls.

He'd torn her jeans. Clutching them round her, arms across her belly, she staggered into the cottage and stumbled upstairs to the children's rooms. But they were safe, asleep. Melissa clasped her ancient teddy and was surrounded by her animal family; Timmy had a small fire engine tucked against his cheek.

Valerie had been too shocked to weep, but now tears filled her eyes as the agonizing terror she had felt began to subside. She blinked them back and blundered across the landing into the bathroom and sat on the lavatory, rocking to and fro and moaning to herself. Then she remembered that the cottage was unlocked; he might return. Somehow she dragged herself to her feet and, clutching the wall at the side of the stairs, groped her way down again. She thrust home the bolts at the front and the back doors. She was trembling now, her teeth chattering. Her throat tightened with nausea and, leaning over the kitchen sink, she vomited up her supper.

She stood upright at last, and her gaze fell on the automatic clock on the electric cooker. She felt as though hours had passed, but it was still only half-past eight.

She shivered with shock, her body cold: dirty.

Who would help her? What should she do?

The police, she thought. They must be told. But the cottage was not on the telephone and to ring them she must walk either to Fell Farm, or up the village to the box in the High Street. He might be lurking in the lane, waiting to pounce again. She couldn't do it. Anyway, she couldn't leave the children.

When at last it seemed that the sickness had passed, she struggled upstairs again and into the bathroom, where she turned on the hot tap and poured into the bath all that was left of a bottle of Dettol. As the water ran, she pulled off her clothes and left them where they lay on the floor, climbing into the bath while it filled. Fiercely she scrubbed herself, every crevice and cranny. When that was done, she ran the water out and refilled the bath until it ran cold, then washed again, and this time

73

submerged her head and washed her hair. She was sure she would never feel clean again.

The shivering had eased with the warmth, but now, as the water cooled, it began again, and she got out and began to dry her poor violated body. She still moaned softly to herself. She hurt.

Slowly she dressed in fresh clothes, loose old wool trousers and another worn sweater. She went on uttering small moans, her body bent over like an old woman's. She combed her wet hair, then went downstairs. Truffles came to sniff at her legs and she patted him absently. The fire in the sitting room was almost out, but there were dry logs stacked in the hearth and she knelt before it, building it up, coaxing it back to life with the bellows, while Truffles lay down nearby. His company was consoling. When the fire was going, she pulled up her chair and lowered herself gingerly into it. She still felt cold, so she got up again and put on her padded anorak.

Brandy for shock, she thought vaguely. She'd bought a small bottle, because she was afraid of her father having another heart attack when he was visiting them. She poured some of it into a glass, and as she sipped it she began to feel steadier.

For a long time she sat there by the fire, getting up now and then to add a log. Whom could she turn to? What should be done? Oddly, she thought of Nigel, but he would not want to hear her troubles in the morning when he was at the office and negotiating, no doubt, a major deal. She could never tell her parents.

The police, she thought again. They'd have to know. But he hadn't killed her. The initial soreness was easing and she did not think she had been really damaged physically. That part was over very fast; terrified though she was, she had realized that it was very brief.

In the morning she had to catch the bus to visit her parents as soon as the children had gone to school; if she cancelled the visit, her parents would need an explanation. The police would have to wait.

She went upstairs and collected the clothes she had been wearing when it happened. She dropped them on the fire where, with a great deal of smoke and an acrid smell, she succeeded in burning them, except for the metal zip from her jeans. Then she scrubbed the bathroom floor where they had lain. After that she fetched the quilt from her bed, stoked up the fire again, and sat in the chair once more with the quilt over her knees.

Towards dawn, she wept, bitterly.

Ronald was only out a little over an hour and, when he returned, Nancy was pleased to see that he seemed brighter. She made some tea later, before they went to bed, and he ate a digestive biscuit. He'd just driven around, he said, and his head had cleared.

He fell asleep within a few minutes of getting into bed. Nancy heard his heavy peaceful breathing, and rolled over herself, in her long-sleeved brushed-nylon nightgown, with her hair skewered under a shiny green net.

The next morning, Ronald felt marvellous. He whistled as he opened the garage, though it was raining and cold. He was in time to catch Lynn before she reached the bus stop on the corner; he often picked her up and gave her a lift to school. She sat beside him, chatting away.

'Seeing that boyfriend of yours tonight, are you?' he asked her genially.

'I see him every day at school,' she said. 'You know that.'

'What's he going to do when he leaves?' asked Ronald.

'He wants to be an engineer,' said Lynn. 'He's good at that sort of thing – mechanical things. He's doing the lighting for the play. We've got a rehearsal tonight.'

'Oh, so you'll be late home, then?'

'Not very, Uncle Ron,' said Lynn.

'How will engineering go with your artistic plans?' Ronald asked. 'Bit different, isn't it?'

'Oh, goodness, I don't know!' Lynn was laughing. 'Peter and I may hate each other in a few years. Who knows? I hope we don't,' she added. 'Only it happens, doesn't it?'

'I suppose it does,' agreed Ronald. 'Your Auntie Nancy and I have been very lucky. And your mother and father, too, of course.'

'Yes.' Marriage was weird, Lynn thought; fancy living with the same person for twenty years! Even for fifty, maybe! She couldn't imagine how one faced the prospect.

Ronald dropped her outside the school gate and watched her join a group of young people walking through. She wore thick navy knee-length socks over her tights; she was very slim. That girl last night was plump; she had felt soft. That part had been nice.

Driving on to Crowbury, he wondered briefly what she would have done after he left. Had she told the police? The thought gave him some uneasiness, but there was nothing that could lead them to him. The knife was under the seat of the van, with the balaclava and scarf. He hadn't worn gloves, but he'd touched nothing; only the girl's clothes and her body. He'd used the point of the knife to unlatch the door and ease it open. His prints would anyway be legitimately in the garage, because he went there regularly. There was nothing to fear.

Besides, no one would suspect a respectable citizen like him of the crime of rape.

A crime. It was a crime. He had committed rape and that was a crime.

But she'd asked for it, wearing those tight jeans and loose sweater with only those tiny pants below, and leaving the doors unlocked. She'd invited it, almost as blatantly as Dorothea Wyatt. If it ever came to it, all he need do was say so: her word against his. Who would believe her, a divorced woman and morally suspect, if she ever accused him? All he had to do was deny what she alleged and declare that she had made certain proposals which he had refused, claiming that her accusations came from spite.

It wouldn't happen, though; there were no means by which his identity could have been suspected.

Ronald felt triumph, working away as usual in the shop; the triumph of achievement. When Dorothea Wyatt came in during the afternoon on her way back from Middletown, where she'd bought a small fluted jug in the market as an excuse for calling to ask his opinion of it, he felt quite calm. She knew the jug was nothing special, unmarked and probably Victorian, but pretty, and cheap at the price if it could be used to restore harmony between her and Mr Trimm.

They discussed it together and agreed that it was attractive.

There were no new jugs in since her last visit. He told her that Nancy had several at home which she was repairing, and Dorothea said she'd pop in again before too long.

She went away, smiling. It could all be forgotten now.

Ronald was smiling too, when she left.

He bought the *Middletown Evening News* before he went home. There was nothing in it about an assault on a local woman.

Valerie was exhausted when she returned from visiting her parents. All day, she had been haunted by visions of the children being attacked, although they were never out alone in the dark. But it needn't be dark: a child molester might waylay them on their way to the Mounts' farm, might spring on them from a barn, might lure them from the school playground. And Primrose Cottage, which she had loved for its isolation, was just the place to appeal to the lawless.

Her parents, though absorbed by their own problems and frailties, had exclaimed at her pallor; and she explained it away by mentioning Timmy's earache, which had only just cleared up, and which had meant some broken nights, and by inventing a stomach upset. It wasn't so far from the truth. Her father gave her a ten-pound note when she left.

She stopped at a hardware shop on the way back to the bus and bought two strong bolts for the garage, an extra chain for the cottage and some further bolts and padlocks for its doors.

She met the children outside the school. Through the shop window, Ronald Trimm saw them all crossing the road together. The little girl skipped along beside her and the boy held her hand. She'd not turned a hair.

By the time Valerie did go to the police, on Friday, she could offer no evidence at all to support what she said, and she would not agree to see the doctor. She'd washed, she said, and would not admit to bruises that might be examined.

8

When Ronald took out his magazines, after he had done the books on Friday evening, he was smiling as he gazed at the glossy pictures. A lot had happened in a week.

Gazing at a naked redhead, he thought first of Dorothea, and then of Valerie. There was no doubt about which was the better memory. He closed his eyes and was able to imagine that he felt Dorothea's clutching hands again and heard the echo of her moans. Valerie, when she stopped struggling, had kept saying, 'No, no, no,' over and over again in a strange sort of voice, and it hadn't been at all the same; it was difficult, and so quick. You'd have expected it to have been better with her; she was younger. But Dorothea Wyatt had wanted it, whatever she later said, and Valerie hadn't. That was the truth.

Ronald did not go to the Plough that evening, but he drove down the lane to the Manor House and stopped outside, the van's engine ticking over. Several cars were parked in the drive; Dorothea had company. He did not linger.

Nancy was pleased to see him home in good time;

she'd made a steak and kidney pudding. They'd just finished eating when Keith Norton from next door came round, looking rather grave.

Letting him in, Nancy patted her hair into place and pulled at her skirt. She had not finished clearing away the dishes.

'I'm afraid the place is in a fearful mess,' she said, edging him towards the armchair that faced away from the dining recess.

'Looks all right to me, Nancy,' said Keith, sitting down and placing his large feet neatly together on the hearthrug. You hardly dared tread on Nancy's carpets.

'Is something wrong, Keith?' Nancy asked.

'Well – not exactly. It's just that I met Dave Gower this evening – you know Dave, Detective Sergeant he is now, at Tellingford. Used to be in Middletown. Said some woman reported being attacked. Raped.'

'Oh dear,' said Nancy, folding her hands together. 'Well?' It was no concern of theirs.

'The police think she's making it up. Women do, it seems. Get hysterical and imagine things,' said Keith Norton. 'But it makes me a bit worried about Lynn, going off to school these dark mornings. Silly, probably. I just wondered if you'd mind running her along to school, Ron, for a week or two, till it gets a bit lighter and this scare blows over. You often do give her a lift, as it is. Fussy, I expect, but you'd feel the same if you had a daughter.'

'I'm sure I should,' said Ronald carefully. 'I'd be glad to take her, Keith.'

'It means such an early start for her, if she comes

with me, you see,' said Keith. 'And the school isn't open then, anyway. She'd have to hang about outside.'

'But in the morning?' Nancy queried. 'Could it happen then? An attack of that kind, I mean?'

'Could happen any time, Nancy,' said Keith. 'Evil doesn't wait for the dark. But, as I said, the police don't think there's anything in it.'

'What do the police do, in a case like that?' Ronald asked. His voice sounded perfectly normal in his own ears. 'When they think it's not true?'

'Oh well, they have to go through the motions a bit, I think,' said Keith. 'Take a statement, that sort of thing. But they're not going to waste time over it. They've got plenty of other things to look into.'

'I see,' said Ronald. 'Where'd it happen? Do you know?'

'Dave didn't say exactly – just said they'd had the report,' said Keith.

'Well, it's all very unpleasant,' said Nancy. 'You're quite right to be concerned about Lynn.'

When he had gone, Nancy set about clearing away, murmuring to Ronald about how upsetting it was to be caught with the plates still on the table. 'Another five minutes and it would all have been out in the kitchen,' she said. 'What will he have thought?'

Ronald, heart pounding, felt an urge to shout, 'For crying out loud, what the hell does it matter? They're only dishes and Keith eats too.' But all he said was, in fact, 'It was wise of him to come round, Nancy, and make arrangements for Lynn. Seeing that he's worried.'

'Fancy people doing such things,' Nancy said. 'Or making them up, if they haven't happened. How very unpleasant.'

While she washed up, Ronald turned on the television. There was a programme about the migration of birds, and he sat staring at it, not taking it in. He'd had a bad fright. But at least he knew what had happened, and that the police would be taking no real action. He soon grew calmer, and began to enjoy the prospect of Lynn as his daily passenger.

Nancy came into the room at the moment a nest was being constructed on the screen. Birds made very little fuss about all that business, she thought, unaware of the reason for much of their noisy springtime song. Some species were so unrestrained, so gross: especially men. She looked fondly at Ronald. He'd not troubled her now for a very long time.

That evening, Dorothea was having a dinner party. She did this sometimes to pass the time, and also to ensure that her friends would not forget her and would invite her back. Her guests were Bill Kyle, her solicitor, who lived in the village, and his wife Eileen, and another couple from over beyond Middletown. Then she'd rung up George Fortescue and asked him, to make up the table; there weren't many unattached men around, and they'd all been friends for years. He'd fit in better than Colonel Villiers, who was over eighty but still quite a racy old boy, or the vicar.

George had demurred at first. It would upset his evening's jog.

'For God's sake, George! Where's your sense? Wouldn't you rather have a decent meal and a bit of company than go hammering round the lanes all on your own in the rain?' said Dorothea.

Put like that, it had seemed unreasonable to refuse. As promised, the meal was good; Dorothea had always been an accomplished hostess. There was an excellent claret to go with the pheasant.

George was about to follow the other two couples when they left at a quarter to twelve, but Dorothea detained him; this was the part she hated: being left, after a convivial evening, on her own.

'Have another brandy, George,' she said. 'I want one.'

She was not drunk, but she had reached a pleasant feeling of detachment, as though she floated somewhere above her own body, watching its actions from a soft cloud. There was no need to get drunk when she wasn't alone.

'We needn't clear up,' she said. 'Mrs Simmons is coming tomorrow.' She could not face the aftermath of a party and, although Mrs Simmons did not normally come on a Saturday, now and then she would, to oblige.

'Very well,' said George, who certainly had no wish to spend the next hour in an apron in Dorothea's kitchen.

She poured them each brandies and they sat facing one another in the sitting room, Dorothea on the settee and George in a wing armchair.

'Doesn't get any easier, does it, George?' she asked.

'What doesn't?'

'Being alone. I've been at it longer than you, and I'm no better. Worse, if anything.'

'Poor Dorothea,' said George inadequately; and then added, with scant tact, 'Of course, it's different for me. Angela will come back.' But Harry, in dying, had not rejected Dorothea, as Angela had rejected him.

'It's sad for you. I hope she does,' said Dorothea. 'Harry and I had such a good thing, you know. We got on so well. I miss it.'

'So do I,' said George, but he had a feeling they were not talking about the same thing.

When he'd finished his brandy, he rose to go. Dorothea stood facing him by the fireplace. She smiled at him.

'Silly old George,' she said, putting her arms round his neck. 'What are you waiting for?'

Valerie knew the police didn't really believe her, though the constable who took her statement was quite kind.

'You should have called us at once, love,' he said. 'Why didn't you?'

'I don't know. It was so late – I felt ill, awful. And it's so far to a phone,' she said dully. 'Then there were the children. And he didn't – well, he had the knife, but he didn't stab me, or that sort of thing.'

'He might, the next person,' said the constable.

She'd gone into Tellingford herself, on the bus, hoping to avoid the police coming out to the cottage, but they sent her home with a woman police constable and Detective Constable Cooley, who drove her in his own Ford Escort and who wanted to see the place where the alleged attack happened.

'It did happen,' she told Cooley. 'I'm not making it up.'

'I'm not saying you are,' said Cooley. She certainly wasn't hysterical, this one, and she wasn't accusing a specific person; but all this about dark clothes and a woollen hood was rather fantastic and had to be suspect.

'He knew I'd got children,' she said, standing in the garage while Cooley looked around. 'He said he'd hurt them, if I didn't—' Her voice trailed away as she saw that Cooley was pointing to a corner where Timmy's fairy bicycle and Melissa's small cycle stood.

She looked relieved at that.

'Oh – of course. I was afraid he might be – might be someone from round about here,' she said.

Cooley made her explain where she had been when the attack came, and how it happened. She tried to speak calmly. The man could have been standing behind her, watching her, for some time; that was terrifying to think of. She told Cooley and the policewoman how the sander had lain on the floor all the time, still whirring. She'd watched it, stared at it, while it went on.

Had he worn gloves, Cooley asked.

She didn't think so. She'd seen the knife, held in front of her face, but she'd looked away from it, down at the floor.

Cooley wanted to believe her. She seemed a nice enough girl. But she lived alone, apart from the children, and he knew well enough that women developed strange fancies; she might simply crave attention. He sifted among the ashes in the big fireplace that was seldom cleared and where she said she had burnt her clothes. He came across definite traces, finding the zip from her jeans. This didn't have to make the rest of her story true.

She'd left the chest she'd been working on unfinished, too, but, if Ronald had turned up to collect it the next day, as they'd arranged, he'd left no message. It was ready for him now. Beautifully smooth all over, there were no prints on it at all but a few of her own.

Long before it was dark, now, Valerie began locking up. The children were intrigued by all the bolts and chains she had fitted to the doors.

But she did not want to frighten them.

'There have been some bad men about,' she said. 'Burglars. If we lock everything up, they won't be able to get in and they'll go off and try somewhere else – that's if they were so silly as to come here at all. We haven't got anything worth stealing.'

'We have,' said Timmy. 'We've got my new bike.'

His fairy cycle, fourth or fifth hand, was his Christmas present from his grandparents.

'That's true,' said Valerie. 'So we'd better keep it safely locked up.'

The children thought it quite a joke, entering with enthusiasm into the new ritual. A week ago, Valerie would have mocked at her own fears. Crowbury was populated by respectable citizens and the few incidents of vandalism that had occurred in the centre of the village – broken windows in the village hall, graffiti on some walls – had been perpetrated by youths who had ridden in from Tellingford or Middletown on their motorbikes.

Valerie knew she would never work at night in the garage again, no matter how much was outstanding.

The children had gone up to the Mounts' farm to play on Saturday morning, and Valerie was out there working when Ronald called. Since it happened, she'd been unable to sleep and had worked early in the morning, finishing not only the chest but some other pieces Ronald had left. The mornings were safe, she was sure; that sort of evil man must be a creature of night who would not come out with the dawn.

Ronald was curious to see her, to discover what signs she bore of what had happened. And he hadn't collected the chest she'd been working on; it had seemed rather pointless. Besides, there was a chance he could have endangered himself by going back so soon. He should be safe now.

He found the garage door locked when he tried the latch. He could not hear the sander but he could see that the light was on inside.

Valerie heard the door rattle and called out sharply.

'Who is it?'

Ronald felt excited.

'It's Ronald Trimm,' he called.

'Oh – just a minute,' came the answer.

He heard the sound of bolts being drawn and a chain unhooked; then the door was opened. He noticed at once that Valerie looked pale and there were shadows under her eyes; she seemed ugly now.

'Sorry – there's been a prowler round, so I'm keeping everything locked,' she said; and then added defensively, 'I left it open on Thursday, though, when you said you'd come for that chest, but I hadn't managed to finish it. I expect you saw that.'

Ronald had made the excuse to his customer that the outworker had let him down. Now he responded smoothly.

'Yes. It was too bad of you, Valerie,' he said. 'I hope it's ready now?'

'I wasn't well that night,' said Valerie in a tight voice. 'Here it is. I've done some more things, too.'

She showed him two pale, softly gleaming chairs and a box. He could find no more fault with her, and together they loaded the furniture into his van which was drawn up outside. She picked up a broom while he counted out her money, and swept up some shavings into a pile ready to clear them away. Ronald put the notes down on the old deal table she used as a workbench, and added two extra pounds. Now he'd paid her for it, he exulted. She'd not been worth more.

'There's a bit extra this week,' he said. 'I expect you can do with it. But don't let me down again, Valerie, there's a good girl.'

'Oh – thank you,' said Valerie flatly. She picked up the money as he turned to go. It was little enough anyway, for all that scraping and rubbing and paring, and she had her materials to buy, the chemicals, wire wool and glass paper. It was not nice to be patronized, but she was in no position to be proud.

Ronald heard her locking the door up after him. If he came at night again, and told her who he was, she'd let him in; not otherwise. So it could not be repeated.

But he didn't want it like that again. It had all been too quick and furtive. He'd have to find somebody else.

9

Last night had really been very embarrassing.

George, getting ready for his day's golf, thought about Dorothea. He was playing in a foursome, teeing off at nine o'clock; he'd be at the club for lunch and have a second round in the afternoon, so the day should be pleasant.

But last night! Dorothea had clamped herself to him, soft and clinging. She'd nibbled his ear, of all things. George was extremely shocked. He had detached her, and pushed her back, none too gently, until she subsided on to the sofa.

'Sorry – can't stay,' he'd said. 'Got to be up early for a game of golf. Thanks, Dorothea,' and he'd bolted.

He was not sure if he was thanking her for the implicit invitation or just the good dinner. Tangling with Dorothea would be madness. Besides, he felt not the least bit tempted. All that sort of thing was rather unimportant. He'd had one or two awkward moments with Angela when it hadn't worked out too well.

It would be good to be out on the fairway with the

other fellows. You could forget about women, and their complicated ways, in the good fresh air.

Dorothea was more amused than annoyed by George's rejection. She had a few more drinks after he left, laughing to herself.

'Poor stupid George,' she said aloud, wandering round the room glass in hand. 'Perhaps you were right.'

It was a pity about him, for there they both were, opposite halves of what could be a pair. But things never worked out so neatly. Her mind ran over the unattached men she knew: apart from the vicar, a pink-faced man of forty who covered the wide area of his various parishes, now wedded together, in an aged Ford, and whose main interest outside his work seemed to be folk dancing, and the elderly Colonel Villiers, there were several perpetual bachelors, spinster men of varying ages and in various professions, but no lusty widower. She sighed. How sad! At last she went to bed and, after a final nightcap, fell asleep.

In the morning, her head was again a thumping lump of agony. Always, when she woke like this, she vowed to cut out the drink, but, when night came once again, and with it the weight of her unhappiness, she would seek the comfort that was always there.

There was a knock at the bedroom door. It was a loud, impatient rap, and Dorothea realized that it was this sound that had wakened her. For a moment she wondered whether George had changed his mind and come back, but then she saw daylight creeping through the gaps in the curtains and knew that it must be Mrs Simmons, who would have let herself in at the back door with her own key.

'Come in,' she croaked.

Mrs Simmons entered, bearing a tray. Her thin lips were folded into an even narrower line than usual and turned down at the corners. The array of empty bottles put out each week for the dustman told their own sorry tale. She deplored her employer's weakness, yet she had an impatient affection for her. She had been coming to the Manor House for years; Mrs Wyatt was a kind and thoughtful employer and it was all the more sad because Mr Wyatt had been such a nice gentleman.

'I brought you some coffee, madam,' said Mrs Simmons. Usually, she addressed Dorothea as Mrs Wyatt; 'madam' signified grave disapproval.

'You're an angel,' said Dorothea. 'What's the time?'

'Gone half-past nine,' said Mrs Simmons frostily. She'd arrived sharp at nine, and spent the first half-hour clearing up downstairs. There was always the chance that Mrs Wyatt might appear under her own steam. But when she didn't, despite much thumping and banging round by Mrs Simmons, action must be taken.

It was a pity young Susan didn't do something about her mother, though, to be honest, Mrs Simmons didn't really know what the girl could have done. The good Lord helped those that helped themselves. It had been a great shock when Mr Wyatt had dropped dead like that, no doubt. Mr Simmons had dropped dead too, in a somewhat similar fashion, but Mrs Simmons had not sat round in tears afterwards, nor taken to the bottle; she'd set about earning, for one thing. But then Mrs Wyatt had been used to having things made easy.

Making excuses for Dorothea, as people had always done, Mrs Simmons had popped bread into the toaster, though it wouldn't be touched, for sure.

Dorothea asked for Disprin from the bathroom.

Speechlessly, Mrs Simmons put two tablets in a glass of water and stirred them briskly while they fizzed.

'Bless you, Mrs Simmons, dear,' said Dorothea, taking the proffered tumbler. It was just as well that George Fortescue wasn't tucked up beside her, she reflected; that would have been too much for Mrs Simmons to accept.

When she came downstairs, Mrs Simmons had finished cleaning up in the dining room and the sitting room. The dishwasher was whirring. The glasses and the silver had been washed by hand and were waiting to be put away. Dorothea helped Mrs Simmons do this job; when she felt well, she liked caring for her house and would spend hours with beeswax and soft cloths going over the furniture. Mrs Simmons liked beautiful things, too; she enjoyed coming from her square red council house to this luxurious place in its lovely setting, but felt no trace of envy: possessions brought worry and responsibility. She knew that Dorothea would be lost without her and that she could take liberties with her, even scold her.

She did so now.

'You shouldn't do it, madam,' she reproved. 'It's not good for you.'

'I know,' said Dorothea, sighing. 'I'm so weak, Mrs Simmons. That's the trouble.'

'Couldn't you open a shop or something?' Mrs Simmons asked. She'd watched a programme on television about setting up in business. If you had capital, it didn't seem too difficult. 'It would take you out a bit.' Out of yourself, Mrs Simmons really meant.

'I can't do book-keeping,' said Dorothea.

'But would you need to? Couldn't the bank do it?' The television programme, it was true, had stressed the importance of keeping proper records.

'Oh, probably. But what would I sell, Mrs Simmons?' asked Dorothea.

'Clothes,' said Mrs Simmons promptly. Mrs Wyatt always dressed so well, and handed on her cast-offs to Mrs Simmons, which enabled her to cut a dash at times, though often she sold them; they were always in excellent condition. 'Or antiques,' she added.

'Antiques! Now, there's a thought! What would Mr Trimm say if I set up in opposition?' Dorothea chuckled.

Mrs Simmons didn't see why it was funny; competition often did a bit of good.

'That Mrs Turner might help you,' she suggested, on an inspiration. 'Her that lives in Primrose Cottage. Rents it from Bob, my son-in-law.' Mrs Simmons's daughter Pearl had married Bob Mount, thereby doing well for herself; Mrs Simmons had met Valerie

Turner several times when visiting Fell Farm; the children were nice little kiddies – well mannered, which was rare today. 'Mrs Turner mends furniture for Mr Trimm,' Mrs Simmons explained. 'It's difficult for her, on her own with the two children; she likes to be at home.' By implication, Mrs Simmons was declaring that things were harder for Valerie than for Dorothea. Dorothea got the message.

'What a good idea, Mrs Simmons,' she said lightly. 'You're quite an agony auntie, aren't you, sorting people out?' She drifted from the kitchen.

'Might as well have saved my breath,' thought Mrs Simmons, crossly folding up a tea towel.

Time hung heavy for Dorothea that day. Sometimes she went into Tellingford or Middletown, or even as far as Fletcham, to browse round the shops, and would cheer herself up by an impulse buy of some sort – a silk scarf, or a shirt, even a dress. But, on Saturdays, everywhere was crowded and parking difficult. Television on a Saturday afternoon offered little; this weekend the ancient movie, the only alternative to hours of sport, was a western. She would have enjoyed some romantic comedy or wartime drama.

In desperation, she put on her coat, tied a scarf over her head, and wandered down the garden. Bulbs were thrusting pale green spikes through the dark soil but there were weeks, yet, before the birds would be twittering and roses putting out shoots.

She strolled on towards the fence separating the lawn from the fields. Without Susan and Leo, she felt no urge for a healthy walk. Soon she could put the kettle on for tea; at six she would pour her first gin. She'd had two before lunch, and hadn't much fancied her bread and cheese.

There were walkers in the field. She saw two children running and skipping about, and a woman. A dog ran ahead, a black spaniel. Dorothea watched them draw nearer, following the path leading to the next stile.

The spaniel saw her and bustled towards the fence, snuffling and wagging its tail; it was rather old and fat, she noticed, like her Sammy, who had died.

'Truffles, Truffles, come here! Bad boy!' called one of the children.

Truffles took no notice. He could not get through the fence into Dorothea's garden because of the wire netting, buried in the ground and extending upwards for two feet, that kept out rabbits, but he sought diligently for a hole. Dorothea watched in amusement as the small girl ran up to him, seized him by the collar and continued to scold. The woman and the little boy added rebukes as they approached, but the dog persevered.

'I expect he's smelled a rabbit,' Dorothea suggested as Melissa tugged Truffles back from the boundary.

'He's bad,' said the child.

'Truffles, bad boy. Come here at once,' called Valerie.

As she approached, Dorothea recognized the young woman Mrs Simmons had mentioned. She was often about the village with the children and the dog.

Dorothea repeated her remark about the rabbit.

'Yes. There are some about, aren't there? But we haven't seen any today,' said Valerie. 'We've been down to the river looking for trout.'

'Did you see any?'

'No. Just a few minnows. I don't think there are any trout down there,' said Valerie. The river that ran through the meadows at this point was hardly more than a stream, but it widened at Tellingford where a bridge crossed it.

'I've got a fish pond,' said Dorothea. 'No trout, I'm afraid, but some big goldfish. Would you like to come and see?'

'Yes, please,' said Timmy at once.

'Do come,' said Dorothea to his mother. 'It might amuse the children. Can you get over the fence?'

The humans made short work of climbing it, but Truffles had to be lifted across. Valerie heaved him up and Dorothea took him from her, lowering him, scrabbling against her, to the ground.

'Have you got a dog?' Timmy asked.

'No.'

'Oh, why not?' Timmy wanted to know.

'I had one, but he died,' said Dorothea. 'I didn't get another.'

'Oh. Did you bury him?'

'Yes. He had a proper funeral,' said Dorothea instantly. 'His grave's under a big tree.'

Joe Cunliffe, her part-time gardener, had in fact dealt with this melancholy task, but Dorothea knew where the corpse was interred and pointed out the spot to Timmy as they crossed the garden.

'You should have a tombstone with his name on,' Timmy told her.

'Yes, perhaps I should,' Dorothea agreed. Timmy had taken her hand and was walking happily along beside her. They came to the lily pond, and among the leaves some fat orange fish could be discerned, lazily flapping their fins. A discussion ensued about whether Mr Jeremy Fisher might be in residence there; Dorothea had seen frogs from time to time, but never in winter. Perhaps they hibernated?

No one knew.

Reluctant to let the little family go, Dorothea asked them in to tea.

Valerie hesitated, looking searchingly at Dorothea, trying to see if she really meant her invitation. The older woman saw that she longed to accept. Why, she's as lonely as I am, she thought.

'Do come,' she urged. 'I'm all on my own.'

'But Truffles's feet make an awful mess,' said Valerie. 'He's filthy.'

'Never mind that. What's a house for but to be lived in?' asked Dorothea.

The children left their boots by the back door and had tea in their socks in the kitchen, the best place for wet hairy paws. Dorothea made dripping toast and found some chocolate biscuits. The young woman looked very tired and at first would eat nothing, but when pressed accepted some toast, and then ate another slice. When they had finished tea, she suddenly shivered and looked towards the window.

'It's getting dark,' she said.

Astonished, Dorothea recognized fear.

'I'll run you home,' she said.

'Oh no! I can't let you do that,' said Valerie. 'It's not all that far, it won't take us long.' But she had no torch, and there were no street lights in Ship Lane.

'It'll be no trouble,' said Dorothea. 'I've nothing else to do. Your cottage is some way out of the village.'

'Well – it seems so, sometimes,' Valerie admitted. She smiled, rather sheepishly. 'Thank you,' she said.

Timmy busily helped with the garage doors. He wanted to know the make of the car, which he didn't recognize. It was quite dark when Dorothea turned in at the gate of Primrose Cottage and the children scrambled out.

Valerie fumbled in her pocket for her keys.

'Mum's been putting bolts on everything,' said Timmy.

'There are bad men about,' said Melissa.

'Well, yes – but we hope they won't come to Crowbury,' said Dorothea.

'Will you come in for a minute?' asked Valerie.

In the weak glow of the car's interior light Dorothea saw once again that expression of fear on her face. The girl really was frightened; she did not want to enter her dark and empty cottage.

'I'd love to,' said Dorothea. 'Thank you. What a pretty place this is.' She followed Valerie inside and added, 'I leave the lights on when I'm out, and the radio. It makes coming home better. But of course you're much later than you expected.'

Valerie had a little sherry left in a bottle she had

100

been given for Christmas. She sent the children up to have their baths and poured some for Dorothea and herself.

'I hear you work for Mr Trimm,' said Dorothea, accepting her glass and sitting down in the one armchair. Her hostess perched on a sagging leather pouffe by the hearth.

'Yes. I strip furniture for him,' said Valerie.

'How do you do it?'

Valerie told her about painting on stripper, scraping off the peeling varnish or whatever covered the wood, rubbing with wire wool, and the various problems on the way.

'Are you doing some now?' Dorothea looked around the small sitting room. But of course there must be a workroom elsewhere.

'I do it in the garage,' Valerie said.

'Will you show me? I'd love to see how you do it,' said Dorothea.

Valerie hesitated, and that closed look came over her face again. Then, with an obvious effort, she said, 'Yes, of course.'

She fetched a large, heavy torch, called up to the children, picked up a bunch of keys and, when they crossed to the garage, there was much to-do over unlocking the various padlocks she'd fixed to the door.

'I expect you think I'm very silly, taking so many precautions,' Valerie said, with a nervous laugh.

'I don't, my dear,' said Dorothea. 'Your cottage is isolated, after all. I think you're sensible.'

It was on the tip of Valerie's tongue to tell her what

had happened. She was kind, and would believe her, Valerie was sure.

But she said nothing. It was too awful, too humiliating, too degrading to mention.

Lynn was waiting at the gate when Ronald backed the van into Sycamore Road on Saturday morning. He got out and opened the door for her, as if she were grown-up; Lynn always enjoyed his doing this – not like most people who left you to open the door yourself, not even leaning across inside the car to do it.

He told her he would take her to school each day in future, at her father's request. She knew the reason.

'It's silly,' said Lynn. 'I'd just run away from someone like that.'

'He might run after you,' said Ronald.

Lynn made a face. 'Maybe,' she said. 'Anyway, those things don't happen in the morning.'

But they did. Ronald recalled at least one case that had been reported of a schoolgirl disappearing on her way to school. It all depended on opportunity.

'It must be awful, something like that,' said Lynn.

'Some women ask for it,' said Ronald. 'Then they make a fuss.'

They drove along in silence for a few minutes. Then Ronald spoke again.

'You'd never take a lift with someone you didn't know, would you, Lynn?' For an instant he glanced away from the road and at her smooth young face beside him.

'Golly, no! Dad would skin me, if he found out,' said Lynn.

'You're growing up, you see,' said Ronald, and he took his gloved hand off the wheel for a moment to lay it on her thigh. Well covered as it was by skirt and duffle coat, Lynn barely felt the gentle pressure. 'You're such a pretty little thing. You always were.'

Lynn had always known herself to be a favourite of her Uncle Ron's, it came of his having no children of his own. She took his affection for granted.

They had a busy day in the shop. People out for a stroll would come in to warm up before continuing. You had to watch out for shoplifters because, though the shop attracted an apparently respectable clientele, objects had been known to disappear, and children were often menaces, picking up things and fingering them while their parents paid no heed to them. Something precious might easily get broken. Lynn jealously guarded the wares, hovering over the browsing customers. She felt very responsible when Ronald was not there.

He went out early that morning, to visit two dealers with pieces he knew they would buy. When he came back, Lynn made him some coffee; later, they had instant soup to reinforce their sandwich lunch, and tea with a digestive biscuit at four o'clock.

Ronald had his tea first; then, while he minded the shop, she, in her turn, took her tea down to the cellar and switched on the electric fire for some surreptitious warmth. The cellar was lit by a strip light on the ceiling above the desk. The room was entirely functional; boxes, sacks and cardboard used for packing were stacked in a corner, and there was no furniture apart from the business desk and two upright chairs. It was kept scrupulously clean; the stone floor was never dusty. Glancing round this afternoon, Lynn noticed a cobweb on the big desk. You never saw cobwebs in the shop; Auntie Nancy was most particular about cleaning everything thoroughly and often. Lynn brushed the cobweb aside with her fingers, but it still clung to the handle of the drawer. She rubbed at it with her handkerchief; then, not consciously thinking of what she was doing, she tugged at the drawer handles. It was locked tight.

She gave it no further thought, scrumpling her grubby handkerchief up and putting it back in her pocket.

When Ronald dropped her outside her own home that night, the lights were on in both bungalows. It was nice to be hurrying in from the cold and the darkness to brightness and warmth, and a waiting meal. Lynn was going to a folk dance evening with Peter and he was coming to fetch her. Under her father's new stringent rules for her safety, she was never to walk alone in the dark. It seemed silly to Lynn, but anyway it was much nicer being with Peter, and he was coming to supper.

Uncle Ron patted her gloved hand before she got out of the van, thanking her for her day's work. He'd already paid her from the till. She barely registered the fact that he brushed against her, leaning across to open the van door for her. She was used to it.

Ronald watched her run up the drive to her own front door, open it and disappear, before he turned in at his own gate. She never turned back to look at him, but he always hoped she would.

He was still thinking of her when Nancy was serving their dinner.

10

The radio forecast sunshine on Sunday, but, when Ronald went into the garden to dig the bare section of the vegetable bed where leeks and savoys had grown, the sky was still overcast. A neat strip of ground, dug to take advantage of winter frosts, bordered the part he was working on; soon he would sow broad beans and plant potatoes there. Ronald pulled out the thick, faded stalks of the savoys and made a heap of them at the bonfire spot.

Nancy was in the kitchen making an apple pie to go with the roast pork for lunch. She'd dusted round, after making the beds; just because it was Sunday, there was no excuse for letting up on standards.

By half-past twelve, Ronald had a hearty appetite. He came in by the back door, took off his boots and left them in the porch, and in his socks padded over the spotless, grey-marbled-effect Marley tiled floor of the kitchen. Even when she was cooking, there was no mess around Nancy: morsels that fell on the floor were noticed at once and wiped up immediately; the stove gleamed as pristine as when it was new, many years ago. An enticing smell filled the room.

'Smells good,' remarked Ronald. He said this at the same hour every Sunday, and it was always true.

'It'll be ready sharp at one,' said Nancy, piling shredded cabbage into a pan. It always was.

Over lunch, as the weather was improving, they decided to go into the country for the afternoon. Nancy had been reading a feature in the local paper about property values, and had noted a village where there were still a number of the original inhabitants living in cottages which might one day be available for modernization. Dewton had not been developed by speculators; in a sense it could be called a dying village, with few young people living there, though there were already weekenders in some of the cottages. There might be scope for some careful knocking, Nancy thought; each year Ronald tracked down a few clocks by calls at spots Nancy had selected. They'd inspect Dewton.

While Nancy washed up, Ronald prepared the van for their expedition. He cleaned the windscreen and rear window; there wasn't time to wash the whole van, a thing he often did on Sundays. He wished they had an estate car. The business was prospering, and it would be a legitimate expense to set against profits. He mentioned it to Nancy as they set off.

She favoured the idea. The shabby van was not in keeping with the true status she felt they had achieved. Sitting beside him in her black and white herringbone-tweed coat, with a yellow silk scarf at her neck and her tinted hair inflexibly arranged, she felt herself to be a prize portrait inappropriately framed.

Dewton, when they reached it, seemed to be just a row of cottages lining each side of a narrow, undulating lane.

'What a dead place,' said Nancy.

Some of the cottages were thatched, the thatch in many cases black and sagging, with mossy patches and gulleys dredged by rain pouring down from eroded ridges. Halfway along the street a cottage had been gutted by fire, and stark, black beams poked up into the pale sky. A cement mixer stood in the front garden, and a builder's sign was attached to the fence. There was one cottage with a spanking new pale thatch, a blonde among the rest; its door and window frames were painted yellow. The white-painted plaster between the beams of the construction shone the more brightly because of its contrast with the drab exteriors of the neighbouring cottages. They might all look like this in ten years' time, fully renovated.

Smoke spiralled from a few chimneys. There were no walkers about, and only two cars were parked at the roadside. It looked promising territory.

'You could try here, Ronald,' Nancy said.

'Yes.'

'Not today. It would be wrong on Sunday. But don't leave it – why not come down on Wednesday?' Nancy suggested. 'You're not going to a sale this week, are you?'

'No.'

'Very well, then.'

They drove past a country mansion which later in the year would be open to the public, regretting that they could not enter now and gaze upon its treasure. Such visits were instructive; they sometimes called at stately homes to look upon rare objects.

'Shall we go back through Fletcham? We might have tea there,' Ronald suggested.

'That would be nice,' said Nancy.

They were soon travelling along the road down which Ronald had followed Felicity Cartwright the week before. He noted the turning to the estate where she lived.

Fletcham Abbey dominated the town. Ronald and Nancy went into it and looked around. Small groups of sightseers trod respectfully on the ancient stone floor and gazed at the tombs of long-dead abbots. Later in the year, tourists would mill about the aisles. A cassocked figure was preparing for an evening service, moving among the pews. A few people sat, either resting or meditating; one woman knelt, head bowed.

Leaving the abbey, Ronald and Nancy walked on, looking in shop windows, strolling; they traversed the length of Market Street and came to an antique shop called the Treasure Box. It had a narrow front, between a dress shop and a chemist. In the window were displayed silver objects in a case and several good small boxes: needlework boxes and, he was sure, the writing box he had sold to Mrs Felicity Cartwright. So this was her place. He felt perversely glad to see the box still unsold. The price tag was turned over so that the figure on it was concealed. It looked as if she specialized in boxes.

As it was Sunday, the cafés were closed, so they

went to the Bell Hotel, where afternoon tea was served in the lounge. Nancy enjoyed walking in ahead of Ronald; they made, she was sure, a handsome pair: no longer young, true, but well turned out and, as must be obvious, quite devoted.

Ronald, ordering tea and toasted tea-cakes, noticed the trim figure of the waitress, her slim waist and narrow ankles. He smiled into her eyes, suggesting cakes to follow.

Daniel Fortescue telephoned his father that Sunday afternoon.

He'd had a long talk with his girlfriend about the split between his parents.

'Couldn't you get them together?' Vivian said. 'A friendly meeting, I mean – sort of casual? After all, neither of them's gone off with someone else. Mightn't they make it up? It's probably all just some silly quarrel and they're both too proud to say sorry.'

'I don't know,' Daniel said. 'Mum's in such good spirits. I don't ever remember her being like this. She looks years younger.'

'Perhaps your father will fall for her all over again,' said Vivian. 'Maybe that's what it needs.'

'We could give it a try,' said Daniel. 'Poor old Dad, having to manage on his own. He lives on frozen food. Mum's very capable and he must miss all that. And there's this jogging he's taken up. He's much too old for that sort of thing.' To Daniel, who saw his parents as well over the hump, it was shocking that they should be behaving in what seemed such an adolescent fashion. After the age of forty, people's parents stuck it out; splitting up, if things didn't work out, was for younger folk, and preferably before they went so far as getting married.

'Let's take them out to dinner somewhere romantic,' Vivian suggested. 'Let's ask each of them to meet us, and not tell them the other one is coming. How about that for an idea? They might refuse, if they knew, and this way, because of us, they'll have to cool it. Won't they?'

'You're a genius,' Daniel said. 'What an inspiration. The Sorrento, eh? When shall we do it?'

They consulted their engagement diaries. Both were involved with university societies as well as work and one another. Wednesday, it seemed, was free, however.

Daniel went to the telephone in the hall of his digs, where this conference had taken place. Despite their unpredictability, it was likely that both his parents would be available to answer the telephone on a Sunday afternoon, though George might be at golf. If so, they'd catch him later. His parents, Daniel thought, were hardly likely to refuse.

Valerie kept her children close to her on Sunday. She cooked breast of lamb for lunch, played cars with Timmy and made a dress for Melissa's doll. In the afternoon they went to Fell Farm to look at the Mounts' new donkey. The children had wanted to go over the fields again; they'd enjoyed their tea with Mrs Wyatt the day before and thought a repeat would be nice. So did Valerie, but she was not going to hang round the Manor House. Mrs Wyatt, when departing the evening before, had pressed her to come again, but Valerie would wait to be invited.

She did a big wash that day, pegging everything out to blow freshly in the cold air, though it was not likely to get dry. She still felt unclean, and she had another fear that filled her with dread. Supposing she were pregnant? The police might believe her, if that turned out to be the case, she thought grimly.

After tea, she played Happy Families with the children. Timmy, still a diffident reader, needed help from time to time, but could identify most of the characters by their pictures. The fire was well stoked up, the doors were soundly locked and bolted, and the chains secured. Truffles lay sleeping in his basket.

Ronald lay awake in bed that night, planning. Beside him, in the other bed, Nancy snored lightly; it was a friendly sound and normally never disturbed him.

It hadn't been right with Valerie. For one thing, she was a young, strong girl and, if he hadn't had the knife, he'd have got nowhere. She'd submitted, straight away, when threatened. There had been her kids, of course; saying he'd go for them had been a good idea. But it had been very different from the interlude with Dorothea Wyatt. There'd been no warm response; it was all so quick.

It occurred to him that Valerie, living alone as she did, might have responded to an open approach, like the women mentioned by the young men in the Plough. How did they do it so easily? According to some, all you had to do was raise your little finger, in a manner of speaking, and there you were. But he'd tried with that Felicity Cartwright and been rebuffed. When you came to think about it, she'd seen him off good and proper. The snub rankled. Who did she think she was?

He thought about her, gazing at the ceiling in the darkness, his mind full of visions. There were other ways than the one he'd used with Valerie.

Nancy had already decreed that he should visit Dewton on Wednesday, and that was close to Fletcham.

He worked out what to do, lying in the dark. He'd need the knife.

Planning it took his mind off Lynn. She was the one he really wanted, but she was too young.

11

Detective Constable Cooley had plenty of cases to deal with; an alleged rape was merely a diversion. There had been a break-in at a shop in Tellingford from which radios had been stolen, an incident of suspected arson, and several burglaries, all of which had to be investigated, besides various outbreaks of vandalism. But on Wednesday, when he was returning to the police station from a farm where a barn had been set alight, and had to pass through Crowbury, Cooley turned aside down Ship Lane.

His boss, Detective Sergeant Gower, had dismissed Valerie Turner's complaint as a fantasy. It was on file, a telex had gone to all stations, but no time would be wasted on investigation of what had been imagined by a neurotic woman who knew a doctor would prove her allegations false. She'd soon be on to them again with some other invented tale – anonymous letters, or obscene telephone calls, was Gower's theory.

But Cooley had been to the cottage, had seen how jumpy Valerie was, had noticed her clenched hands. Gower explained these signs as indications of her neurosis, but Cooley's instinct told him her story was true.

She was working in the garage. He could hear the sander buzzing. It would have drowned the sound of his car approaching, as it would have masked any noise the rapist made that night.

Cooley banged hard on the door and rattled it.

Inside, Valerie sensed some sound above that of the sander and looked up. She worked facing the door now. By her side was a large hammer. She would not be found unable to defend herself, another time. Truffles was with her, too; unferocious, it was true, but company.

'Who is it?' she called.

She was expecting no one. Ronald had been in earlier, collecting finished work, and he brought three painted chests from the house-clearer where he got so much cheap stuff. He'd a busy day ahead, he'd told her, explaining his early call.

'Still locking up, I see,' he'd said, as she undid her bolts and chains to let him in.

'Yes. I expect you think that's silly,' she'd replied, defensively.

'Not at all. You can't be too careful,' Ronald had remarked. 'I'd be annoyed if any of my pieces were stolen from your place, Valerie, and you'd be responsible.'

She hadn't thought of that. Would her insurance cover such a thing?

Cooley announced his identity and looked approvingly at her defences when she opened the door to him. She faced him with an air of defiance, a short, stocky girl, her body stiff, hands clenched by her sides.

'Look, love, I haven't come to badger you with questions,' Cooley said at once. 'I was passing and I just wanted to see that you're all right. That's all.'

Valerie relaxed slightly. She turned away from him.

'Depends what you mean by all right,' she muttered.

'Well—' Cooley sought about for a positive comment. 'I see you've started locking up, for a start. That's good.'

'I've fixed up chains and bolts on all the doors, yes,' said Valerie. 'But I should think anyone who really meant to could still get in. It wouldn't take too much to break these doors down.'

'You could get the crime prevention officer to call,' said Cooley. 'He'd advise you. It's a free service. He'd tell you about locks on the windows and all that sort of thing.'

'I've nothing much worth stealing, if you're thinking of burglars,' said Valerie.

'Everyone has something,' Cooley said. 'A bit of money lying about – a ring – a radio. Some thieves nick things just to use themselves.'

'Do they ever go to the same place twice?' asked Valerie. 'You know – those—' She could not say the word.

'Rapists?'

She nodded.

'I can't remember one that has,' said Cooley, but he could think of several vicious ones who had haunted

116

a particular district. 'Sometimes they'll be prowlers in a car. Yours was probably one of those. He won't come back here. You should put that right out of your head.'

'It's not so easy to do,' said Valerie.

'No, I don't suppose it is,' said Cooley.

'You're acting as if you believed me now,' said Valerie.

'I never said I didn't,' said Cooley promptly.

'Well – up at the station – those other policemen – they didn't.'

'We get a lot of reports that aren't true,' replied Cooley. 'Girls tear their clothes, that sort of thing. Or lead a fellow on and then say he attacked them. It's difficult to prove. After all, you and I are here alone now. What's to stop you running up the road saying I went for you? It'd be your word against mine, wouldn't it?'

She hadn't thought of it like that.

'Male motorists picking up girl hitch-hikers are asking for trouble,' Cooley said. He saw this was a novel idea to Valerie. 'Look, why don't we have a little chat, eh? You've had a while to get over it – something might occur to you that you forgot at the time. How about a cup of tea?'

Valerie looked at the drawer she was working on. She still had a lot to do, to get through what she'd planned for the day, and it would soon be time to fetch the children from school. But she could spare half an hour.

She led the way to the cottage, taking the back-door key out of the pocket of her slacks.

'It's an awful nuisance, whenever I go in and out,' she said. 'But I imagine him inside, lying in wait for me.'

'I'm sure he won't come back,' Cooley said. 'Really, love, lightning doesn't strike in the same place twice, you know.' He crossed his fingers, saying this.

All Valerie knew was that she would never forget it. She had been invaded, defiled: how could she welcome a man within her, ever again? And what man, if he knew what had happened to her, would want her in that way?

Truffles followed them into the kitchen, where Valerie put on the kettle, and they sat at the table among Timmy's model cars and Melissa's plaster models, her new interest.

'He was heavy, the man,' Valerie said abruptly, pouring tea into pottery mugs. 'Sugar?'

'Yes, please,' said Cooley. 'Heavy?' he prompted.

'Yes. He – he pinned me down. It was awful – like an animal.' Her voice was gruff as she tried to speak steadily. 'He was so strong. I suppose he must have been a large man.'

Cooley had asked her earlier if she had scratched him, but she'd said she hardly saw his face.

'I'm sorry to make you talk about it again,' he said. 'But, in the end, it's better if you face it – don't bury it till you've got it all out of your system. Who else have you told about it? A girl friend?'

Valerie shook her head.

'No one,' she said. 'I couldn't. It's too dreadful.'

'Well – if you could – it might help,' said Cooley.

'Suppose I'm pregnant?' Valerie asked. There! It was out!

'Are you? Would you know by now?'

'I'm due,' said Valerie. 'Two days ago.'

'Well – you'll have to go to the doctor, then, won't you?' Cooley said. 'Give it a couple more days – maybe a week – but don't hang about after that.'

'I can't bear to think of it – of that—' Valerie suddenly began to weep. She laid her arms on the table and slumped over them, burying her face. 'I can't sleep,' she wailed. 'I keep thinking I hear someone in the house.'

'That'll pass,' Cooley assured her. But would it? How could a woman get over so dreadful an experience? The man responsible was a monster.

He'd learned nothing new, and would gain no more by pressing her.

'I'll pop by again,' he promised. 'Just to see how things are going. And if you do remember anything – anything at all, no matter how slight – you let me know. Right? I'll give you my phone number at home.' He wrote it for her on a scrap of paper and tucked it under the sugar bowl.

Valerie pulled a tissue from her sleeve and wiped her face, then blew her nose.

'Sorry,' she said, managing the semblance of a smile. Her face was blotchy, but Cooley still liked it. 'Will you really come again?'

'Of course I will,' he said. He'd suggest to the panda patrol boys that they might cruise down Ship Lane from time to time, too; there was nothing like a police car in the area to scare off villains.

'I think you really do believe me now,' said Valerie.

Cooley patted her arm.

'I do,' he said.

But there was not a shred of proof.

Nancy had decreed that Ronald should go to Dewton on Wednesday afternoon, and so he obeyed. He knocked on several doors and bought a bracket clock in a mahogany case for fifteen pounds. To get it, he paid five pounds for a chipped china ewer. He spent quite a while talking to the old lady who sold the pieces to him, and learned about her neighbours.

In a cottage along the road from her, he bought a dower chest and a brass scuttle from a whiskered old man who walked with a stick and peered at him from clouded, cataract eyes.

Then Ronald telephoned Nancy and told her that the van was giving trouble. It wasn't firing properly, he said; a garage was fixing it, but he didn't know how long they'd be, they'd had to send out for a part. She shouldn't wait for dinner; he was afraid he would be late.

When he reached home, he must be ready with an explanation of why he rang her from a call-box, not the garage, just in case she asked.

He drove to Fletcham, went past the turning to Priory Road, where Felicity Cartwright lived in Number 7, and parked in a nearby street. Then he returned to Priory Road on foot: a respectable citizen in his raincoat and tweed hat. He wore his dark scarf wound round his neck; the balaclava helmet, the knife and a small torch were in his pockets, and he had his leather driving gloves on.

It was not yet five o'clock. Felicity Cartwright should still be in her shop, and her house empty. The tricky part would be finding a way of entering it, and he'd thought of one.

No lights showed as he walked up the short path to the front door. He'd seen it done on television, where it looked easy. Ronald inserted his credit card into the door and tried to press back the catch.

He couldn't do it.

He stood there, furious. What now? Blood pounded in his ears.

Most of the door was glass, with a wood surround. He could break the glass and turn the catch, but then his presence would be no surprise, and the neighbours might come running. He stared at the door angrily. He must present a calm rear view in case there was a passer-by to notice anything strange.

His gaze focused on the letterbox. It was a wide, vertical slit, quite near the lock, large enough to admit his hand.

He reached inside the letterbox, felt about, and found the knob. He could just get his finger and thumb round it.

In seconds he was standing in the hall, the door closed behind him, heart thudding now in triumph. He had done it!

He waited for a little while in the dark house, in case he had been seen, but nothing happened. He could return to his plan. He turned on his tiny pencil torch, shielding the bulb.

Basing his reasoning on Nancy's habits, he'd

worked out what to expect. The first thing Nancy did when she returned home was to go into her bedroom and remove her coat, hanging it in the wardrobe or, if wet, in the bathroom to air off. Then she'd see to her hair and all that. A fortnight ago, when he'd come back here with Felicity Cartwright, she'd hurried in, leaving him on the pavement unloading the van, and when he entered the house had called to him from upstairs. Then she'd come down, not wearing her coat. They were all the same. All he had to do was wait for her in her bedroom.

In the light of his torch, he examined the back door. It was bolted from inside, and opened on to a small garden. A rotating clothes line was sunk in concrete beside a patch of grass.

Ronald took off his raincoat and tweed hat. He bundled them up and stowed them under a large bush. Then, with his knife, he cut some lengths of plastic rope from the clothes line and coiled them round. That could be useful.

Wearing his balaclava helmet, with the scarf round the lower part of his face and his hands in his leather gloves, Ronald went upstairs after bolting the back door once more.

It was easy to see which was her room. There was a big Victorian brass bed, covered with a white silk spread, in the back bedroom. There were tortoiseshell brushes on the rosewood sofa table she used as a dressing table, and there was a faint flowery scent in the air. A peach-coloured quilted dressing gown hung on the door and there was a pair of slippers beside the bed. They were the same colour as the dressing gown, and very small: dainty, he thought, smiling. He enjoyed noticing it all by the light of his torch before he settled down to wait, in his black sweater, his breathing a little muffled by the scarf over his face. He had the knife, blade exposed, in his hand as he stood behind the half-open door.

He had to wait a long time. Felicity was busy with her own book-keeping that evening.

It was a quiet road, but an occasional car went by, and as he heard them Ronald tensed, waiting for further sounds that would mean she had entered the house.

They came at last, the click of the front door opening and the glow of the light from the hall.

She didn't come up at once. He heard her moving about below; doors opened and closed and water ran. That was the kitchen. There was no other plumbing on the ground floor of this tiny house.

Then he heard her on the stairs. Stifling already behind the scarf and the woollen helmet, he drew in his breath and tightened his hand on the knife handle.

She went into the bathroom, not bothering to close the door properly, imagining herself alone in the house. Soon he heard the lavatory flush. When she pushed the door open a few moments later she almost took him by surprise, for he knew she would be washing, a nice sort of woman like this. But she was quicker than Nancy at such times.

The bedroom light snapped on and she moved over the threshold away from him, towards the

123

window, quite unaware of his presence which was concealed from her by the door. He watched, breath held, while she drew the curtains. Then he sprang on her from behind and bore her down on to the bed on her back, himself on top of her. He leaned his left arm on her chest and held the knife, in his gloved right hand, at her throat. Excitement surged through his body.

'If you scream, you're dead,' he hissed, in a snarling tone, the same sort of voice he had used with Valerie, quite unlike his normal one.

Felicity had uttered a strangled shriek, but terror left her too little breath for real screaming. She thought her heart would burst with fear.

Ronald flourished the knife.

'Take off your clothes,' he ordered, in his false voice.

She was incapable of movement beyond opening her mouth, and Ronald thought despite his threats she was going to scream, but in fact she was gulping for air. He hit her hard across the face with his left hand, and then took a handkerchief from his pocket and tied it across her mouth, laying down the knife while he did it, still straddling her with his body. He dragged her head up from the bed by her hair, tying the handkerchief at the back, hitting her again as she began making croaking noises. The gag forced her mouth open but held her tongue down. She felt as if she must choke, struggling to beat and claw at him with her hands.

Desperately, Felicity tried to fight him, but his weight lay on top of her, holding her down, and his arms pinioned her. She tore at him again, but he hit her in the face once more, much harder this time. The pain brought tears to her eyes and for a moment she stopped resisting. Ronald picked up the knife and laid it against her throat. She felt the point on her flesh. Breathing was still difficult; her chest rose and fell with the effort. Slowly, Ronald sat back. He hurt her; his weight crushed her.

He felt an enormous surge of power as her resistance ebbed. She was making little guttural sounds in her throat but this merely goaded him on; they were not unlike the lustful moans of Dorothea Wyatt on that magic night. He caught hold of her wrists and forced them up over her head, holding them there with one hand while he laid down the knife once more and pulled the nylon twine from her own washing line out of his pocket. He wound it tightly round her wrists, lashing them together, then secured them to the strong struts of the fine old brass bedstead. That was a bit of luck, her having one like that; he couldn't have done it with a divan or a solid headboard. He tied her firmly so that she could not get her arms free.

Fighting the pain and the terror, Felicity made a supreme effort, kicking at him as he moved back from her and began to fumble with her clothes. Her legs flailed.

But he had the knife in his hand again, and held it against her breast. She could feel the blade pressing down on her. She shrank back then, eyes staring at him frantically above the gag, and he moved the knife away, but still she resisted, more passively now, making her legs heavy as he tried to pull off her boots, keeping her ankles rigid, feet pointing upwards. She kicked out again. It made him angry.

'Stop that. It will be worse if you don't,' he said.

He dragged at her slacks. They were tight, and it was more difficult than with Valerie, for she still mutely resisted, lying stiff, pressing herself into the bed. Rage at her opposition made him desperate. He caught at her legs, meaning to raise her hips, but she writhed and wriggled, still making sounds, and he jabbed her in the side with the point of the knife. As she struggled, she moved against it and it sank into her flesh. Ronald withdrew it so that the point lay on her flat, white belly. He did not see the blood that came from the wound; there was, in fact, very little, but she stopped struggling.

After that it was easy, and he left her sprawled out on the bed, not unlike some of the pictures he had spent so long gloating over, the light still on.

Ronald went calmly down the stairs and out through the back door to where he had left his things. He put on his raincoat and tweed hat and walked quickly along the side of the house and into the street. There was no one about as he strode off down the road.

He felt very peaceful, drained not only by the act itself but by the struggle.

Back in his van, he smiled as he slid the knife, wrapped up in the balaclava helmet, under the seat. Then he drove home to Nancy.

Upstairs in her bedroom, still tied to the bed and still gagged, Felicity stirred a little.

Ronald dwelt mentally on the sensual pleasure and release of his experience as he drove towards Tellingford. Gradually the violence faded from his mind until it was as though that part had never happened. He'd barely touched her with the knife; it had been just a sharp prod, to make her obey him. She'd been punished now, just like Valerie.

Before reaching home, he stopped to take off his black sweater and put on his corduroy jacket, and the tie he had removed earlier. He combed his thick hair neatly, slicking it back past his ears.

Nancy was watching a programme about battered babies on television when he entered the house.

'Terrible, the things people do,' she said, turning it off when he came in, to give him her full attention. His dinner was keeping warm in the oven, and he ate it all up, every bit. Afterwards, he showed her what he had bought in Dewton and she was delighted with his success.

The van seemed quite all right now, he said. Luckily it had failed quite near a garage and he hadn't had to walk far, he told her, before he found help.

He drank three cups of tea, when Nancy brewed a pot before they went to bed.

Felicity's eyes would not focus properly.

The terrible figure in the weird helmet and black clothes seemed to have gone, and the room was quiet except for a strange banging sound. She did not realize that the noise she heard was her own struggling heart.

Her arms, still tied above her head, ached unbearably; her wrists rubbed raw against the chafing twine. She was too tired to try any longer to free them.

He had been so strong, that man, and so heavy, weighing her down, crushing her under him, taking away her strength.

She lapsed into unconsciousness some time before, at last, she died.

12

The Ristorante Sorrento was in a narrow street that led to Fletcham Abbey from the market square. Within, concealed lighting was augmented by candles inside large goblets on each table.

Daniel and Vivian arrived there in good time, on Wednesday evening, for their dinner with his parents. He had sold the idea to his mother as a delayed celebration for her birthday, and she had agreed to drive down after work. She had changed her job again and was now with a small firm that handled sales promotions. By working through her lunch hour, consuming yoghurt in the office, she was able to leave early and reach Fletcham at the agreed hour.

Daniel wore his suit, which showed how important the evening was to him, and Vivian was in a flowing dress of Indian origin, with small animals and emblems in purplish colours printed on a neutral background. Her legs were sensibly encased in her lined boots. Both wore identical shaggy sheepskin coats which they'd bought at a secondhand shop; imperfectly cured, they smelled faintly as the waiter bore them away to a remote cupboard.

The Sorrento was a place to which students at Fletcham University went only rarely, when their grants had arrived or their exams were over, or on other special occasions. Some of the more old-fashioned ones took particular partners there when laying the groundwork for a sexual siege; Daniel and Vivian had been there several times. The menu, pinned in the window, could be studied without commitment, and a plan made in advance to obtain value for money without embarrassment. In fact, this was what the Sorrento supplied: modest pasta dishes, veal or chicken served in various ways, and inexpensive wines from Tuscany at a reasonable cost, though you could go mad, if you wished, *à la carte*. At midday, businessmen from the district lunched there on their expense accounts. The restaurant, a family concern with few outside employees, flourished.

'Ah, good evening, Mario,' said Daniel suavely, as the proprietor's eldest son, the head waiter, greeted them. 'I've booked a table for four. My parents are joining us. Fortescue's the name,' he added anxiously, in case Mario did not remember their earlier encounters.

'Of course, Mr Fortescue. *Bene*. I have this nice table for you,' said Mario, who had lived all his life in England but cultivated a heavy accent. He led them to a table in a corner, partly screened from the entrance by a buttress.

Daniel and Vivian sat down, and Daniel ordered a carafe of the house red wine.

'Plenty of plonk. That'll help,' he said to Vivian, and swallowed half a glass himself as soon as it came.

'Dad'll be first, you'll see. He's always so punctual. But Mum won't be late, exactly. She'll be a bit breathless, though, as if she is. Maybe she'll be five minutes behind time.'

'You're scared,' said Vivian.

'Yes.' Daniel loosened his tie and laughed in an embarrassed way. 'This is a new scene for me – trying to get my parents to kiss and make up.'

'It'll be all right,' said Vivian, patting his hand. 'They're civilized people, after all. Just relax.'

George and Angela were civilized people and, when they met in the market square after parking their cars at opposite ends of it, they realized at once what had happened. They had, in fact, driven along the same road into Fletcham, for George had taken the car to the office in order to drive straight down, but he had found his way directly through the town, while Angela had taken some false turns.

They made no scene. They never had, in their years together.

'They've asked you too?' said Angela, to confirm it. 'Daniel and Vivian?'

'Yes.' George fiddled with the keys of his car. 'Shall I go away?'

'Of course not. That would upset them,' said Angela. Then she added suspiciously, 'You didn't ask them to arrange it, did you?' She remembered the pendant he had sent her; it had surprised her, for it was lovely and unlike any gift she had had from him before. She would send it back, naturally, but had not got round to doing so yet. She decided not to mention it.

'I did nothing of the kind,' said George crossly.

'No. You were never devious. Well, don't let's disappoint them. They must have got everything planned. They'll expect you first since you're always early for things. You go ahead. I'll come a minute or two later.'

'You are punctual,' George said, accusingly. 'You never were, before.'

'I'm quite a lot of things now that I never was before,' said Angela calmly. 'Go on, George.'

'Yes – well – all right.' George had wanted to suggest they might as well arrive together, but gave up the idea. This new Angela might argue. He made an awkward gesture and moved away, wondering, as he walked up the road, if she knew where to go. But she need only follow.

Angela took a turn round the market square. She gazed in some shop windows and wished that the Treasure Box, which had some intriguing objects on display, was open. Eventually she entered the Sorrento, and by then George, who had been pretending with difficulty not to know she was expected, particularly when confronted with a table set for four, was getting anxious. He'd been there nearly ten minutes himself; what could she be doing?

She arrived in a little flurry. Mario glided forward to take her coat and hand it to a minion who was his nephew. Daniel sprang to greet her, bending to kiss her, something he rarely did; her cheek was cold from the night air. He moved in behind her as she followed Mario to the table, to cut off her retreat in case she tried to flee when she saw her husband.

132

But she did no such thing.

'Well, George! What a surprise,' she said, as he stood up. She spoke calmly, not touching him, no kiss or handshake. 'Vivian, dear, how nice!' She kissed the girl, who had risen awkwardly and now blushed. The enormity of their plot, her idea, suddenly overwhelmed her; the quarrel between Daniel's parents was not her business.

Mario was pouring wine into all the glasses.

'Happy birthday, Mum,' said Daniel, raising his.

'How sweet of you to give me a party,' Angela said.

She was so poised. She looked different, somehow. Her hair was done in a new way and it made her seem younger. It dawned on George that she'd had a rinse. She wore a dress he didn't remember, black and slinky, and a cameo brooch that had been her mother's. Now she took charge of the evening, determined not to permit the young people to feel any sense of humiliation by allowing it to become a social failure. She steered the conversation to subjects they could discuss, asking about their studies, seeming informed as to detail. She turned to George now and then.

'You look well, George,' she said. 'Still playing golf?' and between remarks to Daniel or Vivian inquired about the parish council and the Liberal Association, and expressed pleasure that he had found someone to come in daily and act as housekeeper. She knew Mrs Pearson; a pleasant, reliable woman.

'Yes, she's very dependable,' said George shortly.

He did not like this new Angela: she was tough, confident, even aggressive, like those libbers people were always mentioning; like women he met through his work.

He bent to his veal.

'Dad's taken up jogging,' said Daniel.

'No!' Angela laid down her fork and stared across the table at George. He would not meet her eye, concentrating on his plate, mopping up the rich sauce with rice. 'Have you really, George?'

'Yes. It's wise. Promotes good health,' said George brusquely.

'When do you do it?' Angela asked. 'Up in the morning early? Pounding round the houses with the dawn?'

'No. In the evening, after I get home.' He made an effort to defend himself. 'It refreshes me after the stress of the office. I haven't had a cold all winter.'

'How splendid, George,' said Angela. She was trying not to laugh. 'What do you wear? Little shorts?'

'Of course not, in winter,' snapped George testily. 'I have a proper tracksuit, and when it's very cold I wear a sweater as well. And a singlet, naturally.'

'Oh, naturally.' Angela's mouth was twitching. She carefully cut a slice of chicken.

George's control suddenly snapped.

'It's all very well for you to find it humorous,' he burst out. 'Going off and leaving me alone like that! You won't be so amused if I drop down dead and you're left a widow, though you're well provided for by my pension.'

'George, how dare you,' said Angela coldly. 'I haven't taken a penny from you since I left you.'

'Daniel still depends on me. He isn't self-supporting yet, nor will be for some time,' said George. 'I should have thought it only prudent to keep myself fit.'

'Well, I think it's very funny, you running around at your age puffing and blowing,' Angela said. 'As if you didn't get plenty of exercise playing golf.'

'I don't play every day,' said George. 'Only at weekends. And not always then.' Suddenly he could carry on the charade no longer. He stood up, fumbling for his wallet. 'I appreciate what you've been trying to do, Dan,' he said. 'But you can see the frame of mind your mother's in. It's a waste of time.'

He flung a little scatter of five-pound notes down on the table and marched off, demanding his coat. None of the others moved to stop him as a waiter helped him on with the heavy lined raincoat he wore in winter. As he left the restaurant, George thought he could hear them laughing. Angela noticed that George had finished his main course. The plate was quite clean. He would never make a gesture involving waste.

'Well,' she said. 'I'm enjoying myself, anyway, Daniel. It was a touching idea of yours, getting us together, but you'll do better to see us separately. At least you can feel you've tried.' She smiled at the two of them. 'You'll get used to it, and so will George,' she said.

Daniel was staring down at the money on the table, his distress evident.

'I didn't mean him to pay,' he growled.

'He knows that, Dan. But accept it, darling,' Angela advised. 'Or he'll be even more hurt.' For a moment she met Vivian's gaze.

'He minds dreadfully,' Vivian said, in anguish.

'Yes, but it isn't his heart,' said Angela coolly. 'It's his pride.'

'He's alone – lonely,' Vivian persisted.

'And so was I, while we lived together,' said Angela. 'You can be very lonely within a marriage, Vivian. Don't you know that? I'm only forty-four. Do you think I should spend the rest of my life – maybe another thirty or forty years finding little jobs to do to keep me occupied, running coffee mornings for charity and keeping meals hot when George comes home late? I'm a person, too.'

Vivian was unable to answer. She stared at her plate.

'I'll post him the money,' said Daniel, gathering it up.

'No, don't do that,' said Angela. 'Write and thank him for it, or ring up, and use it to take Vivian somewhere nice quite soon. Now, let's enjoy ourselves, shall we? I'll tell you about my job.'

And she set herself to sparkle for them.

George walked down the road in a blind rage. How dare she mock at him like that? How dare she look so youthful and elegant? Why was she not wearing the pendant he had sent her?

He saw her car, the brown Mini he had bought for her, parked a short way from his own Rover. She

136

talked about not taking his money, but she'd kept that. He kicked at one of its tyres. A silk scarf lay inside on the seat. He tried the door. Of course she hadn't locked it. She'd taken the keys, but he had the duplicate set in his pocket on his own ring. He could drive it away. That would teach her to be so uppity.

As he thought this, a policeman came up to him and asked him what he was doing.

'It's my wife's car,' said George.

'I see, sir. And your name is?'

'Oh – drat it.' Why wasn't the fellow out catching burglars? George supplied his name and address.

'Could I see your driving licence, please, sir?' said the constable courteously.

'Oh, God! Is this necessary?' George found it and handed it over. The policeman made notes in his book and handed it back. George had one endorsement for speeding.

'Leaving now, are you, sir?' the policeman inquired. This certainly did not look like your usual car thief but you couldn't be sure.

George was going to be breathalyzed. He could feel it coming. But he'd had only a couple of glasses of that rather ordinary wine. Would that be enough to do it? He kept his head.

'No,' he said. 'My wife's at a restaurant up the road, with my son. She's driving. I didn't feel well – I came out for some air. I was just checking up on the tyres.'

The policeman bent down to look at them. Luckily they were in good order; it would be too much to bear if they were worn and the policeman held George responsible.

'I see, sir. Feeling better now, are you?' asked the constable. This apparently respectable citizen in his good raincoat didn't seem drunk, though he showed signs of distress.

'Yes, thank you,' said George. 'Much better.'

'Don't forget to lock the car, will you, sir?' the policeman reminded him. 'Before you go back to your family in the restaurant.'

'Oh – no. I'll see to it, officer,' said George.

The policeman watched as he did so, and stood there while George walked away, back towards the Ristorante Sorrento. He peered in at the window. He could see Angela and the others at their table; they were laughing at some good joke, not caring at all that he had gone off alone.

He couldn't go back to the Rover while that policeman was about. He walked on, and into the grounds of the abbey, stumbling about among the tombs, for the doors were locked. After some time he decided it would be safe to return to his own car. The Mini was still there, but there was no sign of the policeman.

George got into his Rover and drove off.

Felicity Cartwright never met her lover, Hugo Morton, on a Wednesday. Tuesday, when a friend came to play picquet with his invalid wife, was their regular evening together, although sometimes they missed even that when the friend failed to show.

He could spare little time for the Treasure Box, in which he was a partner with Felicity. His wife approved of his investment in the business; it would be an interest when he retired in a few years' time. Felicity had given up her London job for several reasons; one was because they were able to meet so little. She had played for some time with the idea of a business of her own, nearer to Hugo, but had too little capital to buy a house and to stake a year's rent on a shop. Hugo was delighted to have found a real way to help her by investing in the shop.

Every evening, before leaving the office, he telephoned her when he did not see her, but that Wednesday he made his call later than usual. When there was no reply, he did not worry. She had said nothing, the night before, about going out, but could have made some subsequent arrangement. He was not her keeper; he was pleased to think she might be making new friends in the area. By the time his wife was asleep, freeing him to telephone unobserved from his own house, it was midnight, and too late. He did not want to wake her.

In the morning, when he'd done the post with his secretary, he rang her at the Treasure Box but again there was no reply, nor was there one from the house.

That was odd. If she'd had to go out, and had no one to look after the shop, she'd have put the Ansaphone on.

He asked the operator to check both telephones and, when no fault could be detected, he made some excuse to his secretary and went round to the Treasure Box. The shop was locked and bolted, the mail thrust through the letterbox lying on the floor inside.

Hugo drove straight to Felicity's house. He had his own key, and he found her there, lying half naked on the bed, with her hands still tied to the bedstead.

13

The police arrived very quickly.

A uniformed constable in a panda car was the first, in answer to the 999 call which Hugo made on Felicity's telephone. After the immediate unbelieving, appalling shock, no other course occurred to him. His first impulse was to free her poor arms, tied up above her head, but, when he touched her, she was cold, and he realized he must disturb nothing.

He waited in Felicity's elegant little sitting room, numb with horror and grief, until the constable arrived. Hugo told him briefly what had happened, then took the officer upstairs and waited outside Felicity's bedroom door. He had spent much of the war in a prisoner-of-war camp; he had seen men killed in battle; but nothing he had seen before had shocked him so much.

The constable came out of the bedroom in a very few seconds.

'Please go downstairs, sir, and wait,' he said. 'I'll need to radio in. Who is the dead woman?'

Hugo told him.

'Are you a relative?' Her husband?'

'No, a friend. She has an antiques shop in the town and she wasn't there today. I could get no reply on the telephone so I came round.'

'The front door was open? Unlocked?'

'No. I have a key.'

'I see, sir. Please go and sit down,' said the constable. 'I'll be with you shortly.'

Hugo returned to the sitting room. Soon the constable returned and said that help was on its way. Then he took out his notebook and asked Hugo some more questions. They were quite straightforward – about the time he had telephoned, and when he had arrived, and when he last saw the dead woman. And his name and address.

The scenes-of-crime officer and Detective Inspector Maude arrived while this was going on. Hugo was allowed to telephone his office to say he would be delayed indefinitely, and then he went to Fletcham police station to make a statement.

He was glad to leave the house. More dreadful things must happen to Felicity's poor body now if the police were to find whoever had committed this monstrous crime.

How had she, in fact, died? He had seen some blood on the quilt, but very little. The policemen told him there was a small wound but they could not say what had caused death. By the time the police doctor arrived to certify that life was extinct, Hugo was already at Fletcham police station making his statement.

Real evidence as to the cause of death must wait until the post-mortem, but the police doctor thought it was probably due to internal bleeding; the liver might have been punctured. If she had received prompt attention, the victim might have recovered. It was obvious she had been raped and routine swabs from her body should yield evidence about the attacker. Traces of her might be found upon him, if a suspect could be found.

The body lay there, waiting for the forensic pathologist to arrive. Establishing the time of attack would be important, and might be difficult. She could have lain there, wounded and alone, a long time before she died. Maude looked at her hands, small, with varnished nails. She might have scratched her assailant, trapping skin particles under her fingernails. He had the hands bagged and started the meticulous work which would tell him about Felicity Cartwright's life, and who might have ended it.

He began with Hugo Morton.

Detective Sergeant Dunn and a detective constable went to see Hugo Morton's wife while her husband was being questioned.

A thin, faded, once pretty woman, Rosemary Morton spent most of her time in a wheelchair. She could move around a little without it, using crutches, but her condition was deteriorating and the time would come when she would have to be wheeled or carried everywhere.

She confirmed that her husband had spent the previous evening at home, arriving from the office at about six fifteen as usual. Their daily housekeeper had left the meal prepared, and he had cooked the vegetables, dishing up the pigeon casserole. He was fond of pigeon, said his wife. After that she had watched television, while Hugo had attended to papers in his study.

'You knew Mrs Cartwright?'

'Naturally,' said Rosemary Morton. 'She was a friend of my sister-in-law. We've known her for years.'

Dunn went stolidly on.

'You were aware of the relationship between your husband and Mrs Cartwright?'

'They were business partners,' said Rosemary.

'He had the key of her house in his possession, madam,' said Dunn.

'I know,' said Rosemary steadily. 'Felicity lived alone and my husband would occasionally do little things about the place to help her. He needed to get into the house sometimes when she was out.'

'What sort of things, Mrs Morton?'

'Er – change tap washers. That sort of thing,' said Rosemary.

She was holding a handkerchief in her knotted, swollen fingers, twisting it round as she spoke. Marital loyalty was a remarkable quality, Dunn reflected.

'Is there anyone else who can confirm that your husband was at home all the evening?' he asked.

There was not. Hugo's car, which according to his statement was in the garage all the evening, would therefore not have been seen by passers-by; anyway, he could have walked to Felicity Cartwright's house in fifteen minutes. His wife, watching television and almost immobile herself, imagining him to be in his study, might have been unaware of his absence if he had left the house for an hour.

When the police had finished talking to his wife and her statement had been taken and signed, Hugo was allowed to leave Fletcham police station. He went back to the office to clear a few things that were urgent, and then hurried home, for Rosemary must be told the news before she heard about it from someone else, or the newspapers.

It had not occurred to him that the police would talk to her. He had been questioned in detail at the station himself, but had thought that inevitable if the police were to discover how Felicity's last hours of life were spent; he had explained clearly that he had touched her hands, wanting to free her, had moved about her room. He put his faith in British justice and the efficiency of the police force; they would find clues which would lead them to the killer. Meanwhile, he must somehow submerge his own grief and shock until there was time to examine them, and prevent hurt to his wife, if he could.

She told him about Detective Sergeant Dunn's visit.

Of course the police must confirm his movements; stupid of him not realize that, Hugo thought, bitterly.

Rosemary gripped her poor twisted hands together. There must be frankness between them now, or they were lost.

'I knew about you and Felicity,' she said. 'In a way, I was glad. It made me feel less guilty, because I'm not much of a wife to you now. I'd much rather it was

Felicity than some little scrubber, or your secretary – someone who would laugh at me, be sneering inside if we met. I liked Felicity and she had a lot of guts. I'm so sorry, Hugo. You must be dreadfully sad.'

He made a move towards her, but did not know what to say. Rosemary took a deep breath and continued.

'I'd imagined I'd die first, and then you could marry her,' she said.

But until today she hadn't really known: she'd suspected, feared, but had no proof.

'Oh God!' Hugo began pacing about the room. He thumped his hand against his forehead. 'I never meant to hurt you,' he said.

'Nor I you, my dear,' said Rosemary sadly. 'But we've each managed to hurt the other. Perhaps we should be glad, in a way.'

'Why? What do you mean?'

'You can only be hurt by those you have some feeling for,' said Rosemary quietly. 'It means the love between us isn't quite dead.'

'Of course it isn't,' said Hugo. 'What an idea!'

'You were caught in a trap, when I fell ill,' said Rosemary. 'You might have left me but, being an honourable man, you didn't.'

'I never would have,' Hugo declared. 'You know I wouldn't.' In sickness and in health, he thought; to love and to cherish. He'd tried.

'If you'd gone out last night, I wouldn't have known,' said Rosemary. 'I went to bed early.'

Rosemary had her own bedroom and bathroom, specially adapted for her, on the ground floor of the house. Sometimes she went to bed soon after dinner; she was often more comfortable, warm in bed with a portable television set in her room, than in her wheelchair. She could still undress herself unaided.

'If you did look in before you went to bed yourself, I don't remember,' Rosemary said. 'I took a pill last night and could have been asleep. I didn't tell the sergeant that. He thinks I watched television in here. I told him what the programme was.'

'I didn't go out last night,' said Hugo dully. 'And, if I had, I'd never have attacked Felicity. Why should I do such a thing?'

'I know. You loved her,' said Rosemary. 'But it may not look like that to the police, or even to our friends. We are probably in for rather a difficult time.'

Later that day, Detective Inspector Maude issued a statement to the press about the killing. It was quite short. The dead woman was named and her age given. She had been found tied to her bed and stabbed, the victim of a sexual assault. It was a vicious crime. Various lines of inquiry were being pursued. The journalists hurried off to write their pieces and try to find photographs of the deceased.

Police officers had already called at houses in Priory Road and the surrounding area, asking if anything suspicious, any unusual passers-by, had been seen. It would not be easy to establish the time of the attack, since the victim had not died at once. Detective Inspector Maude was inclined to believe that Hugo Morton had nothing to do with it, for he would scarcely have returned to the scene of the crime if that were so, but there were plenty of questions he wanted answers to before dismissing that idea for good.

Morton's fingerprints were everywhere in the house, including the bedroom. He had clearly been intimate with the dead woman. Residents from nearby houses – the neighbours on each side and two from over the road – had often seen a grey Volvo parked outside, the same one that was there when the police arrived, or its twin.

'She could have become a nuisance. Threatened to tell his wife about their afrair. Wanted money. Wanted to marry him. Wanted security, getting old, as she was,' hazarded Detective Sergeant Dunn. Morton had made no secret of his financial involvement with Felicity; he had explained about the Treasure Box. 'He could be boxing clever – reasoned we'd think it wasn't him, if he came back and found her, and if he made it look like a rape.'

'Well, forensic will have something on that for us, soon,' Maude said. Morton had made no objection to having a blood sample taken; he went so far, in fact, as to say what his blood group was and produced a blood donor's card to prove it. However, the sample was taken all the same. Swabs from the dead woman's body would disclose the blood group of her attacker if, like seventy-five per cent of the population, he was a secretor. In the absence of a husband, Maude had to consider Morton the most likely suspect until proved otherwise. There was no sign that the house had been broken into; there was no sign of a struggle except in the bedroom. She may have known her killer and let him into the house willingly. Against this was the fact that she had been callously left to die. A killer she could name was unlikely to leave her like that, in case help, however improbably, were to arrive. He would stab her again.

The handkerchief gagging her mouth bore no laundry mark. It was a very ordinary kind and could be bought at stores throughout the country. A great many men would be able to produce one exactly like it. Possibly, when examined, the lab would find something of interest on it, apart from the dead woman's saliva.

A neighbour had seen a man walking along the road the evening before. He was of average height, she thought, but had not really noticed. He wore a raincoat and a hat of some sort. She put the time at between half-past eight and nine but could not be more precise; she had gone upstairs to calm her crying baby and had walked about the room with the child in her arms, drawing back the curtain to distract the infant by giving it something to look at beyond its own room. The child was teething and would sometimes settle if put back in its cot with the street light shining through the window. The lights were on in Mrs Cartwright's house at the time, but the Volvo, often outside, was not there. She could not say if the man had come from Number 7. The other neighbours, behind their drawn curtains, had seen nothing.

In the incident room at Fletcham police station the various reports were studied.

Hugo Morton, the dead woman's lover, was

allegedly at home at the probable time of the crime, but an alibi supplied by a spouse was not reliable.

Police Constable Rowe's routine report of his activities when he was on patrol in the town included an investigation into the credentials of a man in a raincoat, but hatless, whom he had at first suspected of attempting to steal a car. The man had given proof of his own identity, and the car was, as he had said, his wife's; Rowe had checked it on the computer at the time. The man, a Mr George Fortescue, had seemed distressed and had said he felt unwell. Rowe's report included the explanation about his wife being in a local restaurant.

A constable went to check the restaurants in the area off the market square. It was soon established that a Mr Fortescue had reserved a table for four at the Ristorante Sorrento that evening. This Mr Fortescue was a young man, a student, known by sight to the management. The older man in the group had left before the end of the meal after, Mario volunteered, what looked like an argument, but the rest of the party, the two ladies and young Mr Fortescue, had completed the evening in good spirits.

Police Constable Rowe had spoken to Mr Fortescue at ten past eight. Once he'd checked the car, he had resumed his patrol, and later that night had noted the Mini had gone from the market place. The witness who had seen a man in a raincoat near the dead woman's house had estimated the time at between half-past eight and nine. At that hour, with little traffic about, the journey by car would have taken only minutes from the market square. Fresh inquiries as to whether a brown Mini was seen in the area must be made, and any brown Minis reported would be investigated.

Officers were exploring the details of Felicity's life, attempting to discover who were her friends and associates. They had been to the shop to look into its financial standing and had spoken to a woman who sometimes worked there. Now they must seek a connection with George Fortescue.

And they would have to talk to him.

14

Ronald had a severe shock when he glanced at the front page of the *Daily Telegraph* over breakfast and saw under the headline WOMAN ANTIQUE DEALER FOUND DEAD that the victim was Felicity Cartwright. He anxiously read the brief report. The paper disclosed that she had been sexually assaulted and stabbed, and that the police were pursuing their inquiries: no more.

It was quite difficult to eat his eggs and bacon after that.

He took Lynn to school as usual, and for once found it hard to think of conversation; but she did not notice anything wrong, prattling on cheerfully about the play rehearsals and the O-level exams she would face next term. When he reached Crowbury, he went into the newsagent's before opening the shop and bought more papers. Nancy permitted only the *Telegraph* into Number 15, Sycamore Road.

Ronald's hands shook as he unlocked the shop and went inside with the bundle of papers. He began reading at once, and learned that the police had been at Number 7, Priory Street all the previous day. The body had been discovered by the dead woman's business partner, Hugo Morton, and there was a picture of him leaving the police station. Facts about Felicity Cartwright emerged. She had moved from London to Fletcham only recently; she had been widowed years before and had had one son who had died in a road accident at the age of eighteen. A sad article had been constructed by the practised crime reporter. There were pictures of the small house in Priory Road and of the Treasure Box, and a shot of Felicity, not at all like her, taken from her passport. It was implied that the police had no lead; the theory that she had been killed by some casual intruder, a burglar surprised in the act of robbing the house, was not rejected.

He hadn't thought of staging a robbery, but he hadn't intended to kill her. He'd meant to bring pleasure to himself and to punish her. Well, he'd done that, all right, though the pleasure had been slight and fleeting – better than with Valerie, but not like that first, amazing time with Dorothea Wyatt. He shut his eyes and tried to imagine it once more, but failed; his mental image became Felicity, her body white and thin, the hip bones protruding, the ribs visible. He could not superimpose Dorothea's plumper, responsive form upon this memory.

He'd barely touched her with the knife. How could she be dead?

He'd thought about her yesterday, imagining her freeing herself eventually. She'd tell the police, of course, but he'd left no clues. He'd worn gloves throughout. Perhaps she had a weak heart, and that had killed her. She'd certainly been frightened, and he had enjoyed that.

There was the handkerchief he'd used for a gag. He'd left it. He panicked, remembering. But it had been clean, spotlessly laundered by Nancy. It was an ordinary handkerchief, plain white, without an initial; he owned no other kind. There must be thousands like it in daily use.

He grew slowly calmer. All he had to do was keep his nerve; the police would be baffled. If they were ingenious enough to discover he had taken that box to Fletcham for the dead woman after the sale nearby, he would insist that this was their only meeting, but he had better admit to going into the house while she wrote her cheque, lest his fingerprints be found. The business nature of their encounter could be proved by the passage of her cheque through his account.

At lunchtime, when the shop was shut, he went out to the van and brought in the knife, wrapped up in a rag. It didn't look bloodstained, but he washed it thoroughly at the sink and then took it back to the van again. He threw the rag into the dustbin in the back yard behind the shop.

He looked at his magazines as usual that evening, after doing the books, but they failed to excite him. He needed the real thing now. When he returned them to the drawer, he put the newspapers reporting Felicity's death under them. Then he went home to the steak pie Nancy had prepared, without calling at the Plough.

She had heard the local radio's report of the killing in Fletcham, and did not know what things were coming to. There were some peculiar people in the world, she said. Had Ronald met the murdered woman?

Yes, he told her, at a sale, and had afterwards sold her a box he'd bought at it.

'Dear, dear,' said Nancy.

When George returned from the office on Friday evening, a police car was parked outside his house.

He ran the Rover into the garage, switched off the ignition and secured the steering lock. He locked the driver's door when he got out of the car; the other doors were still locked, as they had been while the car was in the station yard. He took his time, closing the garage doors and locking them too; you could not be too careful, even in Crowbury.

He could not think what the police might want with him unless to solicit funds for some charity.

Two men in plain clothes were waiting for him as he walked towards his dark house.

'Mr George Fortescue?' asked one, and introduced himself as Detective Sergeant Dunn, based at Fletcham.

Could this be connected with the episode two nights ago? Surely not? The matter had been concluded.

George admitted his identity, hoping they would not keep him long; his schedule would be thrown out if they did, for the next event on it was his nightly jog.

'We'd like a word with you, sir. May we go in?' said Dunn, standing solidly before George, between him and the gate.

George turned and put his key in the lock, fumbling a little in the gloom.

'Certainly,' he said. 'But I'm a busy man, sergeant.'

The two men followed him in, as George put on lights, going ahead into the sitting room where he turned on an electric fire in the grate. The room was warm, the central heating timed to cut in an hour before his return.

'Well?' George took off his raincoat and laid it over a chair. He had left his tweed hat in the hall as they passed through. 'What can I do for you, sergeant?' he asked. 'I can give you five minutes.'

'It will take longer than that, sir,' said Dunn. 'Shall we sit down?'

George wavered. To sit was to place himself at a possible psychological disadvantage. Yet to think like that was foolish; he had done no wrong. Perhaps, though, he had exceeded the speed limit driving from London to Fletcham on Wednesday evening, and been caught by an infernal machine that would record his car's registration number as it went too fast through some electronic barrier. He had hurried, it was true, and there was that endorsement already on his licence. He began to sweat a little as he sat down in his usual chair.

The sergeant took a seat facing him, and the other man one a little apart.

'You were in the market square at Fletcham last Wednesday evening at eight ten p.m.,' stated Dunn. 'You were spoken to by Constable Rowe of C division.'

'I talked to a policeman, yes,' George said. 'I didn't

156

ask his name. He looked at my driving licence. Everything was quite in order. A conscientious officer,' he added. Some flannel might get rid of this one quickly.

Rowe's report stated that George Fortescue was returning to the restaurant where his wife was, which he had left because he felt ill. But he hadn't returned, according to inquiries at the Sorrento.

'After this conversation with the officer, where did you go?' Dunn wanted to know, and waited with interest for the answer.

What could be behind all this? Had Angela done some damn fool thing on her way home, and had her number taken, George wondered. The police would not know she was not living here now; the address on her records would still be this one.

'Well?' Dunn prompted.

George realized that if he said he had wandered about the abbey grounds until he thought the coast was clear to allow him to return to his own car and drive off, his conduct would be thought curious, to put it mildly.

'I went back to the restaurant, of course,' he said.

'Which restaurant, sir?'

'The Ristorante Sorrento, in Abbey Road,' said George.

'You went back there?' Dunn gave him another chance.

'Yes.'

'And how long did you remain there, Mr Fortescue?'

'Till the end of the meal. Another half-hour or so.'

That would be about right, George thought, to allow for dessert and coffee.

'I see, sir. And then?'

'I came home,' said George.

'It's forty miles, but the road is good. It would take about an hour. You'd be back when, Mr Fortescue?'

'I don't know. Between ten and half-past, I suppose,' said George unhappily. That would be if he left, as he'd said, at nine, but in fact, he'd been very late. He'd been so upset that he hadn't come straight back but had driven about aimlessly for some time, raging at Angela and the fates and his own misfortune. Eventually he had gone into a pub somewhere out in the wilds and had had three whiskies. It had crossed his mind to go round to Daniel's lodgings and apologize for the upset to the boy's plans, which after all were well meant. It was Angela's fault that the evening had gone wrong; she had behaved irresponsibly, mocking him, just as her departure had been totally irresponsible. But in the end he'd decided to leave it; the girl would be there, very likely, and it made him uncomfortable to see the blatant evidence of how they lived. Youngsters were quite without morals, it seemed to him, and shameless. Daniel got it from his mother, of course.

But if he told this sergeant that he'd stopped for a few drinks on the way home, could they get him after the event for driving over the limit? Surely not. What could all this be about? He hadn't had an accident on the way back; he couldn't have hit someone, or some other car, without knowing it had happened, surely?

He remembered no near miss. Could some busybody have reported seeing him driving without due care and attention? He might have been doing that, upset as he was after such an evening. He decided not to risk mentioning the pub.

'Can anyone confirm what time you got home?' asked Dunn. 'Your wife?' They must have travelled back together in the Mini.

'No – er – she's away. We went independently to the restaurant that night,' said George. 'I had my own car.'

Dunn nodded.

'I see, Mr Fortescue.' All those inquiries about a Mini near the dead woman's house were now, very likely, a waste of time. He'd have gone there in his Rover.

Dunn asked George next if he knew a Mrs Felicity Cartwright who lived at Number 7, Priory Street, Fletcham. After that the interview became a nightmare.

George denied all knowledge of where Priory Street was, but it made no difference.

'You didn't need to know the name of the street, nor even the lady's name, did you?' Dunn said. 'She'd have let you in, as likely as not, a well-spoken man like you with a tale of wanting to sell her double glazing or life insurance. What is your job, Mr Fortescue?'

'I am in insurance,' said George. But his position was lofty; he did not pound on doors.

It was some time before he understood that this Mrs Cartwright, whoever she was, had been

159

murdered, and the police thought he was involved because he was in Fletcham when she was killed. At one point he was asked what clothes he was wearing on Wednesday evening, and they all trooped upstairs to inspect his wardrobe. The policemen put his suit and his shoes into separate plastic bags which the younger one fetched from the car; they fished in the linen basket for his soiled shirt and socks and put them in bags too.

When they left to return to Fletcham, they took him with them, saying they wanted a statement from him and to ask him some more questions. They would not let him put on his raincoat and tweed hat, putting them into more plastic bags. He was allowed to collect an anorak out of the cloakroom to wear instead, but the detective constable went with him, even there, and stood outside with the door ajar.

Valerie saw one of the more sensational newspaper reports of the attack on Felicity Cartwright. She felt sick as she read it. The woman must have known the same terror as herself, but had not survived. She'd fought, of course, as Valerie would have done, but for the threat to the children.

Could it have been the same man? It was forty miles away and, if so, was just as Detective Constable Cooley had prophesied, in another area altogether. Pity for the dead woman mingled with relief in her mind.

Cooley came round that evening after the children

were in bed, passing, on the road, his colleagues from Fletcham bearing George Fortescue off for questioning. He rang her bell and gave a cheerful rat-tat on the door, then started to whistle, hoping by these signals to impress on her as she came to the door that it was a friend.

After careful inquiry, and first peering round the door as the chain held it, she let him in.

'Don't make so much noise, you'll wake the children,' she said, almost laughing.

He grinned at her. That was better.

'Villains don't make a shindig,' he said. 'I didn't want to scare you, coming round at this time of night.' It was just after eight o'clock. 'We'll have to have a code knock. Then you'll know when it's me.'

'Well, as you're here, come in by the fire,' said Valerie, her tone more welcoming than her choice of words.

She'd been sewing, turning up a hem on a skirt for Melissa made from an adult one bought at a jumble sale. The room was faintly smoky, from a log that had fallen forward while she went to the door, and she pushed it back with a long poker.

'Tea?' she asked. 'Coffee? I'm afraid I haven't got any beer.'

'Tea'd be lovely, I hoped you'd suggest it,' said Cooley, and he followed her out to the kitchen. While she put the kettle on, he bent over a colouring book Timmy had left on the table, a page half done, picked up a crayon and began blocking in a soldier's scarlet tunic. 'I like colouring,' he said.

'Have you got any children?' Valerie asked.

161

'No, love. I'm not married,' said Cooley, colouring on. 'Thought I was going to be, once, but it came to nothing. Not easy, in this job, you see.'

'Where do you live, then?' Valerie asked.

'In digs. Good ones, with an inspector's widow as my landlady,' said Cooley. 'Comfortable.'

'Does she give you a meal?'

'Not now I'm CID,' said Cooley. 'Used to when things were more predictable. She does on Sundays sometimes.'

'Like something now?' Valerie asked. 'What have you had?'

'Fish and chips in the nick,' said Cooley.

'There's cake,' said Valerie. 'Chocolate cake.'

'Yes, please,' said Cooley, and his face lit up when he saw the light, yielding sponge, the butter filling oozing out. 'Did you make it?'

'Yes.'

He was just like Timmy, eating it up greedily without waiting for his tea. Valerie was smiling as she poured water into the teapot.

Cooley accepted a second slice of cake to take with him to the fireside, and asked Valerie if she wouldn't have one too.

'Please do, Valerie,' he said. 'I won't feel so greedy, then.'

Valerie still wasn't eating much. She had lost ten pounds. Perhaps she could manage a small slice of cake. She cut one, and added it to the tray.

Cooley picked it up and carried it in for her. Then he stoked up the fire rather more effectively than she had done, and settled himself comfortably into the one armchair, leaving the sofa for her. He sat back, waiting for his tea.

It was some time before they talked about the attack in Fletcham, but it was in both their minds.

'Could it be the same man?' Valerie asked at last. 'The one who came here?'

'Who's to say, at this stage?' said Cooley. 'They'll find evidence, there.' He did not spell it out: there'd been no bath for the victim. 'They'll get him,' he said confidently. Maybe they would. 'A long way from here, too, Fletcham is, Valerie.'

'He may do it again, though.'

'Yes. If we don't catch him first.'

'That woman was on her own too. Like me.'

'Yes.'

'He'd be looking for that. Someone alone, I mean.'

'Maybe. Well, yes. But a lot of women are alone at times, aren't they? Vulnerable.'

Nothing was too severe a punishment for a man who terrorized women like this, Cooley thought. It was a dreadful thing that a young – or indeed, any – woman could not walk through the streets of Crowbury or Fletcham without risking assault. A knife was common to the two attacks. He contemplated asking her if she could remember any more details, but decided not to risk upsetting her.

'You're looking better, Val,' he said.

'I'm not pregnant,' said Valerie. 'Thank God.'

'I'm very glad to hear it,' said Cooley.

While his colleagues at Tellingford were being informed, as a matter of courtesy, that George Fortescue of Crowbury was on the way to Fletcham for questioning in connection with the murder of Mrs Felicity Cartwright, Cooley settled down to spend half an hour chatting with Valerie. Why not?

15

Much too early on Saturday morning, Dorothea Wyatt's telephone was ringing. Her caller was Daniel Fortescue. In her usual waking fuddled state, Dorothea strove to understand his message.

'Do you know where my father is, Mrs Wyatt?' he was asking. 'I can't get any answer from the house.'

'Oh, can't you?'

'I tried several times last night, and I've tried this morning, but I can't raise him,' said the boy. 'I asked the exchange to check the line and they seem certain it's ringing properly.'

'They're often wrong,' said Dorothea. 'Sometimes it sounds as if it's making the ringing noise, but you can't hear it in the house.'

'I know,' said Daniel.

There was a small silence. He wanted action from her, Dorothea realized.

'It's a bit embarrassing, Mrs Wyatt,' Daniel ploughed on at last. 'My father came over here on Wednesday, and he was rather upset. I just wondered if he was all right, as I haven't heard from him since then. Have you seen him lately?'

Dorothea hadn't.

'Is he playing golf, Daniel?' she suggested. 'He starts early, when he plays, doesn't he? And he goes up most weekends.'

'I know,' said Daniel. 'I thought of that and I rang the club, to ask if his car was there. I had an awful job persuading someone to go and look. It isn't.'

By now, Dorothea was sitting up and her head was clearing. An inescapable duty was being thrust upon her.

'What's worrying you, Daniel?'

'Well – it seems silly, but I'm afraid he may have had an accident,' said Daniel. In his mind was a vision of his father lying on the bedroom floor, having swallowed dozens of sleeping pills. He might have access to them; people who really wanted them seemed to get them all right and Daniel had no means of knowing if his father, in his bereft state, had applied to the doctor for a prescription. He would have to add some explanation. 'You see, Mrs Wyatt, I lured my mother and father over here together, the other evening, hoping that if they met things might be patched up. It was a total failure.'

'Oh dear!' Dorothea saw that she could avoid her task no longer. 'You want me to go round and see if he's all right,' she stated.

'Oh, would you, Mrs Wyatt?'

Dorothea muffled a groan.

'Of course I will, Daniel,' she said.

'I can come over, but it would be quicker, you see, if anything's wrong,' said Daniel.

'I do see,' said Dorothea. 'Sensible of you to ring

me, Daniel. It will take me a little while, though. I'm not properly dressed. Give me half an hour and then ring again. Or can I ring you?'

'Oh yes – there's a phone at my digs,' said Daniel. 'I'm using it now. I'll stay nearby till you call.'

'And, if I don't, you ring me back,' said Dorothea. 'Just in case there is a fault on the line.'

'Right. Thank you very much, Mrs Wyatt,' said Daniel. He gave her the number. 'Goodbye for now, then.'

She replaced the receiver and swung her legs over the side of the bed, grimacing. But once she stood up and began pulling on slacks and sweater, she felt better. She had something urgent to do, nuisance though it was.

She didn't wait to make coffee. George was sure to be at home, doing something in the garden or the garage where he couldn't hear the telephone; with all that keep-fit lark of his, he'd certainly be an early riser at the weekend. She'd take coffee off him and make him ring his anxious son.

She opened the garage, got out her car, and drove round to Orchard House.

There was no answer when she rang the bell. She tried several times, and walked all round the house, but there was no sign of anyone being at home. A bottle of milk stood on the step and the newspaper was thrust through the letterbox. George's Rover was in the garage; she saw it through the window. She walked all round again and tried the back door and the french window, but they were locked. She could see the entire garden from the patio, laid by George's own hand outside the sitting-room window, but he was not there. She looked in the shed, to make certain.

There were several simple explanations. He might be out shopping in the village, on foot. He could be jogging. A friend could have taken him to the golf club.

She went home, made herself some coffee, and then telephoned Daniel.

'He never jogs in the morning,' said Daniel when she put forward this theory.

'There has to be a first time for everything,' said Dorothea. But what about the milk and the news-paper? Could both have arrived after he left on his run? She felt she must put this point to Daniel, who grew more alarmed.

'I wonder if I should ring the police?' he said.

'Oh no, Daniel. George won't thank you if you make a fuss and he's innocently at the butcher's. Though I did glance round the village as I came back,' she acknowledged.

'I'd better come over,' Daniel decided. 'I've got a key.' If anyone had to find his father's corpse, he was the proper person.

'I've got a better idea,' said Dorothea. 'It will take you at least an hour to get here, Daniel. Mrs Pearson must have a key, or know where one is kept. She lets herself in when your father's gone to the office. I'll go and tell her you've rung up and ask her for it. Then I'll ring you back.'

Fulsome thanks came down the line. How wearing all this emotion was, thought Dorothea. Her excursion would give time for George to return from the harmless expedition he was doubtless on, unless a friend had taken him to the golf club, which seemed the most likely answer.

He could be ill. Harry had died, on the bedroom floor, of a sudden heart attack. But not George too, surely? And he was younger, by some years, than Harry had been. All that healthy jogging would take care of George's arteries, wouldn't it? Or was the damage done already? Leo had thought the jogging itself might be dangerous. He could be right.

She had another cup of coffee and a piece of toast, then drove to Mrs Pearson's council bungalow and explained her mission. Mrs Pearson, trustee of the key, insisted on accompanying her back; two heads were better than one, she said, not liking to admit that it would not be right to surrender the key, even to Mrs Wyatt, without authority from her employer. Besides, she was curious.

George was not lying dead anywhere in the house. His bed, the large double bed he'd shared with Angela, was neatly made, the coverlet taut.

The two women looked at one another.

'Golf?' said Dorothea.

'He keeps his things in the cloakroom,' said Mrs Pearson, bustling off.

George's golf clubs were in their place in a corner of the cloakroom, the trolley, folded, by their side.

Dorothea took Mrs Pearson home. Then she rang Daniel. They agreed that he should tell the police that his father could not be traced, though it seemed rather a drastic step to take.

169

Mrs Pearson, meanwhile, told her husband and neighbours that Mr Fortescue had disappeared.

Fibres of a dark, purplish wool, almost black, had been found under Felicity Cartwright's fingernails, but no skin particles so she might not have marked the face of her assailant.

Sitting in the interview room at Fletcham police station as the night wore on and various officers came in and out to talk to him, or left him alone with a silent, uniformed constable, George's nightmare continued. At one stage, when he complained that he had eaten nothing for hours, they brought him a cup of tea and a cheese sandwich. On and on they went, asking him about a house they kept calling Number 7, Priory Road. How had he got in? Where was the knife?

'You were in Fletcham on Wednesday evening?'

'Yes.'

'You left the Ristorante Sorrento at between eight five and eight ten p.m.?'

'I left. I didn't look at the time.'

'You were addressed by PC Rowe at eight ten in the market square.'

'I talked to a policeman, yes.'

'And afterwards? What did you do then? You said you went back to the restaurant but there are witnesses to say that you did not. Where were you?'

On and on it went, with the imputation that he had been to Priory Road, wherever that was, and killed some woman: the same questions, the same answers, for what seemed hours.

For a long time George did not mention his walk

round the abbey grounds. It would sound so foolish. When at last he did, the policeman who was talking to him at the time thought he was making it up. He went on to relate how he had called at a pub after that, but he had not been on the usual road home as he'd driven around a bit, so he could not say where it was.

This was when you called your solicitor, whose advice would be to say nothing. George could not drag his golfing companion Bill Kyle all the way over to Fletcham because the police had gone mad. In the end, truth would prevail.

They jumped on his story about the abbey and the visit to the pub. He'd been disturbed, upset; he admitted that, didn't he? After the row with his wife?

George allowed that he was distressed.

If he'd gone to a pub, he'd remember which one, declared Detective Inspector Maude, who had returned to interrogate him. He'd in fact gone to the house in Priory Road and killed Mrs Cartwright.

It was Detective Sergeant Dunn who remembered that the police in Tellingford had reported an alleged rape at Tellingford, two weeks before the murder. Right on George Fortescue's home patch, that was. And a knife had been used.

A knife was common to both assaults.

Where was it now?

The radio news was on during breakfast. Nancy and Ronald heard that a man was helping the police at Fletcham with their inquiries into the death of Felicity Cartwright.

'Well, so that's that,' said Nancy, putting a kipper on Ronald's plate. He liked a nice kipper, juicy and bursting away from its thready skeleton, not one of your packets of frozen fillets. 'Though I daresay she was no better than she should be.'

'No. Yes.' Ronald did not know what to reply. He picked up his knife and fork and began to dissect the kipper. What could be happening in Fletcham?

Later, he helped Lynn into the van with a hand on her elbow. She could feel his grip even through her coat.

Before polishing the brasses, she helped him set out some porcelain that Nancy had finished repairing.

'She is clever, Auntie Nancy, doing this so well,' said Lynn.

'You should learn from her,' said Ronald. 'It's a useful skill. You can make a living, doing this. You've got nice, delicate hands, you'd be good at it.' He held her hand for a moment, and gave it a squeeze.

'Oh, Uncle Ron!' Lynn giggled. 'I wouldn't be patient enough,' she said.

He didn't go out that morning. Calls to dealers could wait. He still felt a bit edgy.

While Lynn was having her lunch in the cellar, and he was minding the shop above, she stood her hot mug of coffee on the desk, then realized it might leave a ring. She got up and fetched the telephone directory to put underneath it. Somehow or other, she was clumsy, and knocked over the mug that stood on the desk, filled with pencils and pens. The pens and pencils spilled out, and so did a small brass key.

Lynn picked up the pencils and pens from the floor and looked at the key in her hand, about to replace it. She turned it round, glancing at the desk. Did it belong to the locked drawer? If so, it was private. Perhaps there were valuables locked inside: silver or jewels. She went on eating her sandwiches, the key before her.

Then she opened the drawer.

Just newspapers. That was all there was. How dull. She lifted one out, and another. They were faded, old. Then she saw the magazines. She opened one.

Lynn knew about pornography, of course; people were always on about it. It was what you saw in the centre of some of the papers, girls photographed nude. Perhaps there were fellows, too, with their backs turned. Just rude. She'd never dreamed that women would allow themselves to be pictured in attitudes like this. She stared in fascinated horror, turning over several pages before snapping the magazine shut and pushing it back in the drawer. She piled the newspapers on top, and closed the drawer, her cheeks flaming, feeling rather sick. It was nasty, vulgar. Uncle Ron couldn't know what was in the drawer.

But who else had locked it?

Lynn replaced the key in the mug, and put the pens and pencils on top of it. She had not seen the newspapers beneath the magazines, the ones bought the day before, reporting the murder.

Uncle Ron couldn't have bought that magazine, and the others that lay beneath it which she hadn't examined. He just couldn't have. They must have got into the drawer by accident. Probably he thought he'd lost the key.

She tried not to think about it but, when he laid his hand on her knee before she got out of the van that evening, bidding her farewell, she shrank back from him, reaching out for the door handle and letting herself out as fast as she could.

Whatever was wrong with her, Ronald wondered, as she hurried away. Got her period suddenly, perhaps, he thought, and smiled. Dear little Lynn.

16

Daniel consulted the telephone directory in order to discover the number of Tellingford police station. Then, in the midst of dialling, the difficulty of expressing his concern over the telephone occurred to him. He mentally rehearsed the conversation.

'I wish to report my father missing.'

'Missing from where?'

Details would follow.

'When did you last see your father?'

The dialogue seemed fraught. It would be better to do the thing in person, here in Fletcham, speaking to the policeman man-to-man, lest they think it some sort of hoax. The Fletcham police would ask the ones at Tellingford to search discreetly. Wouldn't they?

Because he made this decision, Daniel learned very quickly where his father was, though not the reason, and he was not allowed to see him. Totally bewildered, he importuned the sergeant at the desk.

'Helping with inquiries into an incident,' was the sergeant's answer.

'But what incident?'

Everyone in Fletcham knew about the murder. It

had been headline news in the *Fletcham Gazette*, conveniently happening just before the paper went to press. Daniel, not particularly interested, though appropriately shocked that such a serious crime should happen in what was not, on the whole, an area noted for its violence, knew that the woman's body had been found some time after his disastrous evening with his parents. But it was the failure of that evening that concerned him; not the death, tragic though it was, of some unknown person. He saw no connection.

Because of his persistence, the sergeant at last was moved to action. Daniel was taken down a passage and into a small, bleak room. There was a table and two upright chairs in the centre; no other furnishings. For a panic-stricken few minutes he wondered if he had been arrested; it was no more lunatic a thought than that his father should be here, somewhere in the building. Then a man came in, one not in uniform, burly, with very pale blue eyes and thick, dark hair cut very short. He introduced himself as Detective Sergeant Dunn.

'You met your father here at the Ristorante Sorrento on Wednesday evening,' he stated.

Daniel nodded.

'A woman was killed that night,' said Dunn. He made no allegations; no charges had been brought against George Fortescue and at the moment it looked as though none could be, unless he cracked. It was too soon for forensic to come up with any proof.

'But my father went straight home,' said Daniel.

'Did he?'

176

'He must have done. Why not?'

'He was upset. A constable spoke to him and he said he was returning to the restaurant, but he didn't go back there. Did he?'

'No.' This was puzzling. The sergeant must have misunderstood.

'He can't account satisfactorily for his immediate actions,' Dunn remarked.

'But you can't think he—' Suddenly the gravity of his father's position became clear to Daniel. 'No! You're mad! He didn't know her. He wouldn't! He couldn't! Where is he. Surely he can explain?' Daniel looked round wildly as if expecting his father to peer through bars in the adjacent wall.

'He hasn't yet,' said Dunn.

Police harassment. Daniel had read about it, heard fellow students mention it, but not experienced it. Here it was.

'A woman was killed,' said Dunn. 'Violently. Left bound and gagged, terrified, bleeding to death. Whoever did that is going to pay for it, lad.'

But it couldn't be his father!

Daniel blundered out of the station, his one idea to find Vivian quickly. Something must be done. But he realized, himself, what it should be before he found her, and telephoned Bill Kyle, his father's solicitor.

It took some time to track him down, in fact, since he was on the golf course, and even longer before he was able to rescue George. He drove straight over to Fletcham and at last persuaded the police to let him take George home.

They left the police station by the back entrance to

avoid press photographers and journalists who were clustered at the front. At the moment George was a man unnamed, and his best hope of peace lay in remaining so, but Bill feared he was far from out of the wood.

They dropped Daniel at his digs; he would come over to Crowbury the next day. Bill would let Dorothea know that George was all right, but would conceal from her what had happened; the fewer people to know about it the better. He telephoned his wife, warning her that he would be bringing George back for a meal.

While they ate, Bill and Eileen Kyle urged George to spend the night with them, but he insisted on returning to Orchard House. There was no one about when Bill delivered him to his door and he slunk in, like a dog with its tail between its legs, Bill thought, as he turned the car to drive away. He'd come round in the morning. After a night's rest, George would be able to explain himself more clearly than he'd managed so far; there were huge holes in the tale he had told that must be filled.

At nine o'clock on Sunday morning a policeman called at Orchard House. He was a plain clothes officer, driving his own car, but George recognized him when he opened the door; he had been in the background during the horrors of the previous twenty-four hours.

George had just woken from a heavy sleep; he'd dropped off quite soon after going to bed, for Bill had plied him with several whiskies, though he'd refused to drink any wine; he'd felt slightly sick and hadn't done justice to Eileen Kyle's grilled steak. Then, during the night, he'd started awake with his pulse racing and sweat streaming from him, mindless with terror. When he'd at last calmed down, he'd lain there in the big bed, brooding about Angela, filled with bitter resentment. If she'd been here, in her proper place, looking after him and the house, none of this would have happened. Even if she'd behaved well on Wednesday evening, he'd have been safe; it was because she had laughed at him that he'd left the restaurant. It was all her fault. He'd lain sleepless for a long time; then, when at last he'd relaxed, he'd fallen into a torpor, not refreshing at all, and he woke feeling dull and stupid.

The detective constable at the door wanted to go through his clothes.

'But why? You've taken some already,' protested George. 'Besides, you know you made a great mistake; I can't help you at all. I've told you over and over again.' What redress was there for him, an innocent citizen? He thought about threatening the young man with a complaint to the chief constable. But he felt too weary.

'I want to have a look at your clothes,' persisted the detective constable.

They'd win in the end, George knew. He took the young man upstairs and left him there, while he went down to make coffee. His mouth tasted sour and his head ached; he wouldn't be able to eat a thing.

The policeman did not stay long. He went away taking a dark pullover George often wore for golf; it was one Angela had knitted some years earlier, made in an intricate arran pattern from dark purplish wool,

179

almost black. She was a good knitter. He took some gloves and socks, too.

Daniel and Vivian arrived soon after he had gone, while George was having a shower. Despite feeling dirty and sticky the night before, he'd been too tired to do more than pull off his clothes and fall into bed. When he came downstairs he wore well-pressed dark grey slacks and a pale grey sweater over a checked shirt. The skin on his bald head shone, the surrounding hair neatly trimmed. He always looked smart, thought Vivian.

As soon as Bill Kyle arrived, Vivian made coffee for everyone. She could, at least, be useful in the kitchen.

George told Bill about the policeman's call and the removal of the sweater.

'I didn't do it, Bill. But they don't believe me,' said George. 'I thought they did, at last, and that was why they let me go, but now this!'

'They've got to eliminate you. It's just routine, George,' said Bill. 'Try to be patient.'

Bill's expertise lay in conveyancing and probate, and alas, today, in the murky depths of divorce suits. He had never before had a client questioned in connection with murder and he was worried; George's account of his movements on the relevant evening, after he left the restaurant, was far from satisfactory. 'Have you really no idea what pub it was you went to, that night?' he asked.

'No. I just drove about, and there it was,' said George wretchedly. 'It was your usual country pub. Oak beams and so on. Not very big.'

'We'll have to find it. It'll give you an alibi,' said Bill. But would it? When was the woman attacked? While George was blundering about in the abbey grounds?

'Oh Dad, this is all my fault,' said Daniel. 'If I hadn't planned that evening, you wouldn't have been in Fletcham and it wouldn't have happened.'

'But Dan, you can't blame yourself,' said Vivian. He'd been doing it ever since he discovered what had happened to his father. 'No one can foretell what's going to be the result of some action they may take.' She'd thought of this to comfort herself for her own feelings of guilt.

'Quite right, my dear,' said Bill. What a sensible girl. He sighed. George was his friend as well as his client. It was inconceivable that he should have killed that unfortunate woman. A punch on someone's nose, perhaps, stretching the imagination wildly, in a brawl started by another, but rape – never. On the other hand, who would have imagined Dr Crippen to be such a monster? And there was Haigh. The names of notorious murderers passed through the solicitor's mind. But not George. Where would he get hold of a knife? And why this particular woman? Yet there were knives in every kitchen drawer.

Why had the police taken his sweater? It was one he often wore; Bill knew it well.

'Let's go and look for that pub,' he said. 'We must find it.' The hunt would keep them all occupied, too; otherwise George and those youngsters would sit about all day thrashing it over. 'Eileen's expecting you all to lunch. We'll look for it afterwards.'

They found it, late in the evening, rather by chance, just as George had done. It was the Fox and Hounds at Braycote, well away from any main road, similar to several others George had thought might be the right one, at which they'd stopped earlier. All were closed during the afternoon and they'd had to prowl round them, wondering about them, uncertain.

But by the time they reached Braycote, the law allowed you to buy a drink, and the Fox and Hounds was open. George was sure it was the place.

The landlord, though, was vague. He thought he remembered George, but could not be definite. They did not tell him why they were asking about it, and he thought it must be some trouble at home; a suspicious wife, perhaps.

'We get so many in, you see,' he said. 'I couldn't swear to it. It's not as if you were a regular.'

'Don't worry, George,' said Bill robustly, when they left.

'If necessary we can follow this up. Some of the customers there that night will remember you. Sure to.'

But George wasn't a man you'd really remember, unless for some special reason. He was an excellent example of your Mr Average. And he'd said that, beyond buying his drinks, he'd talked to no one.

Bill dropped them back at Orchard House and went home to his wife. He agreed that George might as well go to the office next day; with luck it would all blow over. The police might have a lead, by now, in the right direction. Bill spoke confidently, but already the names of leading counsel were coming into his mind.

Before Daniel and Vivian returned to Fletcham, George ground out his thanks for what his son had done.

'I'd be locked up by now, if you hadn't got Bill,' he said. 'Thanks, Daniel. And – er – for wondering where I was, in the first place.'

'It'll be all right, Dad,' said Daniel. It was odd to be cast in a paternal role towards one's own father, but this was how he felt.

'Oh yes – certainly,' said George. 'Don't let your mother know about it, will you?'

Daniel had been wondering about this very point.

'No?'

'No.'

George did not want Angela feeling sorry for him, in addition to everything else. Perhaps she wouldn't be sorry; perhaps it would make her laugh.

By the time the young people had gone it was too late, he told himself, to go jogging, though he'd missed exercise now for three whole days. He'd get back to routine tomorrow, when he caught his normal train. Routine was what mattered. With every moment in the day planned for and occupied, there was no time to brood.

All was peaceful at Number 15, Sycamore Road, that Sunday. Ronald cleaned out the garden shed, so that everything would be spruce when it was time for the spring sowing. He sorted through old seed packets, and checked his hose connections; he cleaned all his tools, which were always well kept but could benefit from a wipe down with an oily rag: not for Ronald the earth-encrusted fork or spade; even his trowel gleamed like new.

The black sweater he had worn at Fletcham was still in the van, hidden under the driver's seat with the knife and the balaclava helmet. He'd washed the knife but there might be blood on the sweater.

Nancy had the radio on as she prepared lunch: roast lamb with mint jelly, and steamed syrup pudding. Ronald loved a steamed pudding and, as long as this taste was not indulged too often, it could do him no harm. He was still the same weight as when they married; gardening and heaving furniture around kept him fit.

She heard the announcer say that the man who had been helping the police with inquiries in Fletcham had been allowed to leave.

'They've let him go,' she said, as Ronald made ready to carve the lamb.

'Let who go, dear?' Ronald was sharpening the knife; he ran his finger along the blade to test it.

'That brute who killed Mrs Cartwright,' said Nancy.

Ronald's hands were steady as he made the first incision in the meat. The juices ran the palest pink.

'Oh?' he said, and lifted out a succulent slice.

'There were no details,' said Nancy. 'Just that he'd gone home and inquiries were going on. Talked himself out of it, I suppose. They don't often pick up the wrong man.'

'No,' said Ronald.

He felt no concern at all about an innocent person being in trouble for what he had done. It was as though a different being, not Ronald Trimm of Sycamore Road, Tellingford, at all, had made the assault on Felicity Cartwright. That man, in his hood and black sweater, was charged with physical energy and sexual drive, capable of amazing feats; Ronald Trimm, now carving lamb, was a mild man, a dutiful husband who loved his wife and was blessed in his home life. Nevertheless, good Ronald Trimm had, in middle age, discovered that he could experience bliss, and it was not too late to pursue it. Other men did it all the time – with ease, it seemed. Now Ronald would seek opportunities for finding ecstasy himself, if necessary by force. But he had better wait and see what happened over this Fletcham business; allow the hue and cry to die down.

If someone else was blamed, it would make the next time much easier.

Savouring the lamb, he thought about Lynn. He would be sorry to scare her, yet in a way there was excitement in arousing fear. She'd be much easier to subdue than Felicity Cartwright, because she would be more frightened. She would be soft and warm, not fighting and hostile. He smiled, imagining her young, untried body. But was it? That Peter might have been there. Well, he'd find out. Her youth would not protect her for much longer.

'Excellent lamb, my dear,' he said to Nancy. 'Done to perfection.'

17

Ronald, going to the paper shop on Monday morning to buy the *Sun* and the *Daily Mirror*, felt he must explain his action. He was doing a competition in one, he said, and wanted to read some memoirs in the other.

'Go on, Mr Trimm, it's the cheesecake you're after,' quipped the newsagent. 'We all like a bit of that, don't we?' and he winked.

Ronald, a man of the world, grinned.

'Well—' he said, and let his sentence trail off. How easy some people found it to joke about that sort of thing.

'Terrible about Mr Fortescue, isn't it?' said a woman in the shop, paying for her *Daily Mail*.

'Mr Fortescue? Why? What's happened?' asked the newsagent.

'That murder, down in Fletcham. He did it,' said the woman.

'Mr Fortescue?' exclaimed the newsagent and Ronald, in amazed unison.

'Arrested him on Friday night,' said the woman. 'I heard it from Mrs Pearson, the lady as helps him.'

This was straight from the horse's mouth, if you like.

'Mr Fortescue?' Ronald said again, handing over his money.

'Mr Fortescue,' repeated the woman. 'When his wife left him, I said to my Mavis, you never know with folk. Who knows what goes on behind closed doors, I said. Between husband and wife. Things you wouldn't dream of. His wife leaving after all those years. There must have been some cause.'

'Interesting,' said Ronald, accepting his change.

'Mr Fortescue! Well, I never!' said the newsagent.

Someone else came into the shop then, and had to be told the news. Ronald left them all discussing it. He went back to the shop and read what the *Sun* and the *Mirror* had to say about it. There was little fresh detail: a man had been helping police with their inquiries but had been allowed to leave. That was what had already been said on the radio.

Was the man the police had been questioning really Fortescue? And, if so, why? How had they come to pick on him?

While Ronald was wondering about the police deductions, Detective Inspector Maude and his team were conferring in the incident room.

They still waited for information from the forensic laboratory, where tests were being made on material found at the scene of Felicity Cartwright's death. Now they had a sweater belonging to George Fortescue to match to the wool fibres found under the murdered woman's nails. Efforts were being made to trace the make of the wool, and its outlets. The killer was a secretor, and his blood group had been established; it was the same as George Fortescue's. He remained the prime suspect; Hugo Morton had been eliminated because his blood was of another group.

The murderer had left no fingerprints. There were no bite marks on the body, to be matched to the mouth of a suspect. There was no sign of a forced entry into the house. There had been no robbery. The only evidence of struggle was upon the body; the face was bruised, consistent with being struck, in addition to the chafed wrists and the wound that had brought about death by penetrating the liver, causing massive internal haemorrhage. If Felicity Cartwright had been treated quickly, she might not have died. The fact that she was still alive when her killer left implied that he may not have meant to kill her: if so, he had no fear of being recognized. So he may have been disguised or masked in some way. But a telephone call, anonymously from a box, could have sent an ambulance to help her. The killer must be heartless, and Maude wanted him; but he wanted the right man. Signs led to Fortescue; they must be explored and proved, one way or the other.

Detectives had found, under a bush when they were searching the garden for the murder weapon and for any other clues, a minute strand of fibre attached to a twig. It was so small that it had almost been missed. It was being examined and might not be connected with the crime, even if identified.

Inquiries had been made in Pimlico, where the dead woman had lived before moving to Fletcham. Nothing very helpful had emerged so far. She had lived in a small block of flats near the Warwick Road, and had been on good but not intimate terms with most of the other tenants; their contacts had been confined to chance encounters on the stairs and the occasional residents' meetings. Felicity Cartwright had worked in various museums and, latterly, in an antiques shop not far from where she lived. Two of the tenants in her block of flats had noticed that she had one regular visitor, and identified, from a photograph, Hugo Morton.

It seemed unlikely that her death was linked with this former life.

'Our villain did this on the spur of the moment,' said Maude. 'He saw her enter the house alone. Fortescue fits. He was in a disturbed state that night; he had the time, and he can't give a satisfactory account of his movements after he spoke to Constable Rowe. It needn't have taken long. He's a fit-looking man and she was a small woman. He's presentable. She might have let him in, if he rang the bell with some excuse or other. He could have forced her upstairs at the point of the knife we know the killer'd got. I'd like to have kept him here longer, but we can soon pick him up again. He won't run. We can't charge him, on what we've got. We must hope for something from forensic.'

He could have wrapped a scarf round his face to hide it, and worn a hat. The man seen walking down Priory Road had worn a hat, and one had been removed from Fortescue's house. It might match up with the fibre found under the bush.

A statement was prepared for the press. It said that the police were following various leads and an arrest was expected shortly.

That should make Fortescue sweat.

It was Mrs Simmons who, on Monday morning, told Dorothea the truth about George's absence from home, and she had learned of it from Mrs Pearson. The news that he was missing was already spreading round the village, disseminated by her neighbours, when Mrs Pearson went to the Plough on Saturday evening to buy two bottles of stout for her husband and mentioned her anxiety.

The saloon bar was busy, and Mrs Pearson felt important as she discussed it while drinking a small port to keep out the cold before returning to her husband's uncertain temper, which she knew wasn't his fault, poor soul, with his bad chest.

'He may have gone to see his missus,' said someone, for the whole village knew of Angela Fortescue's departure.

'Or off for a bit of you-know-what,' suggested someone else.

'Without his car?' said Mrs Pearson, playing her trump. 'There it is, as large as life, in the garage.'

Jack Munsey, who kept whippets and walked them through the village every morning and evening, was in a corner of the bar. He sometimes saw George jogging when he was out with his dogs.

'Didn't go out running on Friday,' he remarked,

not looking up from the paper in which he was studying form. 'Went off with the law instead.' He'd seen the police car leaving Orchard House, and George inside. 'Not the local law,' he added. 'Fletcham.' He'd recognized Detective Sergeant Dunn in the car, with another officer; Munsey knew Dunn all too well from the time his boy was in trouble down there last year.

But Mr Fortescue couldn't be in any trouble. Could he?

It took them a little time to work it out. Mrs Pearson knew that Mr Fortescue was to meet his son for dinner in Fletcham on Wednesday night; he'd left a note about it, saying he'd be late home, in case there were any telephone calls or messages for him while she was working at Orchard House. He always did that sort of thing; like an open book, he was, a very nice gentleman. Or so he'd seemed. But on Wednesday night, murder had been done in Fletcham.

Now Mrs Simmons passed all this on to Dorothea, who was appalled. Bill had simply told her that George had been called away unexpectedly and had been out all day. It was nothing to worry about, he'd said, and Dorothea thought it might be something to do with Angela, although that didn't explain why the Rover was in the garage.

'Whoever would have thought it?' Mrs Simmons was saying.

'But it's impossible! It's some dreadful mistake,' said Dorothea. No wonder Bill had been cagey. 'Anyway, wherever he went, he's come back.'

'Mrs Pearson and I were saying you wouldn't credit it, not someone like Mr Fortescue,' said Mrs Simmons. 'But then, things haven't been right for him, have they, since Mrs Fortescue went away? And he has been acting strange.'

'Strange? In what way?'

'Well, all that running about the roads at night. It isn't natural,' said Mrs Simmons.

'It may not be to you or me, Mrs Simmons,' said Dorothea. 'Heaven forbid that we should take up jogging. But it seems to be all the rage now.'

If Mrs Simmons's story was correct, George had been, and might still be, in dreadful trouble. He'd be needing friends.

'That poor woman as was killed,' said Mrs Simmons. 'Lived alone. It's not safe to open your door these days. Don't you do it, Mrs Wyatt, not unless you know who's there.'

'I won't,' said Dorothea. 'Don't worry, Mrs Simmons.'

'It's being said there was a woman attacked in the Tellingford area a while back,' Mrs Simmons produced this titbit like a conjuror with his rabbit from a hat. She'd heard it from her neighbour, whose daughter worked in Tellingford town hall and was going out with a policeman from the local station. 'Unsubstantiated,' said Mrs Simmons carefully. 'They didn't believe her.'

'Really? Where was it supposed to have happened?' asked Dorothea.

But Mrs Simmons did not know. She went off to start her vacuuming, and Dorothea, who was in her dressing gown at the kitchen table drinking coffee, poured herself another cup. There had to be some reason for the police to drop on George. She remembered the night of her dinner party, when George had turned her down, and a remark or two that Angela had made, to which she hadn't paid much heed. Her impression was that, on the whole, George wasn't greatly interested.

But weren't there men who could only get going in circumstances that would make most people shudder?

After Mrs Simmons's revelations, Dorothea did not wait to finish her second cup of coffee before telephoning George.

But once again there was no reply from Orchard House. Had he gone to the office as usual? Surely Mrs Pearson was in the house and would answer the phone?

Bill Kyle would know what was happening. He was George's solicitor. Dorothea rang Eileen, who guardedly confirmed the news. George was a client, she added hastily, and so it was confidential, but she couldn't help knowing what was going on.

'Well, we're all friends, aren't we?' said Dorothea. But what were friends? Weren't they – the Kyles, George and Angela and herself – simply long-time acquaintances, brought together by circumstance, like the members of a family, not from choice? There wasn't time to examine this idea. 'Poor George! It sounds frightful.'

'It's all circumstantial,' Eileen said, and explained what she knew, most of which she'd learned, not from Bill, but from Vivian, while they washed up after lunch the day before. Eileen had not gone with the others when they were looking for the pub. 'Bill is worried,' she admitted.

'Has George gone to the office?' asked Dorothea. 'He's not answering the phone.'

'Yes. Insisted on it. Routine, he said. Maybe it's for the best – it'll take his mind off things.'

They discussed it a little longer, and had just finished their talk when Mrs Simmons came to tell Dorothea that Mrs Pearson had arrived and was anxious for a word.

Dorothea felt she could guess what it was about, and she was right.

Mr Pearson had said that his wife was not to go cleaning for that man.

'He might do me, Mrs Wyatt. That's what Fred said,' Mrs Pearson reported. 'As if I'd let him. A good kick in the you-know-where and that would be the end of any nonsense.'

Dorothea looked at Mrs Pearson, sixty and stolid, in her worn checked coat and thick stockings, her face pouched and lined, rough red hands folded round her capacious, shabby handbag.

'Mr Fortescue was only answering some questions because he happened to be in Fletcham with his son at the time the woman may have been killed,' she said, picking her words carefully. 'He might have seen something suspicious.'

'Oh,' said Mrs Pearson, hesitating. 'He's always seemed a very nice gentleman,' she volunteered. 'Keeps everything neat.'

'You're worried about letting him down,' said Dorothea. She glanced at Mrs Simmons who was standing by, like justice weighing up the conversation. 'I'm sure he's depending on you, Mrs Pearson. He'll be thinking you're round there now, while he's at the office. But, on the other hand, there's Mr Pearson to be thought of.' And a bad-tempered man she knew him to be, retired from the water board, where he had worked in the maintenance department, travelling the district in a little van, his own man, and now confined at home with chronic emphysema. Nevertheless, it seemed surprising that he should be able to impose his authority over this doughty woman. 'He'll know where you are, if you carry on without telling him?'

'He'll know I'm out, won't he?' said Mrs Pearson, and added, 'The money comes in handy.'

'We thought, Mrs Wyatt, if we was to say you needed a bit extra done, and Doris here was helping out,' said Mrs Simmons. 'Fred would never know the difference.'

The two of them had already given George the benefit of the doubt, Dorothea realized; otherwise they'd never have hatched the plot together.

'Just for a bit. Till it blows over,' urged Mrs Simmons.

'Or the police catch the real murderer?' said Dorothea. 'Very well.'

She was not keen on deceit, but it would be Mrs Simmons and Mrs Pearson who were practising it, not herself. She was hardly likely to meet Fred Pearson face to face and have to uphold the story.

Mrs Pearson went off to Orchard House, and Dorothea rang George at the office and asked him to dinner that evening, which had been her original intention. George must have support, particularly if people were going to react like Fred Pearson. How long would the police take to catch the real murderer?

He looked dreadful when he arrived that evening. He hadn't been out jogging.

'I should think not, George,' said Dorothea. 'You've been having a frightful time. You need rest.' And it would be folly, straight away, to expose himself to possible insult in the village. People loved a scandal.

'It was awful, Dorothea,' he said. 'All those questions. On and on. The same ones over and over again. You begin to wonder what the truth really is.'

Dorothea poured him a stiff drink.

'Get this inside you, George,' she said. 'You need it.'

George felt better after a couple of whiskies. Dorothea really did know how to make one feel comfortable. She produced an excellent meal, pork chops in a tasty sauce, with a bottle of claret, and she talked brightly about a plan to visit Cyprus in the spring.

'New horizons, George. That's what I need,' she said. Or a new man. She'd enjoyed cooking the meal this evening, even though it was only George who would share it. You needed to get outside yourself; George did, too. 'You'd better have a holiday too, George, when all this is over,' she advised.

George hoped she would not propose that he should accompany her to Cyprus. He was thinking vaguely of a golfing week at St Andrews in the summer. He'd always hankered after that, but they'd gone to Cornwall every year when Daniel was young; and the last time he and Angela had been away together was for a fortnight in Tenerife, where it had rained a good deal and they had found less and less to say to one another. George preferred to forget their more intimate moments during that fortnight: the humiliation, and the shame. If the police only knew! It had been all right at first, when they were young, but gradually he'd lost interest; there were other things in life that were more pleasurable, like hitting a straight drive down the fairway or sinking a difficult putt. Or even eating this good meal, with Dorothea looking quite decorative and bent on making a fuss of him. She was a good sort and it was a rotten shame about Harry. Pity she was a bit fond of the bottle; that had only happened since Harry died. She was sloshed the other night, of course: that explained her conduct. She was lonely, he supposed, rattling about in this big house on her own. She should do more in the village – help with the old people, that sort of thing. She was really rather selfish, he decided.

Valerie Turner heard the talk about George when she went to fetch the children from school. The other mothers, discussing it while they waited at the school gates, all knew Orchard House, and most knew George Fortescue by sight, for though Crowbury had grown in recent years, the old Edwardian house was a landmark, and George was active in the village. His parish council activities, and his enthusiasm for keeping the village streets tidy so that Crowbury might compete for the title of best-kept village in the county, won attention through the summer; all winter he'd been seen, in the evenings, pounding round in his track suit.

'Bit old for it, isn't he? That jogging?' one young woman remarked. Her own husband jogged, but early, before breakfast, and not far, just round their immediate area, half a mile or so. And he was only thirty. By the time you were bald and your children were at college, you should hang up your running shoes, she implied.

Valerie, like all the rest, had seen George Fortescue about the village; he'd run the tombola at the church fête last summer and been sympathetic when Timmy had found it hard to understand the system.

Could he have been the man who attacked her?

He'd been allowed home. He had been taken to Fletcham police station and interrogated, then let go. On bail, said someone, but another said that wouldn't happen in a murder case.

Valerie was meeting Jill and Johnny Mount as well as her own two. She felt an urge to talk to someone about the news and, instead of letting the children run on from Primrose Cottage to the farm, she went with them. Pearl Mount welcomed them all into the big kitchen where she was baking, and asked them to stay to tea.

It was easy to bring up the subject of George

Fortescue, for Pearl was eager to talk about the murder. She told Valerie that she had heard from her mother about George. Her mother often made a detour past the farm on the way back from Mrs Wyatt's; she had done so today. Pearl repeated what her mother had said.

'Mrs Wyatt's sure he can't have done it,' she reported. 'But there's no smoke without fire, is there?'

'They let him go,' said Valerie. If he'd done it, and been released, he could kill a second time. Even only rape again. Only rape! What a way to think about something so frightful.

And he lived nearby. He could come again, if it had been him, that time. Could it have been? How could she tell?

'Maybe they hadn't enough evidence,' said Pearl.

'What made them think it was him?'

'He was in Fletcham that night, seeing his son who's at the university. Mum says he's been upset – his wife left him, you know – he could have flipped.'

'Yes.'

It was possible. You went through a variety of moods after a marriage died, Valerie knew. But to commit murder?

Cooley had been to see her only a few evenings ago. He'd not mentioned George Fortescue at all, but he'd asked her to let him know if she remembered anything about the man who had attacked her.

That evening, when the children were in bed, Valerie willed herself to relive the dreadful night. Deliberately, she conjured up the memory of her attacker. There was the head, in its dark woollen hood, the black jersey, the scrabbling hands, one at her waist and the other round her throat. She saw the knife clearly: or rather, the blade. It was short and sturdy.

And she saw the hand holding it, without a glove: a stubby hand, with sparse ginger hairs on the back.

There had been no smell: no masculine, sweaty smell; no aftershave, either.

Perhaps she should tell Cooley about the hand?

It was weird, Lynn thought, sitting in the van beside Uncle Ron on her way to school, how she seemed to have gone off him all of a sudden. It was seeing those magazines in the desk. They were really nasty. Since then, she'd noticed how he seemed to brush up against her whenever he had a chance; he was always touching her. His polite way of seeing her into the van and then getting in himself, which she'd always liked, now seemed polite no more, for she would feel his hand on her arm, or on her thigh as he tucked her coat in to stop it from getting shut in the door. She'd giggled about that sort of thing with other girls at school; groping, they called it; but this wasn't funny, for it was Uncle Ron who was doing the groping. She couldn't mention it to her parents; they'd laugh at her, tell her to stop imagining things. She couldn't tell them about the horrible magazines, either, because she shouldn't have unlocked that drawer.

She'd stop taking lifts with him. There'd been no more scares in the town and her father would have to relax his rule. Other girls' fathers weren't so strict.

And she'd look for a new Saturday job. It would be all right if she just kept away from him.

On Tuesday evening, George came home to find three anonymous letters among the mail which had arrived after he left for the office, and which Mrs Pearson had stacked on the hall table. All were obscene. How had people discovered that he was the unnamed man whom the police had interviewed? They must be sick, to write in such terms. He felt sick himself, after reading them.

The previous evening, Dorothea had given him a Mogadon tablet to take when he went to bed; that, on top of the good meal, the whisky and the wine, had been enough to defeat his inner panic, and he had slept well. The day in the office had passed calmly, like the day before; it was strange to move from a world of horror to the normal atmosphere of business, but it would not last if his colleagues discovered he had been held for questioning. Unless the real murderer were soon found, it would be only a short time before the vile letters pursued him to the office. This first batch must be from people in the area who had heard gossip in the village; someone may have seen him in the police car.

He'd told Dorothea that he was surprised Mrs Pearson had turned up for work as usual. Surely the village grapevine would have been busy and she'd have discovered what had happened?

Dorothea had crossed her fingers before replying.

'Maybe she has heard rumours, George, but your friends will stick by you,' she said. 'She's got too much sense to pay attention to spiteful talk, if there is any. Just hang on. It'll pass.' Then she'd asked if he'd told Angela.

George explained that he hadn't, and that he had made Daniel promise not to do so. In that moment, Dorothea found herself liking George. This awful business, once it was over, might be the making of him. Her mind rushed ahead and she imagined Angela seeking a reconciliation after she had tried her wings in the wider world for a while. But then she looked again at George, with his hangdog expression, and banished the fantasy. He was dreadfully worthy and dull; that wouldn't alter. Angela wouldn't return.

She telephoned him on Tuesday evening, and he said he had had some unpleasant letters. Because he sounded upset, Dorothea got out the car and went round, without telling him she was on her way, so that he couldn't ask her not to come.

The letters were on the coffee table in the sitting room. Dorothea saw block capitals in purple felt-tipped pen and read one before he could prevent her.

'Oh George! How awful! How cruel!' she exclaimed. 'You should burn them. Don't open any more letters, unless you know what they are. You don't have to put up with this.'

She was still there when the telephone calls began, and she told him to leave the telephone off the hook. Daniel would get in touch with her, if he wanted his father and could get no reply, as he had before.

18

Dorothea, on her way to the butcher's two days later, paused to look in the window of Nanron Antiques. There was a small jug on display that had to be Wedgwood black basalt. She went inside.

What had happened between her and Mr Trimm left her mind as she asked him about the jug. His wife had just finished repairing it, it seemed. It was hard to see what she'd done. Ronald told her that Nancy had used one of her mixes; probably, in this case, plaster of paris and powdered gelatine, to build up the missing lip of the jug. Then she'd painted it. What with, Dorothea wanted to know. She used different things for different items, said Ronald; possibly for this one dry powder paint, mixed with a few drops of varnish, but he wasn't sure. All that side of things was her department, he said; she was the expert.

'She's very skilful,' said Dorothea. She didn't like buying mended pieces for her collection, but she had several that had been repaired and this was a pretty jug.

While she examined it, making her mind up, Ronald watched her. He knew what she looked like beneath that expensive tweed skirt and sheepskin coat. She wasn't always Mrs High-and-Mighty, asking condescending questions, deigning to spend ten or fifteen pounds on a whim in the shop. People in Crowbury would be amazed if they could see her as he had done. He shut his eyes to recall her arms round his neck, the softness of her body.

'Mr Trimm, are you feeling all right?' Dorothea asked. 'You've gone quite pale.'

Ronald opened his eyes again.

'Yes, quite all right, thank you,' he said.

'I'll take the jug,' said Dorothea. 'I'll give you a cheque.'

He watched while she wrote it out, the jug wrapped in tissue paper for her to take away, and he clipped the cheque into the till as she picked up the parcel. His hands behind his back, he bowed her from the shop while he plotted what he would do.

Those other times, best forgotten now, he hadn't planned well enough. And they were different, those two women: cold, unyielding. Like Nancy, he realized. But Nancy must not be compared with anyone. Some women asked for it, didn't they? Even from strangers. Mrs Wyatt had asked for it, that first time, then turned proud; well, he'd teach her a lesson.

Maybe afterwards he'd stop thinking so much about Lynn; she was seldom out of his mind for long. She'd been quiet in the van, these last few mornings: had a row with that Peter, maybe. He ached to touch her.

It would have to be done on a Friday, the only

night when he needed no elaborate excuse for Nancy.

So, that Friday evening, Ronald went to the telephone box and called Nancy to say he had found a discrepancy in the books and must untangle it. He wanted to clear it that night, however long it took; it didn't do to hold things over, prolong errors.

Nancy agreed that it must be done, and expressed surprise at what had happened. He was always so careful, she told him; he took such pains.

He'd already done the books and put them away, before talking to her. Now he could begin. There was no need for mere magazines tonight.

First he went into the Plough. He ordered half a pint and some ham sandwiches to take away. Then he looked round the bar. If she was there, it would be a sign that his plan was meant to succeed. It was because she was in the bar at the Plough, that other time, that it had happened at all.

She was sitting at a table talking to the bank manager, just as she'd been doing the evening it all began. But she wasn't as far gone, this time. He'd no way of knowing how long she'd stay, but that didn't matter.

He swallowed his beer, picked up his packet of sandwiches and told the publican he had to go back to his books. Then he left. He'd already taken his black sweater, the hood and the knife from their hiding place under the van seat and put them in his desk. Now he changed into the sweater. He put the knife, his small pencil torch, the hood and the scarf in the pockets of his raincoat, and the tweed hat on his head.

It was lucky that Nancy had never learned to drive, he reflected; she couldn't come looking for him, checking up on him. Leaving the cellar and lobby lights on, as if he were in fact working at his desk, he went out by the back way and hurried down the road to the Manor House. The van was still parked in Church Lane, if anyone looked.

His luck held, and he met no one. People were eating their meal behind drawn curtains, or watching television, or whatever else they did in the evenings. He'd already noticed how quiet the village was at this hour. Later, people would be leaving the pubs, moving about. But he wouldn't think about that now: that was for afterwards.

The porch light was on at the Manor House, and the garage doors were open. She'd driven to the Plough again. How lazy she was! She even took the car for her little shopping trips, less than half a mile.

Her headlights would warn him when she was coming back. He'd be waiting: ready. The success of his plan depended on finding a time when she was out, for, as he knew, her door was held on a chain; she'd peered round it when he'd called so filled with hope. He wouldn't be able to get in by force against that. But he could open that solid, old oak door in her absence, for he'd seen what she did herself. He went to the water butt, and there, as before, was the large key.

He let himself in, then locked the door again from inside. Swiftly he walked through the house to the back door. Like the woman's in Fletcham, it was bolted from inside. He undid it, let himself out, closing the door to keep in the snug warmth of the well-heated house, and hurried round the side of the house to the water butt. He had to use his small torch but did it with care. He put the key back in its hiding place; then, before entering the house again by the back door, he took off his raincoat and tweed hat, and hid them under a bush, as he had in Fletcham.

As soon as he was back in the house, he put on his hood and the scarf; he was already wearing his gloves. He held the knife in his hand, the blade out ready. He'd wondered where to wait for her. That other time, she'd gone straight to where she kept her drink. She might do that again, not go upstairs at first.

There was plenty of space behind the long curtains in Dorothea's sitting room. He could watch the room through a chink between them, and he'd see the lights of the car without being seen, for the window looked out at the side of the house.

He might have to wait some time for her, but he didn't mind that. He felt quite safe, standing there, thinking only of how he would surprise her.

Dorothea was tempted to have another drink. She'd already had three, or was it four? But the bank manager had left soon after she joined him at his table, and there was no one she felt able to talk to. She was not drawn to the group of younger people by the bar counter. Her lack of an escort made her feel self-conscious and uncomfortable; she must either drink more, to overcome such sensations, or she must leave.

This time, she chose to go.

During the short trip home, she switched on the car radio. She did not like the silence after she had turned it off, got out of the car, and was locking up the dark garage with the chain and padlock, the key of which she kept on a ring with her car keys. But the porch light fanned out over the gravel sweep and she knew that, although the curtains were drawn across most of the windows, the lights were on inside the house. She went to the water butt, groped beneath it, and found the large key.

As she opened the front door, she could hear the radio playing light music, quite loudly. Once in the house, she turned the key in the front door from the inside, shot the bolts, and put up the chain. She stood in the hall for a moment, shoulders sagging. What now? There was no Harry, sitting in his study reading, or calling out to ask her if she'd like a drink.

But a drink was easily available. After a while, it would bring the familiar numbing of her pain. She would never get used to it; she would never stop missing Harry, looking for him in the chair he often used, thinking she saw him walking across the garden, imagining she heard his footsteps coming into the kitchen while she was preparing a meal, putting his arms around her while she worked, even after so many years, and kissing her.

She shivered, standing in the hall.

Other women had to cope with this, this sudden solitude: it was a fact of modern life that women, in the main, outlived men.

You did too much for me, Harry, she condemned

him silently; you were too good, too kind. I'm too old to cope alone.

But she wasn't old: not yet.

Upstairs were the Mogadon tablets, plenty of them in a bottle. She'd thought of it before: of swallowing them; of quitting. But poor Susan and poor Mark, if she were to do it; they'd feel guilty, fearing they had failed her. She mustn't let despair defeat her.

She took off her coat and laid it, with her gloves and handbag, on a chair in the hall. Then she went to pour herself a drink. She took it into the sitting room, passing close to the curtain which concealed Ronald as she crossed to the hearth to make up the fire. She stoked it up well, building logs across it, putting small nuggets of coal beneath them.

Ronald opened the curtains a fraction to watch her. He saw her bending down, moving; he saw the glass on the floor beside her. He stepped back sharply as she stood up, but she was still turned away from him. She straightened the pile of glossy magazines on the sofa table, and moved a small porcelain vase that held winter sweet and yellow jasmine into a better position.

Dorothea, her hand still on the vase, remembered that she had always planted bulbs in bowls when Harry was alive: hyacinths and daffodils. Somehow she'd never had the heart to do it since.

The room was warm, but she felt suddenly cold, shivering as she had done in the hall. She crossed her arms over her body, hugging herself, shuddering.

Food. That was what she needed. She hadn't had much lunch – a few drinks and some bread and cheese – and she'd forgotten to plan anything for this evening. She should have pulled a chop or something out of the freezer earlier.

Taking her glass with her, she went away to the kitchen. It wouldn't be the first time she'd grilled a rigid chop.

When she had gone from the room, Ronald slipped out of his hiding place. Was she upstairs? If so, he'd follow her.

He went into the hall, hesitating. Then he heard sounds from the back of the house: another radio, relaying a different programme from the one in the sitting room. He moved down the passage. The kitchen door was open and he caught sight of her moving back and forth across the room. She might see him, if she turned, and he would lose his chance of surprising her; besides, it could not happen in the kitchen. There must be some soft surface on which they could both lie, preferably her bed.

She'd built up the fire and left the lights on in the sitting room; she must mean to return there. Would she go upstairs first?

He retreated into the doorway of the sitting room and, as he did so, Dorothea came out of the kitchen, crossed the hall and went into the downstairs cloak-room.

When she emerged, her chop was grilling and her frozen peas were boiling nicely. I'm getting quite like George, she thought; I'll be having boil-in-the-bag meals soon. It might be no bad plan to have a few in stock.

Ronald, heart excitedly thumping, had peered in

through the kitchen door while Dorothea was in the cloakroom, and he saw her preparations. There was a tray on the worktop near the stove. Where would she eat her meal? In the dining room?

He went back to the sitting room, hovering in the doorway, his knife, the blade extended, in his hand, wondering what to do. Then he heard the kitchen radio snap off.

He was back behind his curtain in seconds, his breath held as Dorothea came into the room carrying her tray.

She stopped for a moment just inside the doorway, looking round. Once again she felt shivery. I must be getting a cold, she thought, moving on again, setting her tray down on the coffee table in front of the sofa.

She picked up the newspaper that lay on the sofa and glanced at it; perhaps there would be something worth watching on television, though Friday was notoriously a poor night. Television was better company than the radio; you could at least look at the news readers, for example, and pretend that you were not alone.

She switched off the radio and turned on the big colour set; then she turned off the main light in the room, so that it was illuminated only by the lamp on a small table at one end of the sofa. She stacked some cushions as a back-rest, kicked off the shoes for which she had exchanged her boots while she was in the cloakroom, and arranged herself on the sofa, feet up, to begin her meal.

Ronald could see her quite well from his place behind the curtain. There was a bottle of wine on the

211

tray. He felt no hunger himself, though he had not eaten for hours; he had thrown his package of sandwiches in the dustbin.

He waited, watching her.

It had begun on the sofa that other time. Perhaps it could happen there now. She'd want it, even though, like the others, she would be frightened. He wanted to frighten her: she had to be punished for turning him down. It was her fault that he had had to hunt elsewhere; it was her fault that other stupid woman had died.

Stop that, he told himself: don't think of her.

He parted the curtains slightly so that he could watch her more easily. He could see the back of her head, and her legs, very shapely in their pale, sheer tights, stretched out on the sofa, her tweed skirt a little rucked up. Now and then she stretched out an arm for her glass; he noticed her ring catching the light from the lamp.

She had finished eating. The last of the wine had been poured into her glass.

It was time.

Ronald could scarcely breathe for the excitement that caught his whole body as he moved forward from the shelter of the curtains, keeping in the pool of shadow behind Dorothea. Holding the knife in his gloved hand, moving silently, he came round to face her.

Dorothea was feeling pleasantly woozy after plenty to drink and her hot meal, which in the end had been quite tasty. She was not paying much attention to the drama on the television screen, almost dozing. Suddenly there was a figure in some sort of mask and helmet standing very close to her. The coffee table was pushed aside and the wine bottle fell from it, rolling over the floor, spilling dregs.

Terror filled Dorothea.

She saw a black-clad arm and a gloved hand waving a knife. Eyes, above a dark scarf, glittered at her.

Both hands came up to her breast and she gave a shocked, choking shriek.

At once he hit her on the side of her face with his gloved left hand; the knife, in his right hand, still pointed down at her.

'Be quiet,' he snarled.

Tears of pain filled Dorothea's eyes. She put her hand to her face. Blood pounded in her ears; she felt sick and giddy with horror.

Ronald grinned behind the scarf that covered his face. He had learned the effect of pain.

'Lie back, Dorothea Wyatt,' he said in his assumed voice. 'Lie back, and you won't he hurt.'

He knew her name.

'What do you want?' she croaked, almost petrified with fear. She made a huge physical effort to breathe deeply, attempting to steady herself. This was a burglar. Was he alone?

'Lie back,' he repeated, still looming over her.

'The silver's in the dining room,' she said, her voice shaking.

'I don't want the silver,' said Ronald. 'You know what I want, Dorothea Wyatt. Undo your blouse.' He'd see them again in a moment, those white, soft breasts. He moistened his lips under the concealing scarf. He'd wrench it off later; he'd have to: this time, he meant to experience bliss.

Very slowly, Dorothea moved her hand to the top button of the wool blouse she wore under a heavy mohair cardigan. There were several silver chains around her neck.

The man meant to rape her.

She was still trying to clear her head but what she had drunk, and now shock, made her confused. She struggled to think coherently and into her muddled brain came the memory of the raped and murdered woman in Fletcham, about whose death George Fortescue had been questioned.

This was some dreadful sick joke. Someone who knew her had dressed up to frighten her, make her think he was the murdering rapist.

Who could do such a thing? Could it be George? If it were, all she need do was laugh and tell him to stop being silly.

But it couldn't be George. George would never have hit her. And George knew he did not have to threaten her.

'How did you get in?' she asked, and she tried to sit higher against the cushions on the sofa.

Ronald laughed. It was a harsh, eerie sound, quite without humour, and Dorothea, listening to it, was more frightened than she had ever been in her life. This was physical terror, basic and primitive.

'You showed me where you kept the key yourself,' said Ronald, and forgot to alter his voice.

Dorothea was staring at him. She saw the glittering eyes and the knife still pointing down at her. Then she remembered: she recalled fumbling for the key under the water butt and Ronald Trimm accompanying her into the house; she saw herself pouring him sherry and his hand reaching out for the glass; and she saw his hand at the till the day before, snapping her cheque into it, a squat hand with pale ginger hairs on the back.

She had turned him down, and this was his revenge. It was Ronald Trimm who stood here, frightening her, trying to make her think he was the murderer of that other woman. She'd been stabbed, so he'd brought a knife, and he'd disguised himself to add to the terror: very successfully.

Working this out brought a warm surge of relief, but it also brought a feeling of immense rage. How dare he scare her like this?

'Mr Trimm!' she exclaimed, and she sat upright. 'How silly, dressing up and trying to frighten me. Well, you've had your little joke. Now take off that ridiculous hat. How foolish you look.' And she laughed, a brittle, nervous laugh, but a laugh, none the less.

He had given himself away! He had mentioned the key and she knew who he was! And she had stopped cringing in terror. She was laughing at him! It was all going wrong.

'You turned me down,' he said.

'Let's talk about it,' said Dorothea, struggling to control her laughter, which was bordering on hysteria. She'd got herself into this, acting recklessly that time. Somehow she must save this idiot's face, and any honour she might have left. He couldn't mean to force her at knife point.

But he had hit her. And he was pointing a knife at her now.

Thoughts crowded into her mind. The woman who was murdered had been an antique dealer. Ronald Trimm dealt in antiques. But surely he could not have been the killer? She wouldn't be frightened of Ronald Trimm.

Yet there was madness in those eyes as they glittered at her.

'You need a lesson,' he said. 'Undress.'

Ronald Trimm, Dorothea told herself; that's who this is: Ronald Trimm. She would not be vanquished by Ronald Trimm, whatever he may have done, and she could not think about that now. She struck out with her left fist, hitting his arm hard in the crook of the elbow with the side of her hand, at the same time drawing her legs up to her body, preparing to kick him.

The knife fell from Ronald's hand and he had an awareness of her coiling herself up like a spring, resisting him.

Behind her head, the lamp on the table burned.

Ronald picked it up and crashed the base of it down on her head. It was made of marble, and one blow was enough to silence her for ever. In the last long second of her life, Dorothea knew that this was the killer the police were seeking.

19

Ronald stared down at her. The blood seemed to be everywhere. She lay quite still, mouth open, her blue eyes staring at him. Her arms had fallen back; her wool blouse clung to her body.

He was still holding the lamp.

He let go of it, simply opening his hand round it, and it fell to the ground, the bulb shattering. The lamp rolled a little way.

Ronald looked round, in panic. What now? Was she dead? He bent over her, and could detect no movement, but he did not touch her. He hadn't meant to kill her, only to silence her, to stop her mocking laughter. But she'd recognized him; she'd attacked him. Now she couldn't tell anyone about it.

He'd backed into the coffee table, and Dorothea's tray had fallen from it. The empty wine bottle lay, on the floor, the glass nearby. A thin trickle of burgundy oozed over the carpet. Apart from this, and the lamp lying on the carpet with the broken glass from the bulb around it, the room was orderly. Should he make it look like a burglary? Break open a window somewhere? Ransack the place and take some of her precious objects? But what would he carry them away in? A burglar must come equipped with bag or holdall. He did not know that an experienced thief would probably use pillowcases from the beds.

He wouldn't know what to do with the stuff, if he did take anything. He couldn't get rid of it through his normal contacts. And the sooner he got away from here the better. He'd go home as fast as he could; Nancy would say he had been at the shop, at work, and had come straight home, if anyone asked. But they wouldn't. No one would suspect him. They thought George Fortescue had killed Felicity Cartwright. They'd think he'd killed Dorothea Wyatt, too.

Ronald folded his knife and put it into his trouser pocket; then, not looking at Dorothea again, he went from the room into the hall, unlocked the front door, and let himself out.

He stood there in darkness. She'd turned off the porch light when she came home. He took his small torch from his pocket but he did not dare turn it on. He must get away, fast. He felt hot, suddenly sweating inside his dark clothes.

His raincoat and hat! He'd almost forgotten them!

He groped his way round the side of the house to the rear, and found the bush where his things were hidden, forced now and then to use the torch sparingly. He put on the raincoat and hat. It wouldn't be safe, after what had happened, to risk meeting anyone in the village; he must go over the fields, but he'd never been that way before.

He picked his way over the garden to the fence by

the tiny light of the torch which he turned on and off for quick peeps at the ground.

He was walking across the field when he thought of the unlocked front door. If he went back and locked it from the outside, what would he do with the key? Drop it in through the letterbox? Surely that would look odd?

Perhaps, when she was found, the police would think she had left it open for someone she knew to come in; George Fortescue, for instance. Wasn't that likely?

He felt better, thinking of that, and walked on, stumbling over the field, shielding the thin beam from his torch with his hand, using it only to avoid the worst pitfalls in the rough ground he crossed. A hedge loomed up black in front of him, and he had to work his way along it before finding the stile. In one field some steers blundered up to him, puffing and snorting, following him, their breath warm and sweet, their tread heavy, alarming him.

He reached the last stile, and saw the headlights of a car coming down the road. He snapped off his torch and crouched down, waiting until it had gone by. Then he climbed over and hurried back to the shop by the back way, meeting no one.

His shoes and trouser ends were covered in mud. He washed the shoes at the sink and removed his trousers to soak off the mud; better to explain damp trouser ends to Nancy, if he couldn't somehow hide them from her, than muddy ones. He unlocked the bottom drawer of the desk and put the black sweater inside it, with the knife and the balaclava helmet.

Then he went home. It wasn't yet ten o'clock, but it felt as though most of the night must have passed.

Nancy came out to meet him when she heard his key in the door. He must have had a bad time with the books; he'd never been as late as this on a Friday before.

'You must be hungry, dear,' she said, as he took off his raincoat and hung it up in the hall.

'I slipped down to the Plough for some sandwiches,' said Ronald. 'Just to tide me over.' It was his alibi, so that the truth of his working late would be established if anyone asked. 'I found the mistake in the books. It was a silly one and meant so much cross-checking. I must take care it doesn't happen again.'

Nancy knew she could have found it herself in half the time. She was a much better book-keeper than Ronald; in fact, she was better at most things than he was, but a good wife didn't draw attention to her own superiority in the interests of preserving masculine pride.

'I'll get you your dinner,' she said. 'Though it's quite dried up in the oven. And I'll make some tea.'

'I'll just go and wash,' said Ronald.

While she was putting the kettle on, he quickly changed his trousers. He bundled the damp ones into the airing cupboard, and his shoes too. She wouldn't go looking for anything in there tonight and he would take them out in the morning. The shoes were good ones, so they'd probably be not much the worse for their treatment when he'd given them a good polish.

Later, having eaten his fish pie and peas, followed

by plums and custard, he undressed in the bedroom while Nancy creamed her face at the dressing table. She patted her fleshy jowls, a small plastic cape round her neck, in a green quilted dressing gown above a long-sleeved frilled pink nightdress. She believed in keeping herself pretty for Ronald. He was very tired, physically tired, after his walk across the fields, but he felt safe. It was good to be here at home with Nancy, who always took care of him.

Later still, in bed, he heard her even breathing as she slept. She gave her familiar little snore. It was as if nothing at all out of the way had happened.

He was still unappeased. He did not sleep for some time, bothered by lusts of the flesh which seemed much worse now than ever before.

In the small hours of the morning, heavy clouds massed in the sky and later it began to rain, obliterating the traces of Ronald's passage over Dorothea's lawn to the fence separating the garden from the field.

It was still raining in the morning. George had planned a game of golf with Bill Kyle, who thought he should be kept occupied in as normal a way as possible but, with the heavens spilling, they had to agree to cancel it.

George wondered how to spend the day. It was no use washing the car, a task that could be spun out some time by anyone determined enough to make it last. The paperwork for his committees was all up to date, and he'd delivered the Liberal Association's news letter.

Daniel telephoned after breakfast. Because of the weather, plans he'd had to take Vivian for a country ramble had gone wrong. She'd grown up in an urban area and her ignorance about country ways, though in a sense charming, must, he felt, be corrected. But Crowbury was rural; her education could be pursued whilst at the same time they checked up on his father. They planned to come over, he said.

George had been thinking that he'd go along to the golf clubhouse for lunch; now he abandoned that idea quite cheerfully. He'd go up the village and buy food for the young people, sausages or something easy to cook. The girl would do it.

He set off in the car, because it was raining so hard, and with a certain bravado, not sure if he would be greeted with snubs. He'd not been out in the village since those letters came. There had been some more, but there were none this morning.

There was a small queue at the butcher's. George tacked himself on to the end of it. His turn came at last, and he bought two pounds of the butcher's own special make of sausage, and a large piece of veal and ham pie. They might stay overnight, together, he surmised, in the modern way, in Daniel's room. He supposed they knew what they were doing.

While his sausages were being weighed, a young woman whom he knew vaguely by sight was attended to by the butcher's assistant. With her, there were a small boy and girl who were behaving unusually well for modern children, standing quietly, the boy holding a shopping basket. George was aware that the woman was staring at him. He took no

222

notice, paying attention to the sausages he was buying. She might be an anonymous-letter writer.

But, as he accepted his parcel and turned to leave the shop, he glanced at her warily, and saw that she was gazing at his hands, in which he held the sausages and pie. She looked up then, and caught his eye, and smiled. Her pale, thin face was transformed by the radiance of the expression she now wore.

'Good morning, Mr Fortescue,' Valerie said. 'Terrible weather, isn't it?'

George was amazed at being spoken to, for even the butcher had been quite perfunctory in his manner. He responded warmly and they walked out of the shop together. Valerie said she was going to the greengrocer's, and George realized that he should go there too; Daniel and Vivian would want fruit and so on. He held the door open for her and, when he had bought some apples and bananas, gave each of the children a banana. People in the shop looked very surprised. He drove home feeling almost cheerful for the first time since Angela's departure.

After unpacking the shopping, he thought that it might be a good idea to invite Dorothea over to lunch. She'd really been very good to him. If she didn't care for the menu, she could do something about improving it.

He tried her on the telephone, but there was no reply. It was unusual for her to be out and about so early; perhaps she was in the bath. He waited a while and then tried again. After several attempts, there was still no answer, and George felt a niggling unease, though he couldn't explain it to himself. She had probably broken with custom, got up early, and gone off for the day.

At half-past eleven, he drove round to the Manor House to make sure.

As he turned up towards the house, he noticed the curtains were drawn at all the windows facing the front. Was the lazy woman still in bed? She might have been plastered the night before and be sleeping it off. Well, if that was the case, it was time she roused herself. She was going to pieces, he decided. What she ought to do was get a job to give her an interest; other middle-aged women seemed able to do it. He snapped off this thought, as he remembered Angela's defection.

No one came when he rang the bell.

He walked round to the back door. It was securely locked. A bottle of milk stood outside, the cap nipped by tits and the milk level lowered.

George went back to the front door and tried ringing again, but nothing happened. The curtains were drawn at the window of the bedroom he thought was Dorothea's, overlooking the garden, and feeling rather foolish, he threw gravel up at it, but there was no response.

She must be sleeping very heavily. He'd called her name, and generally made some noise.

He went back to the front door and tried the latch. The door opened.

George went in, and saw that the lights were on. He could hear the radio from the sitting room. She must have been in a state to go to bed and leave things like this.

'Dorothea?' he called.

No answer.

Pausing from time to time to call again, George went upstairs and, with some trepidation, opened the door of the room that must be hers.

Her bed was made; the coverlet neatly drawn up. George frowned. He went from room to room, repeating her name, but she was not to be found.

He went downstairs again. What he had thought was the radio seemed very loud, and as reached the hall he heard a familiar jingle; it was the television. He went into the sitting room. In the corner, the screen flickered. Seeming to watch it, Dorothea lay on the sofa, but where her head should be there was a sickening mess of blood: and more than blood.

He put his hand to his mouth to hold the cry that rose in his throat, that hand which Valerie had noticed in the butcher's shop, a large, well shaped and apparently hairless hand.

George made himself look at her closely, to confirm that she was dead; she had to be, with a wound like that.

She was cold.

He went straight to the telephone.

While he waited for the police, he realized with dread that he would be asked a lot of questions.

He'd walked all round the house, touching things. He might even have blood on his clothes.

George sat in the room with Dorothea. The damage was done now, and he would not leave her alone, his poor, unfortunate friend. But he did not look at her.

Before taking George away to Tellingford police station, Detective Sergeant Gower found out from him about Dorothea's next of kin. It wouldn't take the press and the rest of the media long to discover that a violent crime had occurred in Crowbury and to tell the news to the nation; the relatives must be informed before this could happen.

George mentioned Dorothea's son Mark up in Yorkshire, and Susan, her daughter, in London. Their telephone numbers might be in Dorothea's book.

The news could not be telephoned, he was told. A police officer must call.

Dorothea's address book, in her walnut desk, disclosed the necessary details, and arrangements were made for the news to be broken by local police.

'The girl – Susan – has a boyfriend. Leo something-or-other,' said George. 'A sensible sort of fellow. Works in a merchant bank. It might be as well to get hold of him.'

However, Dorothea's records did not disclose Leo's surname or address, or not in a manner easily found. The Metropolitan Police, who would be seeing Susan, were told of his existence.

After performing this final service for Dorothea, George was driven away. He concentrated on the knowledge that Daniel would be arriving in the village at any time now, and would, for the second time, do what he could for his father. A feeling of inescapable doom filled George as he got into the back of the police car. He had not killed Dorothea, but he knew that he could be suspected of it just because he was found with her, and after what had happened at Fletcham. He was a marked man.

This time, they took away his car.

Mark Wyatt was out when a constable called. Charlotte, his wife, preparing a dinner party for ten people that evening, saw that he had come with bad news, and at first was afraid that Mark had had an accident on the way to get the drink for the evening. She bundled the children out of the sitting room and sat down to listen.

In a way, when the constable told her what had happened, the news that Dorothea had died came as an anticlimax, but she felt shock: her mother-in-law was not old, and seemed healthy. What had happened?

The officer broke the news gradually. There had been an accident, he said. What sort of accident? Well – she'd been attacked. In the end Charlotte knew the bare facts.

She was horrified. How dreadful! Poor Dorothea! She had found her difficult, though she could not say quite why; since Harry's death, Charlotte had felt guilty about not pressing her to visit them more often, easily accepting the excuse of distance, which was silly, since Dorothea had a good car and drove well.

She said she would tell Mark when he returned, but the officer said he must be present and he'd wait in the car. This was quite a hard nut, the young man thought, walking back across the gravel, cap in hand. He'd expected tears; even hysterics. But shock took different forms and it wasn't Mrs Wyatt's own mother, after all. She was a pretty woman, young Mrs Wyatt, and the house was nice; quite large.

He could have done with a cup of tea, while waiting. Maybe she'd get round to it, if the husband was some time.

But Charlotte was busy returning to the freezer her dinner-party ingredients; it would have to be cancelled now. She could not start telephoning the guests until Mark had come back and heard what had happened. He was sure to be very upset. Dorothea must have surprised a burglar; she'd got rather sloppy, she'd probably left a window open or something. Mark would have to go down there. She'd better tell him bluntly; there was no sense in trying to cushion him. Luckily, the children were young enough to be told simply that granny had gone to heaven.

20

Leo drove Susan down to Crowbury. She was numb with shock. You read about such things in the paper, but they didn't happen to people that you knew, least of all your mother. The police officer who had called to tell her what had happened had telephoned Leo from her flat, and he had come round at once, abandoning instantly a plan to go motor-racing that day. In the midst of her incredulous reaction to what she had been told, Susan had registered this single fact.

'You needn't – I'll manage – Mark will come,' she said, when he arrived, and added, 'What can we do? Nothing, really.' But Leo swept such protests aside.

'You'll want to go down, and I'm taking you,' he stated. 'It's dreadful.' He was as shocked as Susan, though attempting to conceal it. Nice middle-aged ladies like Dorothea Wyatt simply didn't get attacked and killed in their homes, though they might be mugged in the streets. He had liked Dorothea and thought her an attractive woman, though a bit over the top. 'There will be things to arrange,' he went on.

'It was a robbery, I suppose. She surprised a thief. You may have to tell the police what's missing.'

As soon as they reached the village, it was obvious that news of some drama had leaked out. People were standing about in groups, murmuring together; a police motorcyclist was at the crossroads. There was a row of cars outside the Plough, but that was often the case on a Saturday morning. The road to the Manor House, however, was cordoned off. When Leo told the policeman on guard who Susan was, they were allowed through, but were asked to park outside the gates of the house, where several other cars, including two police cars, were drawn up. And a plain, dark van.

A police officer led them through the gates towards the house, and a man of about forty, in a raincoat, came out to meet them. He introduced himself as Detective Chief Inspector Hemmings, head of CID for the division, and told Susan he was very sorry to meet her under such circumstances. He led them quickly through the hall, where Leo noticed a man in a black leather jacket using what looked like a paintbrush on the sitting-room doorpost, to the room that had been Susan's father's study. Here, he asked them to sit down, sat down himself, and then said there was very little he could tell them so far. There appeared to have been no robbery; at any rate, there were no signs of that sort of disturbance.

'Who found her? Mrs Simmons?' asked Susan.

'Who is Mrs Simmons, Miss Wyatt?' asked the detective chief inspector.

'Mother's cleaning lady,' said Susan. 'She sometimes comes on Saturdays, if there's been a party or anything the night before.'

'No, it wasn't Mrs Simmons. It was a Mr Fortescue,' said Hemmings. 'It seems he telephoned Mrs Wyatt, and could get no answer, so he came round, found the door unlocked and walked straight in.'

'But Mummy always locked the door! She was rather nervous on her own – locked everything, and bolted it, once she was inside and it was dark,' said Susan. 'She wasn't so fussy before Daddy died.'

'I see,' said the chief inspector.

'Oh – poor George,' said Susan, who had been thinking what a dreadful experience it would have been for Mrs Simmons. 'Mr Fortescue,' she added, in explanation. 'Where is he? Is he still here?' But he wouldn't be, after all this time. He'd have gone home.

'No. He's at the station,' said the chief inspector.

'The station?'

'Tellingford police station,' said Hemmings.

Susan looked puzzled.

'Why?'

'He's just answering a few questions, Miss Wyatt,' said Hemmings.

'Oh,' said Susan. 'I suppose he had to tell you about – about finding her.'

'That's it,' agreed Hemmings. It seemed the girl did not know that Fortescue had been questioned about the Fletcham murder, or she would have referred to it.

'It must have been awful for him, finding her,' said

231

Susan. 'They'd known each other for years. More than twenty, I should think.'

She appeared calm: calm enough to be helpful.

'Your mother might not have been quite herself last night,' Hemmings suggested gently.

'You mean she may have been at the gin?' said Susan bluntly. It was no good pussyfooting about at a time like this.

Hemmings's men had already discovered a great many empty bottles in the house, and there was a strong smell of alcohol around the mouth of the dead woman.

'Perhaps a few drinks,' Hemmings acknowledged.

'She was drinking too much,' said Susan. 'It worried me, and my brother, but we didn't see what we could do about it. We hoped she'd get over it, after a while. It's only been since my father died.'

'Suppose she'd had a little too much last night?' hazarded Hemmings, relieved that he did not have to spell it out.

'And?'

'Got into an argument of some kind,' Hemmings said cautiously.

'You don't mean with George? Oh no, inspector. That's quite impossible,' said Susan. She hesitated, and then said, 'How did she – what killed her?'

'A blow on the head, Miss Wyatt. Done with a table lamp, we think. Death would have been instantaneous,' Hemmings said.

'Not—?' Susan could not bring herself to utter the word when the victim had been her mother. She tensed, waiting for the inspector to answer.

'She hadn't been sexually assaulted, no,' said Hemmings. The pattern differed here from the Fletcham murder. Fortescue, though, knew Dorothea Wyatt. Fletcham CID had been unable to prove that he had ever met Felicity Cartwright before she was killed. 'Suppose Mr Fortescue made certain suggestions to your mother which she'd found unacceptable,' Hemmings went on primly. 'What do you think would have happened?'

'You mean, if George made a pass?' Susan's eyebrows rose. 'Not old George,' she said. 'He wouldn't. And if he did, Mummy would have hooted with laughter.'

'Are you sure?' said Hemmings. 'I mean, that Mr Fortescue wouldn't?' The girl's brave and honest response made it easy to pursue this line.

'Well, I suppose it's not impossible,' said Susan slowly. How did you know about such things among older people? 'But I can't imagine it. George isn't exactly – I don't know how to put it. I suppose I mean sexy.' She frowned, looking thoughtfully at the inspector. 'I don't quite see what you're getting at. You can't think George may have done this.'

'Mrs Wyatt was a very good-looking woman,' interposed Leo, holding the chief inspector's eye. He remembered meeting Fortescue, and he could understand any man who thought he had a chance trying to make it with Dorothea.

'Whatever you say, I'm sure George wouldn't hurt Mummy,' said Susan stoutly. 'I don't believe he'd hurt anybody, not physically.'

'Well, we'll get it all cleared up as quickly as we

can,' said Hemmings. 'Your mother's solicitor has been here, and he left a message to say that he and his wife would be glad to put you up for the night. I'm afraid we can't let you stay here until we've finished, and we'll be some time. I'll just ask you to check your mother's jewellery, to see if anything's missing. If you'd wait a moment.' He went to the door and spoke to someone in the hall. A few minutes later another man appeared carrying Susan's mother's leather jewel case. Susan looked inside. Her eyes blurred with tears as she saw the familiar pieces she had loved to play with as a child, decking herself in rings and necklaces and her mother's clothes.

'I don't see her engagement ring,' she said. 'A big sapphire with little diamonds all round.'

'She was wearing that, Miss Wyatt,' said Hemmings. 'And some necklaces – silver chains. They will be returned.'

'I see.' Susan closed the box and handed it back to the chief inspector. 'You haven't arrested George, have you?' she asked.

'No. He's just helping us,' said Hemmings. 'You want whoever did this caught, don't you?' he added, in a sterner tone.

'Yes, I do. But it can't be George,' she insisted. 'Does Daniel know about it? Daniel Fortescue? He's at Fletcham University. George's son.'

'Yes. He's at Orchard House,' said Hemmings.

'We'd better go and see him,' Susan said to Leo. 'Poor Daniel. He'll be pretty upset.' She turned to the chief inspector. 'I suppose my brother's coming? I couldn't get hold of him on the telephone before I left London.'

'He's on his way,' Hemmings confirmed. 'I'll let him know you're at Orchard House when he gets here.'

'I suppose, with police all over the village, we're none of us likely to get mislaid,' said Susan. 'I still think it must have been a burglar, Mr Hemmings. Mother surprised him. Had she been out?'

'Yes.' Door-to-door inquiries had already revealed that the dead woman had been to the Plough that evening.

'Well, then,' said Susan. 'There you are. She caught him before he'd taken anything. She was quite gutsy, you know. She might go for him with a handy poker or something.'

'We'll bear that in mind, of course,' said Hemmings, glad she had not asked where her mother had been. In time she'd learn that Mrs Wyatt had visited the Plough, alone, the night she died. Would she take that information in her stride?

'She's still in there,' Susan said to Leo as they went back to the car. She glanced at the dark van, its significance now clear to her.

'Yes.' Leo knew that someone would have to identify the dead woman officially, although there could be no doubt, in fact, about who she was. He had been afraid that Susan would be shown the body. But not here, where it had happened, surely?

It was certainly not a job for Susan. Her brother, who had managed to shuffle off so much of the worry about their mother on to Susan, should be the one to deal with that side of things and Leo determined to see that he did.

It all seemed unreal. So short a time ago he had been here, washing the car for Dorothea, eating her excellent food, taking it all for granted. Never again.

He took Susan's hand and pressed it.

'Let's go and find Daniel,' he said.

Daniel and Vivian were in the kitchen at Orchard House when Susan and Leo arrived. Several photographers had taken pictures of them driving away from the Manor House in the Porsche, but the press were not in Crowbury in force so far, and there were no reporters at Orchard House. There were some policemen, though, and Daniel and Vivian were not allowed to leave the kitchen.

'They're searching Dad's things,' said Daniel. 'Looking through his clothes. Oh Susan, it's awful. Your poor mother. I am so sorry. She was great.'

Susan put her arms round Daniel and gave him a hug.

'Dan, your father couldn't have – it's just not on. It's quite impossible,' said Susan.

'I know. Thank God you see it that way,' said Daniel. 'But there was that other business, you see, in Fletcham.'

'What business?' asked Susan.

As Daniel explained, Susan stared at him in amazement.

'It's not possible,' she said. 'He didn't even know that woman. How on earth did he get mixed up in it?'

'Well, he was upset, you see, and this policeman

saw him behaving a bit oddly,' said Daniel wretchedly.

Leo glanced at Vivian, whom he had never met
before, in her Indian dress and hairy sweater. They
exchanged embarrassed grins. What did she think
about all this? There were plenty of cases where
murders had been committed by apparently kindly
men.

Vivian had her hand on the kettle.

'What about some coffee?' she said.

'We could do with something stronger,' said Leo.
'There must be something in the house, isn't there,
Daniel? Your father wouldn't mind, in the circum-
stances, would he?'

'No, but it's in the dining room and we've got to
stay in here,' said Daniel.

'Unless we want the loo,' said Vivian, and she
giggled. 'We ask the constable in the hall, then. We've
had to because of the coffee.'

'I'm sure they'll let us have some whisky,' said
Leo, the confident merchant banker. 'I'll ask them.'

He went to the door and a mutter of voices was
heard as he approached the officer in the hall. Soon
he reappeared with a bottle of brandy and a bottle of
whisky, one in each hand, and some small bottles of
ginger ale poking out of his pockets.

'Well done,' said Susan.

The sausages that George had bought earlier were
on the kitchen table, still wrapped up. Vivian, who
had examined the parcel, turned back a piece of the
wrapping and showed them surreptitiously to Leo.
She was getting hungry, and he, the other outsider,

might be too, though possibly Daniel and Susan were beyond noticing such mundane things at the moment.

She was right. Leo, having doled out drinks in tumblers from the kitchen cupboard, rallied them. They'd need their strength, he said, and suggested searching for some chips in the freezer.

'We can't go out,' he said bluntly. 'The press will be in the pub. Luckily your father had got provisions in, Daniel. When we've eaten, we'll see if there's anything useful to be done.'

There must be relatives to tell, and so on, but that could wait. How dreadful if it turned out that Daniel's father was responsible for what had happened. Surely a burglar was the more likely answer? But what about the murder in Fletcham? There had been no arrest.

A grim time lay ahead, and Susan would need all the support she could get. Leo resolved not to be found wanting, but Daniel's plight was serious too.

A prudent action he might take occurred to Leo.

'Have you got hold of a solicitor for your father, Daniel?' he asked. 'It might be a good thing to do.'

'Yes,' he said. Bill Kyle had heard about Dorothea's death earlier in the day when Mark Wyatt had telephoned him before driving down from Yorkshire, asking him to see to things. He was Dorothea's solicitor too. If Bill hadn't managed to get his father released within twenty-four hours, Daniel would tell his mother what had happened. He found it hard to hold back tears; the grown-up games had gone beyond his league.

The police cars on their errands back and forth between the newly set-up murder room at Tellingford police station and the Manor House did not pass Primrose Cottage, and Valerie, back from her shopping trip in the village, knew nothing about what was going on. She had a lot to do because she was taking the children to see their grandparents that afternoon; they were having an early lunch and catching the one-fifteen bus from the High Street. Valerie intended to tell her parents that she was going to move to Middletown. She knew that she could never be happy again at Primrose Cottage, after what had happened to her there; the isolation that had been its charm now frightened her. If she found a flat in Middletown, she could take a proper job; her parents would look after the children for the time between school and the end of her working day. She would lose much of her once-prized independence, but independence now seemed a lot less important than plain safety.

She wouldn't be sorry to exchange stripping furniture for some sort of office job. Ronald Trimm was very hard to please. When he had come round on Wednesday, he'd collected a chest that, on his instructions, she'd rubbed down with methylated spirit and steel wool and he hadn't liked what she'd done. He'd never shown her how to do the work: just told her what to use; she'd taken books from the library from which she'd done her best to teach herself. He'd stood in the garage in his raincoat, handing her notes from his wallet, not troubling to take off his gloves as he thumbed them from a wad.

The thought reminded her that she hadn't yet told Cooley about that stubby-fingered hand. She had rung his digs twice, and each time he was out. If she telephoned the police station, some other officer would be sure to answer. She couldn't tell anyone else, for they hadn't believed her before and they would think she was making it up. She'd hoped that he would come round again; perhaps he would soon.

There was a lot of activity in the village when she and the children went to catch the bus. A police motorcyclist was standing in the road where it branched for Middletown, and there were many more cars parked in the High Street than was usual, even though Saturday was always busy. Perhaps there was a wedding on. Valerie had no time to find out what was happening, as the bus was already coming. She hustled the children on to it.

Later, when the police officer who was making door-to-door inquiries in Ship Lane knocked on the door of Primrose Cottage, he found no one there.

In Nanron Antiques they heard the police cars go past, sirens sounding and lights flashing. Lynn wanted to find out what it was all about, but Uncle Ron said, quite huffily for him, that such curiosity was vulgar.

Later they heard that the police were at the Manor House, but no one knew what had happened. Robbery, it was supposed, but there was a rumour that Mrs Wyatt had been hurt.

A uniformed officer called in the afternoon. Lynn

watched while Uncle Ron went smoothly forward to see what he wanted.

He asked if Ronald knew Mrs Dorothea Wyatt and, being told that she was an occasional customer, asked when he had last seen her.

'Now let me see,' said Ronald. 'I sold her a little jug – Wedgwood. She collects jugs.' He was pleased with himself for remembering to use the present tense. 'That was on Thursday – yes.' He'd have to go on, speak frankly: he must hide nothing that others might reveal. 'But I saw her yesterday, too,' he added.

'And when was that?' asked the officer.

'In the evening, at the Plough. I was working late – I always do on Fridays, doing the books,' said Ronald. 'There was a discrepancy which took me some time to sort out, so I popped into the Plough for a drink and some sandwiches. Mrs Wyatt was there, in the saloon bar.'

'What time was this?' asked the constable.

'Oh – about seven. Earlier, perhaps. Around then.'

'Was she alone?'

'I really couldn't say,' said Ronald. 'I didn't talk to her.'

'Was she with anyone, Mr Trimm?' persisted the officer. Ronald told him that she had been talking to the manager of the National Westminster Bank.

'Did you see Mrs Wyatt leave the Plough?'

'No. I didn't stay long and she was still there when I left,' said Ronald. 'What's this all about? Is she missing?' Some curiosity would be natural.

'No. There's been an accident,' said the policeman. 'Thank you, Mr Trimm.'

When he had gone, Ronald felt an instant's panic. Was she not dead? If she recovered, she could name him. But he calmed himself. No one could survive, with injuries like that; he'd seen bone, and brains.

Lynn had listened to the conversation and when the shop was empty again she asked Ronald what could have happened.

'I couldn't say,' said Ronald coolly. 'We'll know soon enough.'

Lynn was sorry if it was anything serious, but she would not let distractions deflect her from what she meant to do later, which was tell Uncle Ronald she was giving up the job after today. Oddly enough, that morning he'd done none of the things she'd been finding so annoying lately. He had seen her into the van without brushing against her or leaning over her, and he hadn't hovered around her in the shop. The relief of it made her light-hearted, and she was merry, humming under her breath as she tidied round and dusted, giving him his coffee with a wide smile. It made her feel bad about her decision to leave, but she wasn't going to change her mind about that.

Ronald watched her whisk about, skirt swinging round, her gently swelling hips, legs in white knee socks over her tights, shining hair bouncing on her shoulders. Young as she was, she wasn't innocent any longer; she was asking for it, like those others. He longed to put his hands, ungloved, on her soft young body. He held them before him: short, square hands with stubby fingers and pale ginger hairs on their backs; strong hands: the hands of death.

He went out after the policeman had called, not

telling Lynn where he was going, and was gone some time.

She slipped down to the cellar while he was gone. She'd just look at those magazines again and see what date was on them. If they were very old, maybe she'd think it over. They could have been bought by someone else and put in the drawer long ago.

She must be quick, and listen hard for the shop bell, which you could hear all right from down there for it rang at the top of the stairs.

She tipped out the pencils and pens and found the small brass key. She undid the drawer.

A black sweater, crumpled anyhow, lay on top of the newspapers. Frowning, Lynn pulled it out. There was a woollen hood, too; it was the one Uncle Ronald sometimes wore in the garden, when Auntie Nancy got after him to wrap up well. She and her parents laughed about it; Nancy coddling him, her parents said it was, and remarked, when they thought Lynn wasn't listening, that she was like a mother to him. Lynn didn't really understand what they were getting at; she thought it rather sweet that Uncle Ron and Auntie Nancy were so wrapped up in one another.

Under the sweater and the hood there was a penknife. Or at least it was a knife; it was large and the blade was folded into the big bone handle. How peculiar. Lynn lifted out the old newspapers and came to the magazines. They were recent, two a month old and one a little older. She didn't look at any others, and she did not find the newspapers reporting on Felicity Cartwright's death that were hidden under them. She put everything back and locked the drawer again. She had just hidden the key and replaced the pens and pencils in the mug when a customer called. Lynn sold her a stripped-pine chair.

After that, she made herself some tea. Throwing the teabag into the dustbin later, she noticed a square package in it, in a paper bag. It was a round of ham sandwiches, gone rather dry. Weird.

She did not tell him until they reached Sycamore Road that evening, when she had her hand on the door catch, opening it before the van had stopped. She was out, in the road, as Ronald put on the hand-brake.

She leaned in through the open door.

'Uncle Ron, I won't be coming to the shop any more,' she said. 'I'm sorry if you think I'm letting you down, but you'll easily get someone else. It's a lovely job. I need wider experience and I'm arranging a change of employment.' The stilted phrases had come into her head during the day.

She banged the door of the van shut before he could speak. He'd looked as though she'd struck him; his whole face had crumpled. Lynn hurried down the drive to her own home before guilt could make her change her mind and turn back.

Blood pounded in Ronald's head as he watched her go. How could she, after all he'd done for her? Taking her to school each day because her parents were afraid for her; giving her a job before she knew a thing about it; giving her treats and playing with her when she was a little kiddie. His little Lynn! What had come over her?

It was that boy, of course: Peter. He'd put her up to this for some reason. Well, he'd see what her parents had to say about it when they heard. He was certain they knew nothing about it. Why, only the other day Keith had mentioned how grateful they were for the fact that she had such a pleasant Saturday post. A change of employment, indeed! What sort of change? As a barmaid? That would be the next thing.

He crashed the gears, moving off, and still felt quite shaken when he went into the bungalow, so much so tha Nancy noticed and asked him what was the matter.

Ronald told her, wrathfully.

'What an ungrateful girl,' said Nancy. 'Still, she's young and has no sense of obligation, I suppose. That's what's wrong with the world today. Hilda will be most upset, I'm sure. But I don't expect she'll be able to make her change her mind. Parents nowadays have no control over their children. Lynn will soon find she's made a bad mistake. Working elsewhere will be much harder, that's certain. Don't worry, dear. I'll come in on Saturdays, as I used to, until you find someone else.'

'Thank you, my dear.' He had to have help on Saturdays, when he bought and sold the clocks which brought in so much of their income and never featured in the shop.

'You know you can rely on me, dear,' said Nancy. 'Dinner will be ready when you've washed. Perhaps we might have a glass of sherry this evening, as it's Saturday?'

Nancy knew nothing about the police activity in

Crowbury and Ronald did not tell her. She'd find out, soon enough. It was sure to be in the papers.

He'd transferred, that morning, the trousers he had worn the night before from the airing cupboard to the van. On Monday he'd take them to the cleaner's for express processing. They'd be restored to the wardrobe before Nancy noticed they were missing.

21

The interview room at Tellingford police station was shabbier than the one at Fletcham, which had been built some fifteen years ago and was clinical in design. George had plenty of time to make comparisons, sitting at another small table on another hard chair. He repeated his account of finding Dorothea, pointing out that his car must still have been warm when the police took it from outside the Manor House to be examined. He'd been shopping that morning; people would have seen him in the village. There was the pleasant girl with her children, for instance, for whom he'd bought the bananas.

No one could believe that he had stayed all night beside Dorothea's body.

But the police had an answer to this. He could have visited her on foot the night before, approaching unobserved.

'You had a quarrel. You struck her. Then you went home and changed. You returned in the morning,' Detective Sergeant Gower thundered at him.

'No,' said George, for the umpteenth time.

'Tell me again how you spent Friday evening,' Gower invited.

George had returned from London on his usual train. He had not gone jogging, his usual practice at that time, he explained, and he gave an invented headache as an excuse. He'd showered and changed into leisure clothes, eaten boil-in-the-bag braised kidneys, with frozen peas, followed by cheese and biscuits, drunk one whisky and soda and watched television. Then he'd gone to bed. He told them all this.

There was no proof of the truth of what he said.

'I put it to you that you went to see Mrs Wyatt. You made certain suggestions to her which she turned down. You were angry, picked up the lamp and struck her,' said Gower.

'No, no, no,' said George.

It continued late into the night. He was taken to a cell for a few hours' rest – how could he sleep? – and then it began all over again on Sunday morning, with the detective chief inspector asking the questions.

Both the glasses found in the room with the dead woman – the wine glass and the tumbler – revealed her fingerprints, and traces of lipstick; no one else's prints were there. Whoever had killed her may have been cool enough to wash and put away a glass he had used himself. George would know where such things were kept in a friend's house.

'No,' George repeated, when this was propounded.

It went on and on. His head reeled until he began to wonder if he had, after all, done as the inspector suggested and then blacked out to forget it. But he had no wish to go to bed with Dorothea; if he had, on her past form she would have needed no persuading.

He could not say so. He could not blacken the reputation of the dead woman. Everyone had low moments, and Dorothea, when she made her crude approach, was a bit down. He must hold firm. In the end, innocence would prevail.

Cooley called on Valerie early on Sunday morning. When he discovered that she had been missed in the house-to-house inquiry, as she was out, he was determined to talk to her himself. This incident, happening in the village, would be bound to upset her, even if she did not know the victim.

She was having breakfast with the children when he arrived. Timmy heard the car draw up, looked out of the window and recognized him, and was already undoing some of the bolts and chains on the door before Cooley rang; he could not reach them all.

Valerie looked surprised to see him, but quite pleased, and Melissa made a space for him at the table beside her. He saw a brown teapot, boiled eggs in blue and white cups, a home-made loaf. He grinned.

'I'm just in time,' he said. 'I like an egg myself. Most people don't seem to bother these days – it's all toast and cornflakes.'

'Haven't you had any breakfast?' Valerie asked.

'Well – a bit. I could manage some more,' said Cooley.

'Two eggs?' said Valerie. 'How many minutes?'

'Four and a half, please,' he said promptly.

Valerie poured him some tea. He felt absurdly pleased when she put sugar in without asking if he took it.

'You were out yesterday,' he said.

'Yes. We went to see my parents in Middletown,' said Valerie. 'We were quite late back. Dad ran us home.'

That would be another thing, after they moved: she'd have the occasional use of her parents' car. They'd been overjoyed at her plan and had asked no questions about why she wanted to leave Crowbury.

Cooley asked about her parents, and she told him while he ate the two large brown eggs she boiled for him. Her father had been a minor civil servant in the administrative area of the post office until forced to retire early after his illness. He learned about her mother's operation; but she said nothing about her own marriage. Cooley, in turn, revealed that he came from Devon, where his father had a small dairy farm.

'I'm glad you called,' she said. 'I was going to ring you.'

'Oh?' She might not know about Mrs Wyatt's death, he realized. She had been out the day before, and had probably seen no Sunday paper.

'I've remembered something,' she said. 'It's probably not important, but you'd better hear it.'

'I want to ask you something, too,' he said, and glanced at the children.

'Oh – you weren't just passing by,' she said, feeling oddly deflated.

'Well – not exactly. It's a bit early for a social call,

Valerie,' said Cooley. 'But maybe you'll ask me to breakfast another time. Although in my job it's difficult to know when you'll be free. Things crop up, especially when you're CID.'

'Something has cropped up?'

'Yes.'

Valerie stood up.

'Timmy, would you like to sail your boats in the bath?' she suggested. 'And Melissa, how about making some models?'

Melissa usually mixed her plaster of paris in the kitchen, but Valerie sent her up to use the bathroom as a studio this morning, thus getting both children out of the way and in one room. The mess would be awful, but you couldn't win all the time.

Timmy beamed. Boat-sailing in the bath was a rare treat, since tidal waves from hurricanes were inevitable, and often overflowed on to the floor.

Valerie tied Timmy into a plastic apron with a picture of Paddington Bear on it, and went upstairs to control the depth and temperature of the potential ocean. Cooley sat back, waiting for her. She was a nice girl, with a lot on her plate without all that trouble. He wondered about her husband. Fancy leaving a girl like her.

He asked her why it had happened, when she came back.

'People always think it's that way round,' said Valerie. 'But I left him. I couldn't carry on any longer pretending to be something that I'm not – a smart executive wife. He's got one like that now. He'd been carrying on a bit with her before, but I don't think it had gone all that far; she'd have been too careful. Hedging her bets, you know. He's much happier now.' And so had she been, until a few short weeks ago. 'I sometimes wonder about the children. If it's too hard on them,' she said.

'Well – it happens, doesn't it?' said Cooley. 'Kids are tough.'

'What did you want to ask me?' she said.

'Did you know a Mrs Dorothea Wyatt? Of the Manor House?' asked Cooley.

'Yes, I know her. Not well. She's nice – we all had tea there a bit ago – she saw us walking in the field and asked us in,' said Valerie. 'Why do you want to know? Has something happened to her?' She went suddenly pale. 'You said, did I know her – not do I—?'

'You hadn't heard?'

Valerie shook her head.

'That man – has he—?'

'It wasn't quite the same,' said Cooley. He'd better be blunt: get on with it. 'I'm afraid she's dead.'

'Oh no! Oh, how dreadful! Why – how?'

'She was attacked some time on Friday evening, in her house. She wasn't raped. She was hit on the head with a table lamp,' said Cooley.

Valerie simply stared at him, her face ashen.

'We've been making inquiries round the village to get a picture of her movements that night. Someone came to see you yesterday, but you were out. So I came today,' said Cooley.

'But that's—' Valerie did not know what to say. 'I can't believe it,' she whispered. 'Not dead.'

'Had you seen her lately?' Cooley asked.

'I can't remember when I did,' said Valerie. 'I saw her car in the High Street – when—? Thursday, it would have been, when I was coming back after meeting the children at school. I didn't actually see Mrs Wyatt. Just her car. I know it, it's a Saab. She brought us back here in it, when we went to tea that day.'

'I see,' said Cooley.

'Oh, poor Mrs Wyatt!' said Valerie. 'Was it a burglar?'

'We don't think so,' said Cooley. 'Nothing was taken.'

'Could it have been that man – you know?' Valerie shivered. 'The one who came here? You think that was the man who killed the woman in Fletcham, don't you?'

'There's no evidence for it,' said Cooley. 'It's only a hunch I've got – because of the knife threat to you, and she was stabbed. Mrs Wyatt wasn't stabbed.'

'When was she found?' asked Valerie.

'Yesterday morning,' said Cooley. 'By a neighbour – a Mr George Fortescue. He went round to see why she wasn't answering her telephone. Or so he says. Found the door unlocked and walked in.'

'Oh, poor Mr Fortescue, after all that other trouble,' said Valerie. 'What a shock for him. It's been the talk of the village. Of course, you don't want to believe all you hear in a place like this, but the woman who cleans for him said he'd been taken in for questioning. Anyway, he was let go.'

'Yes, but that was for lack of evidence,' said

Cooley. There'd been plenty of time for another killing.

'Well, if it was the same man who came here – the one who did that murder – it wasn't Mr Fortescue,' said Valerie firmly.

'Why do you say that?'

'That was what I wanted to tell you,' said Valerie. 'I suddenly remembered something. It was his hand.' She shuddered, thinking of it. 'I'd looked at the floor – at the sander – somehow I couldn't look at it. The hand, I mean. But then I suddenly saw it in my mind's eye, holding the knife. It was horrid – short and stubby, with little ginger hairs on the back. Not thin.' She looked at Cooley's hands, which were on the table; he was playing with a spoon, digging with it in the sugar bowl. If Timmy did that, she'd make him stop. 'Not like yours,' she said. Cooley's hands were large and smooth – quite like George Fortescue's, but bigger. 'Sort of plump,' she added. 'Mr Fortescue's aren't like that at all. I noticed at the butcher's, yesterday.'

'That's important,' Cooley said.

'But you can't think he killed Mrs Wyatt,' said Valerie. 'Why should he? They were friends. Besides, he's a nice man. He wouldn't do a thing like that.'

'He was there. He was mixed up in the Fletcham business and there's no lead to anyone else. He has to be eliminated,' Cooley said.

'But the real murderer will be miles away,' said Valerie. 'You'll let him get away with it.'

'I hope not,' Cooley said. 'If Fortescue's innocent, we'll find out. But it all takes time.'

After he'd gone, Valerie wished she'd told him of her plans to move to Middletown. Still, why should he be interested? He'd only come today for information.

Well, he'd got some.

For want of evidence, and because of assurances from his solicitor that he would not disappear, George Fortescue was allowed to go home on Sunday evening. Clothes removed from his house the day before showed no obvious sign of bloodstains; they had been sent to the laboratory to be examined. There had been no recent bonfire in the grounds of Orchard House, nor in any fireplace in the building, where incriminating items could have been destroyed.

He'd soon have nothing to wear, he told Bill Kyle, with wry, unlikely humour.

'There will be more letters. More obscene telephone calls,' he said wearily.

'Burn the letters and leave the telephone off the hook, as you did before,' said Bill.

'Some people are accident prone. I seem to be murder prone,' said George, making in the space of minutes only the second attempt at a witticism Bill had ever heard from him.

'It'll all blow over,' he said soothingly. 'It takes time to prove things either way.'

Bill was certain that George was not involved with the Fletcham case, but this time he wasn't so sure. Being questioned about the other business might have tipped him over in some way, for he had been under a lot of strain since his wife went off. Dorothea might have provoked him. Bill had seen her behaving with some abandon when she'd had a drink or two and there were men around. There was no harm in her if you knew her and took it lightly, but George might have called her bluff. If he was charged, on what was likely to be slim evidence, he might get away with manslaughter, Bill calculated gloomily.

George insisted that he must return to the office the next day. He'd go mad otherwise, he told Bill, with nothing to do but brood about what might happen next. Because the police still had his Rover, they arranged that Bill would take him to the station the next morning.

Daniel and Vivian had returned uneasily to Fletcham, ready to come back instantly if they were needed. Susan and Leo had gone back to London, and Susan's brother Mark had returned home, though he would have to attend the inquest, arranged for Tuesday. No funeral plans could yet be made. It was a dreadful business, thought Bill, as he drove away from Orchard House at last, sighing over the conflicting obligations of friendship and professional duty.

22

The Trimms spent a quiet Sunday.

News of the Crowbury murder was prominent on the front pages of the Sunday papers.

'In Crowbury!' said Nancy. 'Just fancy! No one's safe. Burglars, I expect. You said she had some lovely pieces, dear.'

'Yes,' said Ronald. 'I sold her a jug only on Thursday. That black basalt one you mended so nicely, dear. She was very taken with it.'

'It made her last hours happy, I expect,' said Nancy, threading a needle with maroon wool. She was making a tapestry cushion cover.

Ronald gave the van a good clean after breakfast, taking the vacuum to the floor of it, and polishing the bodywork. His soiled trousers were safely stowed under the driver's seat. In the afternoon, he and Nancy went for a walk, through the park and beside the river. It was cold and raw, but the days were drawing out. Spring would not be long.

Ron looked about for Lynn when they reached home, but he did not see her, though her father was in the garden, doing some digging. They talked for a while across the fence. Keith Norton was disturbed by the news from Crowbury. There had been no mention in the papers of the alleged rape in the Tellingford area some weeks before, but Keith felt there could be a connection and was worried about Lynn.

'I'm sorry she's being so foolish about the job,' he said. 'It doesn't seem right to expect you to give her a lift in the mornings when she's behaved so badly.'

'Don't worry about it,' said Ronald. 'Young people are hard to understand. I expect she'll change her mind quite soon and want to come back.'

'I hope so,' said Keith. 'I'd be glad to feel she was having a lift in the mornings, just until this business is cleared up.'

'Of course. As long as she doesn't keep me waiting,' Ronald said, and went into the house, humming.

But the next morning, when Ron got the van out, Lynn was not to be seen, and her mother came running down the drive when Ronald blew his horn impatiently.

'I'm so sorry, Ronald,' she said in a worried voice. 'I don't know what's got into Lynn. Peter came and they went off together ten minutes ago.'

Ronald drove off, scowling. He was still scowling as he stopped at the cleaners with his trousers.

Mondays were always quiet at the shop. He rearranged the window, putting to the front some Delft ware and a glass case containing some medals he'd bought recently. Old Colonel Villiers might be interested in them. It gave him a chance to look out at the village street but, though there were still cars about that belonged to the press, and an occasional police car went by, no one came in to ask him more questions. He went across to buy the *Sun* and the *Daily Mirror* but neither had any theory about the crime. They mentioned that the body had been found by a neighbour, Mr Fortescue, who had made a statement at the police station and had refused to comment when he left.

Ronald smiled when he read that.

Detective Chief Superintendent Brownley was the officer in charge of the CID for the area that included C division and Fletcham, and D division, covering Tellingford.

On Monday morning he faced the unpleasant fact that there were two unsolved murders in his area. Neither was your run-of-the-mill attack on a prostitute or battering of a wife by her husband in a domestic brawl; each was the death of a woman of good character, middle-aged or older, from a respectable, even prosperous, background. They did not seem to be connected.

Routine investigations were proceeding in both cases but with no good result so far. In the first case, a man named George Fortescue had been held for questioning but had been released. It was this same man who had found the body of the second woman.

It must be more than mere coincidence.

Brownley called a conference in Middletown for Monday afternoon. Detective Chief Inspector Hemmings from Tellingford and Detective Inspector

Maude from Fletcham were bidden there to meet him.

Nancy got through her work in good time on Monday. She finished a repair to a large, rather ornate Victorian teapot that had taken some time because she had had to make a mould for the handle. It looked good; she was proud of it.

In the afternoon she did the ironing, the washing having whirled itself automatically round during the hour after breakfast while she cleaned the house.

When the ironing was done, she looked through Ronald's clothes. There might be a button to stitch on more firmly, something to wash that she'd over-looked. Sometimes, when he put his sweaters away, he didn't fold them as neatly as she would like, and the things he wore for gardening needed attention from time to time. She knew exactly what he owned.

She could not find the black polo-necked sweater he often wore at weekends, nor a pair of trousers he'd been wearing to the shop for the last week. He'd had a different pair on today, the dark brown ones that looked so good with his corduroy jacket. She hunted in the wardrobe in case the hanger had somehow got wedged between others, but the trousers were not there. His knitted balaclava helmet, the one she had made for him, which he wore in the garden on very cold days to protect his ears, was missing too, and a scarf. That was odd. She must ask him about them when he came in. Perhaps he had torn the trousers, or spilled something on them, and didn't want her to know. How silly! As if she'd be angry with him!

She'd just scold him gently for carelessness. It was funny about the other things, though; he wore the helmet only for gardening. Perhaps it was in the shed. He might be wearing the scarf today, as it was cold, but she hadn't noticed it when he went off and she always looked him over before he departed, making sure he was neat. You couldn't trust men, she thought fondly, tucking a sock foot inside the leg so that it was folded ready to put on.

George felt so tired. He had had a dreadful forty-eight hours. His colleagues at the office commented on his pallor; some had seen in the newspapers that he had discovered the dead body of his murdered neighbour. His secretary, who had a kindly nature and had been with him a long time, suggested he should go home early on Monday. He had had a shocking experience, she said, and it would take time for him to recover.

George wanly smiled at her. What would she think if she knew the police suspected he had killed Dorothea Wyatt, who had been his friend?

He took her advice and caught the four-forty train, where he sat with a book about maritime adventures in the time of Nelson open on his knee, not taking in a word.

At Tellingford, as he crossed the footbridge over the line, he could see a police car parked in the station yard. Blind panic hit him.

He saw it all. An officer had been sent to arrest him at work, had learned he had left early, and they were intercepting him. Two officers, very likely, one to clip on the handcuffs which so far he'd been spared. They'd be waiting by the ticket-collector's sentry-box. They'd have found some new way of connecting him with poor Dorothea's death.

Something inside him snapped. He turned back the way he had come, across the bridge to the down-line platform. There must be a way through the fence somewhere along the line. He hurried, hoping to make his escape while the train still blocked the vision of those on the other platform. Passengers crossing the bridge looked surprised as he mumbled something about leaving his glasses on the train, hurrying past.

He ran down the platform as the train moved forward. There was a wooden fence at its side, extending beyond it, and mesh wire after that, but George ran on, fleet of foot from his months of jogging, until the wire gave way to more fencing at the ends of gardens, and at last there was a broken piece, visible in the light from the railway. He scrambled through, into the garden beyond.

There was no sound of pursuit.

George made his way towards the house, a black mass at the end of the short garden with cracks of light showing between drawn curtains. He caught his leg against a cold frame and hurt his ankle. He hobbled on. There must be a way round the house and into the road. He moved quietly, and found a gate at the side of the garage. He unlatched it and went through, and met a line of washing which flapped in his face. A cat ran between his legs and yowled loudly. George, in alarm, almost yowled too, but he bit back his yelp, beat his way out of the washing and ran on, down the front path and into the road.

A door opened behind him and he heard voices. There was a shout. He'd been seen.

He ran on blindly, fast, not knowing where the road led and without a plan.

The police officer driving the car which he had seen at the station was not waiting for George. He was meeting a colleague who had been in London to give evidence in a case being heard up there.

Ronald, too, cut short his working day, closing the shop early. He had three missions.

First, he went to the cleaner's in Tellingford to collect his trousers. He put them, on a wire hanger in their cellophane bag, into the back of the van. Next, he bought Nancy some flowers, a bunch of bronze chrysanthemums; she'd like those. He placed them, wrapped in the florist's green and yellow printed paper, beside his trousers.

Then he drove to the school gates.

He might be too late. Most of the pupils went home before this; he had seen some of them walking through the town as he did his errands. But Lynn sometimes stayed on for a music lesson, or a play rehearsal. He'd wait an hour. If she didn't come, he'd try tomorrow. In the end, he'd get her.

No one else should have her. Afterwards, he'd have to kill her. It was a pity; she was so fresh and sweet; but it would be necessary. She would be a sacrifice, and by that he would be purged. She was small and slender and would be light to carry; he could leave her in a ditch. Then he would be safe: safe from discovery and safe from torment.

It began to rain as he sat there in the van, watching the school entrance. A few girls came out together, none of them Lynn, then a group of boys on bicycles. After that a car drove out of the gates. Then there were two boys and three girls, in a laughing group.

A girl was coming out alone. It was Lynn!

If she tried to refuse his offer of a lift, he'd point out that her father would think it odd of her, when he'd particularly wanted her to avoid being out alone in the dark. Ronald would tell her father, he would say.

But Lynn didn't refuse.

In a way, she felt quite pleased when she saw Uncle Ron's van in the road and he called her through the window. It was never nice going home in the rain; she'd get wet, waiting for the bus. And she did feel bad about him. She'd tried to stop thinking about those magazines, and the clothes. People did dress up, act kinky; she knew that. She had a lot of theoretical knowledge. She hadn't told Peter about the things she'd seen in the desk; somehow she couldn't. She'd just asked him to meet her on the way to school that morning, so that there would be no problem about going in the van; but she'd felt several guilty pangs since at going off without a word.

She climbed in without protest, smiling and uttering thanks.

Uncle Ronald had not got out of the car to open the door for her; he did not touch her as she settled herself beside him. They'd soon be home.

But he turned left at the end of Tellingford's main street, instead of to the right, in the direction of Sycamore Road.

Lynn said nothing at first. Perhaps he had someone to see on the way home. She sat beside him, silent, while the windscreen-wipers scraped to and fro before them both.

As the traffic thinned, Ronald began to drive faster. He smiled, grasping the wheel in his gloved hands. He asked about her day.

Lynn told him that she had been painting scenery for the play. The performance would be in two weeks' time.

They had left the town behind now. Ronald turned from the main road into a minor one where there weren't even any cats' eyes in the middle. Lynn hadn't been able to see the signpost on the corner.

Uncle Ron had begun to hum under his breath. She had never heard him do that before. It was an odd, tuneless sound and she did not like it.

'Where are we going, Uncle Ron?' she asked him. 'This isn't the way home.'

'No, my dear,' said Ronald. 'I've got something to attend to first.'

He resumed his humming. Then he took off his gloves, first one, pulling it with his teeth to free his fingers and tucking it under his chin until it was loose enough to shake off. The other was shed in the same way. All the while the dirge-like noise continued.

The road they were on was a quiet one; they met

no other traffic. Lynn felt troubled. He had not answered her question about where they were going. Still, it wasn't late; her parents knew she would be busy with the scenery after school and they wouldn't expect her home just yet, so they wouldn't be worried. Whatever Uncle Ron had to do wouldn't take long.

'Where do you have to go, Uncle Ron?' she asked.

'You'll see,' he said, and he patted her knee with his bare stubby hand with the ginger hairs on the back.

At first, he'd been content, just driving along in the van with Lynn while he anticipated what was to happen. He'd planned to park in a lonely spot. Afterwards, he could simply leave her there. But it would be difficult in the van, and uncomfortable. Suppose she struggled? He hadn't brought the knife. She must be made to cooperate, or it wouldn't be nice; he'd found that out. Only once in his life had he known it as it should be; that single time with Dorothea Wyatt. He tightened his grip on the wheel and the humming ceased. Lynn glanced at him; she could not see his expression in the darkness, but she felt the change of mood and she began to feel frightened. Grown-ups could behave so strangely.

Ronald turned down another road and went faster. The headlights cut through the darkness and after a mile or so Lynn saw a signpost as they passed. It indicated Crowbury.

'You're going to the shop,' she said.

'Yes,' he agreed.

Why hadn't he said so, at the beginning of their journey? Why had he come this long way round, instead of taking the usual road?

'Did you forget something?' she asked anxiously.

'Yes,' said Ronald, and began to hum again. There was no time to waste now. He knew what to do. He would take her down to the cellar, where from the pile of packing sacks he could make them a bed. Afterwards, he would bundle her up, put her in a dower chest that was waiting to go to Will Noakes and take her away again. That bit could wait till tomorrow, for he might need help from the greengrocer's son to lift it into the van. Sometimes the greengrocer's son did lend a hand when something was too heavy for him alone.

But Lynn wouldn't be heavy.

He might need the knife at first, to make her obey him, but he wouldn't use it afterwards. There mustn't be any blood. He flexed his hands on the wheel and imagined them round her throat: her little neck. She wouldn't suffer; anyway, not long.

They reached the shop and he parked outside.

'Come along, Lynn,' he ordered, getting out and moving round to the passenger door.

'But you won't be long. I'll wait here, in the van,' Lynn said.

'Nonsense, my dear. It's warmer inside, and I'll be ten minutes or so. Time for coffee. You shall make it for me. Come along, Lynn, it's raining and I'm getting wet.'

Lynn was by nature a docile girl, and mistrust was alien to her. The habit of obedience was strong in her, and she obeyed him now, getting out of the van and walking into the shop ahead of him.

He closed the door behind them both and pushed the bolt home.

'Go ahead, my dear, and make the coffee,' he said.

Slowly, reluctantly, Lynn did as she was told, moving to the lobby at the rear, filling the kettle and plugging it in. It was an automatic one that boiled fast. She heaped instant coffee into two mugs, and put sugar in Ronald's; he took two spoonfuls.

Ronald came round behind her, watching her. There was milk still left in a bottle on the window ledge and he passed it to her, smiling.

She didn't like his smile; it was somehow different from his usual one. Best hurry with the coffee-making; then he'd finish whatever he had to do and they'd be on their way home, she decided, willing the kettle to boil.

'I've something to do in the cellar, Lynn. Bring it down', will you?' he said.

'Yes.' That was good: that meant he'd get on with it.

When he'd disappeared downstairs she did, just for a moment, contemplate leaving the shop, running off down the road. But it seemed so stupid. How would she explain when he told her parents what she had done, as he certainly would? And how would she get home? She was forbidden to hitch-hike, and she did not know the times of the buses. She'd get soaked, waiting at the stop, and Uncle Ron would soon find her there.

She went down the cellar stairs, a mug of coffee in

each hand, carrying them carefully so that she didn't spill them, concentrating.

His voice came from behind her when she reached the small room with the desk and the chairs, and the bundle of sacking and cardboard stacked in the corner.

'Put them down on the desk, Lynn dear,' she heard him instruct, and she did so.

The cellar door closed and she turned.

He was standing there, smiling, a strange, terrifying sort of smile now, and he held a knife in his hand as he moved towards her.

'Just a kiss to begin with, Lynn, my dear child,' he said. 'Don't be frightened. Uncle Ron's never hurt you, has he? It's you who've hurt him, by wanting to leave. Now, we can't have that, can we? Just a kiss, little Lynn. It'll all be quite easy, if you do as you're told.'

She opened her mouth to scream, backing away from him, stopped by the desk behind her.

'No!' she cried. 'No, Uncle Ron,' on a rising note that became a shriek.

'Not a sound, my Lynn,' he warned. 'I don't want to hurt you.'

But he must, as he had those others. He struck her across the face, and it silenced her, just as it had the other two women, but this time he hated to do it.

'Dear little Lynn, it won't hurt at all. You'll see. You'll be happy,' he said. 'But no more noise. I won't stand for that.'

Lynn groped behind her on the desk, without a plan, just reaching for something to help her. A mug of coffee spilled and the hot liquid splashed her hand.

Ronald seized her arm, turning her round as he twisted it up behind her.

'No, Lynn,' he said. 'No tricks. I'm far stronger than you are.'

And he was. He gagged her with a clean white handkerchief which he took out of his pocket, and he tied her arms behind her back with the twine he used for packaging.

Then he tied her legs together and bundled her on to the floor while he prepared their bed of love in the corner.

During Monday afternoon the post-mortem report on Dorothea Wyatt came through. It stated that she had consumed the equivalent of four double gin and tonics, and half a bottle of red wine shortly before her murder. The time of death was between seven thirty and ten; because of the central heating in the house and the fire in the room where she died, which may have stayed warm all night, the pathologist could not be more precise.

She had left the Plough at half-past seven, according to a number of witnesses; this evidence narrowed down the time when she could have been attacked. She left alone, and presumably went straight home.

According to George Fortescue's statement, he had been at home all the evening, but there was no witness to the truth of what he said. So far, though, no single shred of evidencee had been found to

270

connect him with the killing. If he was guilty, he might break in the end. He would not run away; the police could pick him up at any time.

Cooley had reported what Valerie said about the hand of the man who attacked her, and his report had duly gone on file. It contributed nothing to the investigation; only if a link could be proved between the attacks would it be significant. At the moment Cooley was the only officer who believed the attack on Valerie had even taken place.

Turning over in his mind what he knew about the murders, Cooley saw that, if George Fortescue was not the killer, there was no trace of a lead to anyone else. The forensic evidence might produce one; or there might be another killing.

His thoughts turned towards Valerie. She was a comfortable sort of a girl to be with and she seemed to trust him. She was attractive, too – not stuck up, and not a bit tarty. But to touch her would be disaster. It would be a long time before she would be able to accept, much less respond to, anything like that. Yet her nature was warm, he was sure. He sighed a little. Well, he'd keep on seeing her, anyway, even when all this was over, as it must be eventually. He'd no other female who stuck in his mind in quite the same way just now, and she could do with a hand. That Timmy was a cute little guy; he'd had a fine time sailing his boats in the bath the day before. When the weather was better, it would be an idea to take him on the river, in a real boat. With Val too, and Melissa, of course. Val would put up a great picnic, for sure. He could tell she was a good cook of the wholesome sort; that bread of hers was the proof.

Detective Chief Superintendent Brownley had ordered a lot more probing into George Fortescue's activities and his connection with both the murders in the area; both the women were of a certain age, and a similar background. Other links might be traced – for instance, that Fortescue was acquainted with Mrs Cartwright, though he had declared he had never met her. She had a lover, Hugo Morton; George Fortescue might have been his predecessor and could have killed her from jealousy. Overlapping features in each case might be found. Officers must search in the Manor House garden for traces of fibre which might match the fragment found at Fletcham, thought to be from a piece of tweed. All the reports must be combed for possible links, and there must be conferences between the officers investigating each case. Detective Chief Inspector Hemmings and Detective Inspector Maude must maintain constant touch.

Cooley brooded. George Fortescue and the killer of Felicity Cartwright shared the same blood group. So far no traces of blood which could be that of the murderer of Dorothea Wyatt had been found, though some might be discovered on her clothing. This would indicate whether or not she had scratched her attacker; that large ring she wore, for instance, might do damage.

If the same man killed those two women, he could also be Valerie Turner's assailant, but in that case George Fortescue was innocent.

Cooley stretched out his own large, well-shaped hand, which Valerie had seemed to admire. True, it was almost hairless, but he had a lot of dark hair on his chest. What would she think about that? She could learn about it gradually, if he took the kids swimming. There'd been a woman who had once seemed to like it quite a lot.

Detective Chief Superintendent Brownley had wanted to know why forensic were being so slow in coming up with any firm evidence from the Fletcham case. They reported that the wool fragments found under Felicity Cartwright's nails were a match with the dark sweater taken from George Fortescue's house but, since the wool was of a common variety, a good barrister would make mincemeat of that unless it was supported. What about this second case? What about Fortescue's Rover? A tiny drop of blood in it – Felicity Cartwright's, or Dorothea Wyatt's – would be enough, but it would take time for the laboratory to find it.

And someone else might die first.

George ran through the falling rain, faster than his normal jogging pace. His town shoes were not as comfortable for running in as his plimsolls, and the overcoat he was wearing because his raincoat was with the police was bulky. Luckily he had a spare tweed hat, an old one, but now he had to take it off and carry it, lest it blow away. His bald head, exposed to the weather, felt cold. There was his brief-case, too, a handicap. He must look ridiculous.

He slowed to a walk. There was no pursuit. He put

on his hat and walked briskly, eyes looking to the front.

He continued this for some time, passing rows of houses with cars parked outside or garages tight shut, lights behind curtains at most windows. People were living happy lives in these houses, George reflected; men with wives who would be content to have someone coming back to them each night, paying the bills, doing their duty.

Dorothea had been one of those contented wives, until Harry died. She hadn't wanted to break out, like Angela. Poor Dorothea. No woman deserved such a dreadful death.

He walked on, past a shopping precinct supplying daily needs. It seemed a peaceful area. Then he met a group of boys, all with motorcycles, gathered on a corner near a bus shelter. Some were inside the shelter, seeking cover from the rain, no doubt. The engines of two bikes were revved as George passed. He thought he heard mocking cries. That would be because he was a neat-looking establishment figure. Yet all youngsters weren't so disrespectful. Daniel, for instance, had been grand through all the recent trouble, and the girl too, despite her strange floating garments and untidy long hair.

Hadn't he promised to telephone Daniel this evening? If he didn't, and Daniel called him and got no answer, he'd be anxious.

But the police wanted him.

He'd be allowed to telephone, if they took him in. He was entitled to make one call. He was getting to know the form. They'd find him in the end, for he had nowhere to go; they'd only to send a few cars out looking for him. He'd done no good by running away.

George saw a bus approaching. Its destination was, he read, Middletown. It must pass through Crowbury and would take him home. He hailed it, and because the night was wet the driver, though between stops, slowed down to let him on.

They'd come for him at Orchard House, but George no longer cared.

Cooley had spent much of Monday at the Manor House in Crowbury, helping sift the place for possible clues. The search of the grounds for fragments of fibre must wait until first light on Tuesday, and soon after six Cooley left the Manor to return to Tellingford. He had had only a sandwich lunch, and as he approached the Plough in Crowbury High Street he decided to stop for a pint and something to eat. Maybe they did chicken and chips.

He parked outside the pub, got out of his car and locked it. Across the road was the butcher's shop where Valerie had noticed George Fortescue's smooth hands. Over there was Nanron Antiques, for whom Valerie worked so hard stripping furniture in her cold garage. There was a light on in the shop, and a small van was parked outside.

Ronald Trimm had been among those in the Plough on Friday evening when Dorothea Wyatt was in the bar. He had left before her, Cooley knew from the reports. He had worked late that evening, normal practice for a Friday, Cooley remembered reading. He was working late tonight, too. He didn't live above the shop, but in Tellingford. Cooley had never, to his knowledge, met him.

A pint of bitter would go down well, and a ham sandwich, if there was no chicken and chips, would do, thought Cooley, still looking over at the shop. The street lighting was effective and the sign, Nanron Antiques, stood out.

Felicity Cartwright had dealt in antiques.

While his mind was registering this fact, Cooley strolled across the road. He might just glance in at the window of the shop, see the sort of things they sold, besides Valerie's furniture. The rain beat down as he approached the shop and he turned his collar up against it.

The blind was down on the door and a sign stated *Closed*. Cooley could see that the light came from somewhere at the back of the shop, where there must be some sort of second room. There were china ornaments in the window, and a case containing medals. He turned away, and his eye fell on the van. *Nanron Antiques* was painted on the door.

Cooley walked round it and shone his torch through the rear window. Its light fell on a dry-cleaner's polythene bag printed with the name of the shop in Tellingford, and a cone-shaped parcel that was obviously flowers. Coming to the front of the van, he looked at the tax disc, which was in order. Then he walked round it again, examining the tyres. It was not a reasoned action, just something he had done automatically before transferring to the CID.

One tyre at the rear was worn rather smooth, smoother than was legal.

Antiques, thought Cooley.

Valerie Turner's attacker could have known from the cycles in the garage that she had children, but she was connected with antiques. Ronald Trimm, who employed her, might know she sometimes worked at night. He would certainly know that she worked in the garage; would know how to approach it unseen; would be able to open the unlocked door unheard above the noise of the sander, peer in and seize his moment.

Cooley knocked on the door of the shop.

Nothing happened.

He knocked again, loudly, rattling the handle, making quite a noise.

'Open up,' he called sharply. 'Police.'

Everyone in Crowbury knew that the police were active in the village, investigating the murder. Only those with something to hide need fear their probing.

Cooley rattled the door again. There might be another way in at the back, perhaps unlocked. As he thought this there was a movement in the shop, and a voice called, 'I'm coming.'

The door opened. Cooley saw a middle-aged man with thick greying hair, dressed in a corduroy jacket and a white shirt with a light brown tie. In the light that fell on him from the street lamp outside, his face was a trifle flushed.

'Mr Trimm?' asked Cooley.

'Yes. What do you want? I'm busy,' Ronald said testily. Then he added, with an effort to speak more civilly, 'I'm going through the catalogue of a sale I have to go to tomorrow.'

'Detective Constable Cooley, D division,' Cooley said flatly. 'Is that your van?'

'Yes. It's all right there, isn't it, officer, for an hour or so? I don't usually park it there, I normally leave it in Church Lane.'

Church Lane, where the foot-path across the fields past the Manor House emerged.

Cooley's gaze dropped from Ronald's pale blue, anxious eyes to the hand that held the door open. The street light nearby shone steadily down and he saw squat fingers, a plump back to the hand, and pale ginger hairs.

He stepped over the threshold.

George got off the bus at the stop beyond the Plough in Crowbury High Street. The bus moved on, a lighted monster lumbering noisily towards Middletown, as he walked through the rain to the turning that led to Orchard House. The police were probably waiting there.

He moved slowly, tired and wretched; so many shocking things had happened within such a short space of time that he could barely comprehend them all. The personal horror of being suspected of committing a capital crime – two capital crimes, it now seemed – was enough on its own, but he was still stunned and shocked by the fact of Dorothea's terrible death.

He would miss her. She'd been a good friend to him.

But he wouldn't be living in Orchard House; he'd be in some prison, sewing mailbags.

Submerged in his own misery, George trudged on, barely aware of his surroundings. He heard the sudden wail of a police siren, and halted.

Here they were, on their way for him. He might as well make it easy for them.

He stepped forward into the road as the car tore towards him, its light flashing, on its way to the aid of Cooley. The driver jammed on the brakes and swerved, but he could not avoid the figure which had appeared so suddenly before him, and the wing of the car struck George hard, throwing him to the side of the road, where he lay inert.

Ronald was late again. It couldn't be the books this evening. Nancy frowned, sitting in her chair, drumming her fingers on the arm with impatience. What could be holding him up? He knew her whole day was geared to the peak moment of his return.

She turned the oven down, and resumed her vigil. After a while she heard a car outside, but it wasn't the van. It stopped in the road. Hurrying into the hall, Nancy drew the curtain back a fraction and looked out.

A police car was parked in the road, and while she watched a woman police officer in uniform, and a middle-aged man in a raincoat walked down the path of the Nortons' bungalow next door. What could have happened? Making sure she had only opened the curtains enough to peer through a chink, and couldn't possibly be seen, Nancy waited.

Quite quickly, she saw Keith and Hilda Norton leaving the house with the man and the woman officer. They drove away in the police car. Whatever could be wrong?

Nancy decided to pop round to see if Lynn was in the house on her own; then she'd learn why the police had called. Surely the Nortons weren't in any trouble?

But she found there was nobody at home.

She went back and turned the oven down still more, waiting for Ronald.

By the time a second police car arrived in Sycamore Road, Nancy was really worried, and when this time her own doorbell rang, she knew that Ronald must have had an accident.

Two uniformed officers stood on the step and asked if they might enter. She stood aside to admit them, and led them both in by the fire. At first she could not make sense of what they told her. Ronald was being held at Tellingford police station, they said, to be charged with abducting a minor, and wounding a police officer while resisting arrest.

The older officer talked on. Things had been found at the shop: a black sweater and a very dark purple balaclava helmet, handknitted, and a scarf. Yes, Nancy admitted; she'd noticed these things were missing from Ronald's wardrobe, and a pair of trousers too. The policeman was mentioning Ronald's raincoat, and his tweed hat.

They asked if Ronald was often home late, and she said almost never. Once, not so long ago, she recalled, he had taken Mrs Wyatt home from the Plough when she felt unwell. There had been two other occasions quite recently, and she remembered the dates; he'd been held up on a Friday with a problem over the books, she said, and another day the van had given trouble.

Had he ever met Mrs Felicity Cartwright, they inquired, an antique dealer fatally attacked in Fletcham?

He had, Nancy knew. He'd sold her a box. It was a few weeks ago now; she could check the date as she kept a diary of the sales he attended.

It was a long time before she understood the reasons for their questions, and that Ron had intended to harm Lynn. The girl was safe, Nancy learned; simply shocked.

'But it was that other man – that Fortescue man,' she said.

'Mr Fortescue wasn't involved,' said one of the officers. 'And in fact he was injured this evening in a road accident. Hit by a car. Some concussion, a few cracked ribs and bruising, but he'll be all right. He was lucky.'

So was the officer driving the car. He'd had no chance of totally avoiding Fortescue, as the man stepped into the road, hand aloft, but if Fortescue had been killed by a police car speeding to effect an arrest it would not have looked good in the press.

Cooley had sustained a flesh wound in the arm. It was painful but not serious.

'Ron had everything a man could want,' said Nancy. 'I did everything for him. Why should he do such terrible things?'

Why indeed?

The older officer told her that Ronald had bought

her some flowers today. They'd been in his van and he'd mentioned them very particularly after his arrest. There was no reason why she shouldn't have them; he'd send an officer round with them later.

Ronald, he had to explain, wouldn't be coming home: not for a very long time.